BANG

A NOVEL
BY
DANIEL PEÑA

Arte Público Press
Houston, Texas

Bang: A Novel is funded in part by grants from the City of Houston through the Houston Arts Alliance and the Texas Commission on the Arts. We are grateful for their support.

Recovering the past, creating the future

Arte Público Press
University of Houston
4902 Gulf Fwy, Bldg 19, Rm 100
Houston, Texas 77204-2004

Cover design by Victoria Castillo

Names: Peña, Daniel, 1988- author.
Title: Bang : a novel / by Daniel Peña.
Description: Houston, TX : Arte Público Press, 2017.
Identifiers: LCCN 2017027801 I ISBN 9781558858565 (alk. paper) I
    ISBN 97811518504488 (epub) I ISBN 9781518504495 (kindle) I
    ISBN 9781518504501 (pdf)
Subjects: LCSH: Mexicans—United States—Fiction. I Immigrant
    families—Fiction. I Illegal aliens—Fiction. I Drug traffic—
    Fiction. I Texas—Fiction. I Mexico—Fiction. I Domestic fiction.
Classification: LCC PS3616.E522 B36 2017 I DDC 813/.6—dc23
LC record available at https://lccn.loc.gov/2017027801

♾ The paper used in this publication meets the requirements of the American National Standard for Information Sciences—Permanence of Paper for Printed Library Materials, ANSI Z39.48-1984.

17 18 19 20   5 4 3 2 1

TABLE OF CONTENTS

For my wife, Sophia.
I wrote this for you. But then again,
I wrote everything for you.

"What thing is the body when it's lost?"

—Sara Uribe, *Antígona González*

FLYING MEXICANS

MISPLACED IS THE WORD Araceli would use. Like her husband was a lost set of keys or a good pair of scissors she doesn't want to return to the neighbors yet. *Misplaced*. First in the spring when he was deported, when the earth was full of holes and the air was spiced with baby citrus trees starving to be grounded. Then in the summer when the rattlesnakes multiplied at the end of the great drought, when the rains brought the crops back from the dead and still her husband hadn't arrived.

He told her he'd return today, just like he said he'd return back in the spring. And so Araceli waits at that spot on the culvert where he was picked up by the police. That's the place he said he'd be. She said she'd meet him there.

In her hands, she holds a portable transistor radio that she's modified to pick up police radios, EMT radios, border patrol radios and twangy, redneck rag chew coming in over the CB airwaves. She listens for any news of her husband, trying to make sense of the garbled English blaring from the transistor's speaker. The radio cuts in and out. Static.

The jagged, kinked lengths of copper wire from her modified radio jangle out over Araceli's knuckles as she tries to fix what's wrong. Araceli is good with electronics, gears and generally anything than can be broken and fixed again. She can make or repair anything. She's frustrated with the failing radio, though she's just as frustrated with the general situation of things. She gets that way sometimes—if one thing goes wrong

1

in her life, everything goes wrong in her life and she has trouble making sense of anything at all. Everything gets tainted by that feeling, by that frustration too.

Out by the road, she takes the positive end of a wire and circuits it through a capacitor that's hooked to a spool of copper wire wound around a rolled up, glued up mess of refrigerator magnets. She flips the radio off, then flips it back on to amplify the signal again. She tunes into the 5,000 kHz band. Nothing. She takes a step to the left, does it again. This time she hears something.

She turns the volume up high. She listens to the rag chew coming in over the airwaves, listening for any news of her husband. She listens so hard, trying to make sense of the English. She can't tell if the voice coming in is a cop or a truck driver. She understands very little of what's being said—it all sounds the same to her. *Fuck this*, she says to herself in perfect English. Nearly twenty years in Texas and the one thing she's mastered is *fuck this*. She loves to say it. It feels good.

She wraps the loose, kinked copper around the busted transistor radio and throws the whole mess out into the road. She waits for a car to run it over, crush it into a million, little pieces, but there's not a single car in sight. Her little creation just sits out there in the road, taunting her. She gets busy ignoring the radio by staring past it, thinking of her husband. He said he'd come today. For all of her husband's lies, she still believes in him.

Ten minutes go by. The radio remains uncrushed. Araceli can't stand the sight of it. She turns toward the milk jug behind her, the same jug her husband dropped the day he got deported. It lies where it was originally dropped in the culvert. Araceli remembers that he'd bought the milk from the Texaco on the corner. The earth grew brown around where the milk spilled when they took him away. Araceli thinks about moving the jug but then thinks against it. *Might be bad luck.* She believes in those kinds of things.

She wears a Catholic scapular around her neck to ward off evil, though she stopped believing in God after her first child, Cuauhtémoc, was born. Her change of heart wasn't informed so much by disbelief than by her incredible belief in luck, both good and bad, and the way those forces had always ruled her life.

She carries her lucky wool Zapotec purse across her body, under her clothes. Araceli remembers that her mother gave her that purse before she died. She said it was full of treasures but Araceli found it filled with only five square fabric samples ripped from a salesman's binder advertising for Quinceañera dresses: bengaline silk, lace tulle, organza, satin, chiffon. She feels a slight pang when thinking back on the simplicity of her mother, that woman she was trying so desperately to escape. Her mother's family in Guerrero pushed her to Texas as much as her husband took her. Her mother loved the bengaline silk (Araceli's least favorite), but her husband loved the satin (her favorite).

She was sixteen when she met her future husband, thirty-two, at a horseracing track in Guadalajara. She thought he was American by the dumb, bleached Panama hat he was wearing. She remembers he was rangy—long arms and no paunch. He was slightly sunburnt, his skin a glowing bronze.

She was selling *tejuíno*, a fermented, corn drink, from a cart and brought him one to slurp down. He paid her and only once he opened his mouth did she realize he was Mexican, from the north.

"Where?" she asked, refusing to leave his side.

"Chihuahua."

"Are you visiting?" she asked.

"I'm betting."

From under her dress, she unlatched the wool purse and brought out her lucky, satin square. She rubbed it, and he rubbed it. His horse won. And from this mutual love for the same square of fabric bloomed a marriage, a home, two children and work in an orange grove in Harlingen, Texas, all before she was twenty-three. She's thirty-nine now. She holds on to that little square of satin now and looks at the milk jug, looks out into the road. To the right, nothing. To the left, the bright red, LED display over the Texaco with the digital American flag glowing between gas prices. Ninety-two degrees tonight. Seven o'clock. Monday, June 1st, 2015. Her youngest son Uli's birthday. She takes the chiffon patch from her purse and rubs that too between her thumb and index. She remembers Uli loved chiffon as a baby. Her oldest son Cuauhté-moc, too, though he loves anything lush, it seems: alcohol, cigarettes, salty foods. Everything bad for you.

She looks for him, too, out in the road in his father's blue pickup truck, which her husband left behind. She was supposed to go with Cuauhtémoc to the Texaco to buy Uli's present but she never steps past the milk jug these days. After her husband was deported, she couldn't take the risk. She's close enough to the grove property where she could jump back behind the fence, even with her hobbled foot. She wonders, sometimes, why her husband didn't do the same. He's the one that taught her the rules of private property in America. He taught her about warrants and police and calling the ACLU lawyer from that little pre-paid Cricket phone she always forgets to carry.

She gets stir crazy standing out there. She looks out to the left again, then the right. She looks at her mistake of a creation out on the road—that shitty transistor radio turned scanner.

She knows her husband is coming from San Miguel, which is in Chihuahua, which is in the northeast part of Mexico—right next to the thumb of Texas. He'd drive south and then east toward Harlingen, which is west of the milk jug. Araceli creates a map in her head to figure out which side of the road she should be staring down. She decides to stare down the right side of the road. She sees nothing. She wishes she could lie down in the middle of the road, next to that radio, and wait for whatever luck comes her way.

She gives up once the stars come out, though she lingers a bit more after that to wait for her sons, her tiny frame bolted to the place where her one good foot rests on the earth, the three remaining toes of her bad foot sloped up on her ankle. The big toe and the small one are gone, lobbed away with gangrene, though the rest of her is healthy. Slim fingers and slim toes, a healthy belly and a healthy face that's constantly flush. Apple face, almond eyes. Along with the fabric squares, she carries a damp rag around in her wool purse that she touches every now and then with her hot and pink little hands.

Uli, her youngest, should be home from high school track practice right now. Cuauhtémoc should have been home from the Texaco too, but knowing Cuauhtémoc, he's out for a drink with Ronnie, the grove boss' son.

Ronnie is the one who taught Cuauhtémoc to fly planes. Cuauhtémoc learned after Ronnie's older brother crashed his Pawnee on a stall. After he died, the grove boss looked to train Cuauhtémoc because he was undocumented and a high school dropout, which meant he was disposable.

Like Uli, Cuauhtémoc was a track star once—he had a college scholarship lined up anyway. But Cuauhtémoc had to drop out of school three months short of graduation when he killed a boy.

Cuauhtémoc was playing basketball in the high school gym. He checked a boy hard in the chest, and the boy's heart stopped. Cuauhtémoc busted the boy's sternum with chest compressions trying to start his heart again, but the boy's blood pooled on the underside of his body. The coach had to pull Cuauhtémoc off him. Said it could have been a birth defect, could have been drugs, could have been anything. But Cuauhtémoc knew, in his heart, that it was him. It was a hard check, a mean check—the kind he'd been meaning to give someone for a long, long time. And that anger turned to shock turned to sadness.

The sheriff sent out some folks from the county to investigate, and being undocumented, Cuauhtémoc couldn't go back to school the next day or the day after that. He went to work flying crop dusters in the groves illegally with the grove boss' blessing. Ronnie taught Cuauhtémoc everything about crop dusting, and with Ronnie, Cuauhtémoc let his mean streak grow.

Araceli thinks you pick friends you secretly want to be like. And that's why Ronnie and Cuauhtémoc are so close, she thinks. Cuauhtémoc wants to be American and Ronnie wants to be free, like all libertarian rednecks in Texas want to be free. Ronnie wants to "live off the grid." Ronnie wants to keep out of the watchful eye of the federal government, and Cuauhtémoc just wants to be a part of anything American (or what he perceives to be American, anyway): see Cuauhtémoc with a twelve-string singing "Free Bird"; see him shoot two guns with one hand; see him douse a shop rag in aviation fuel and watch it burn blue; see him throw a coke bottle, a Molotov cocktail, into a drain tunnel by the tracks; see the flames roll across the ceiling like a thousand burning hills inverted and curling with a whoosh hot enough to draw the slack skin tight over your face.

In the red glow of the Texaco station, Cuauhtémoc appears about a mile down from Araceli's line of sight. He's driving the blue Ford Lobo pickup with cancer patches over the hood. The headlights of the truck shine weak in the pale twilight.

A calm comes into Araceli's heart as she watches the pickup lumber toward the grove. One son back, one to go. Her husband too. Being that she's isolated in the groves—undocumented, and therefore always afraid to leave for fear of being caught—family is the most important thing for her. She does everything to keep it intact, even if all she can do is wait.

She takes a step back from the spot on the road with the milk jug in the culvert and pivots on her good foot, making her way back to the house. She throws up a hand to wave at her son. She stops. She notices the headlights on the truck flip between high-beams and low, the difference between the two just dim and dimmer. The headlights flip once but then they keep flipping. As the pickup nears, Araceli hears that the engine's been cut. Steam pours out from the edges of the hood. Cuauhtémoc's driving off momentum. Just the sticky sound of the tires over asphalt and then dirt as he glides onto the grove property from the shoulder of the road to park the truck in its spot on a bald patch of earth next to the trailer where they live.

Araceli takes the warning and moves out of the way as he glides past her, riding the momentum from the road onto the grove property. Pivoting herself to follow the truck, Araceli loses her footing on a loose patch of dirt and slides into the culvert. A thud in her ears from where her butt hits the dirt. Her own momentum slides her down a foot or two. It's then that she's glad for the drought. No water in the culvert. Just that milk jug behind her. She reaches around and picks it up, cradles it while she catches her breath.

Araceli's official position on Cuauhtémoc's drinking is that she's opposed to it (she says that to him, anyway), but she also knows the booze mellows him out, makes him less like who he's becoming: older, sober, but angrier these days. Secretly, she thinks, *if only he drank a little more booze.*

He was an athlete once and he's trying to get there again. Between flights, he runs the length of the groves in his worn out Lucchese boots. He's dropped weight, gained muscle. Cuauhtémoc says he's faster than his brother, though they've never raced. Araceli won't have it. His soft edges have all gone hard. She knows he's trying to make something of himself. Trying to decenter his life from what it is, or at least what it's been so far. Cuauhtémoc tells Araceli he'll run track for Mexico— long distance. Nothing that requires speed. He'll medal but not too well. Bronze maybe. He'll be known as *the Olympian*. Not the boy killer, not the illegal boy who flies the illegal planes over a grove in Texas.

The pickup door swings open and there's only the smell of too-strong cologne and the smoke-soaked vinyl over the bench seats. She drops the milk jug about the same time his Lucchese boots hit the ground.

Like his father, Cuauhtémoc has a flat head of curly hair. He's rangy and lean and tall. He's got his mother's almond-shaped eyes but his father's small, serious mouth. Tiny ears and no chin. His head almost slopes into his neck so that when he smiles, there's a slight wrinkle in his chin just like he's got now.

He's in a good mood. It's only when he shuts the door that Araceli sees he's got a puppy tucked into the crook of his arm. An ordinary mutt. Black and brown fur. Something between a schnauzer and a dachshund with an orange bow on top of its head.

"You got him a dog?" Araceli says to her son, completely sidestepping the fender of the smoking pickup. She only sees her son and the puppy.

"We've never had one," says Cuauhtémoc with his crooked, little smile.

"For a reason," says Araceli. "They cost too much money."

"It's chipped. It's got all of its shots."

"You can't bring that into the house," she says firmly.

"It's potty trained."

"You mean housebroken."

"Whatever," says Cuauhtémoc.

"You've never had a dog. Neither has your little brother. It's too much responsibility. Take it back before he comes."

"Why?"

"Because your brother hasn't seen it yet. He can't get attached."

"I don't have another birthday present," says Cuauhtémoc.

"Get one," she says.

"How?" he says and nods to the steaming truck. Araceli takes the dog from her son's arms. She searches the collar for a name tag but there's nothing.

"It's a girl," says Cuauhtémoc, rounding the back of the pickup to search for the water hose in the grass. He finds it and unwinds the broach faucet that feeds that hose from the side of their trailer home, a modified school portable with a '4' stamped on the side. The water slicks over the ground as Cuauhtémoc walks toward the truck cabin with the hose in hand. He unlatches the hood and pushes it up above the windshield.

"Does she have a name yet?" asks Araceli.

"I was thinking Roo," says Cuauhtémoc, putting his thumb over the hose and spraying down the engine. A cloud of steam escapes from under the hood as the water sizzles over the cast-iron block.

"Where'd you get that name?" asks Araceli, waiting for the steam to clear, but it never does, just sits there and hangs for a while.

"Roo. Kangaroo. She jumps a lot. She's still teething," says Cuauhtémoc. "Could also be Cajun or something. I don't know."

At this, Araceli imagines the near future: ripped blankets, chewed up wiring, frayed wooden table legs, shredded shoes.

"If she doesn't have a name, she's not ours yet," says Araceli as if to settle the matter.

The dog squirms in her arms. She jumps up and licks Araceli across the lips. Araceli arches her head back, disgusted, before spitting into the grove dirt.

"Dog's mouth is cleaner than your mouth," says Cuauhtémoc laughing. "It's science."

"I don't eat my own shit," says Araceli, feeling the dog's saliva drying tight over her skin.

She looks the puppy in the eyes. No denying, now, how cute it is. Even Araceli can admit this. The puppy yawns and then digs her nose into the space between Araceli's arm and her ribs.

"Let's go inside," she says, turning toward the cabin with Roo in her arms.

She waits for Cuauhtémoc to follow, but he stays where he is, spraying down the engine block.

Araceli sets Roo down just inside the threshold of the door. The puppy sniffs around where she's been placed. Roo does a circle and lays on her paws. Araceli looks into her sad, sleepy eyes as she hobbles toward the stove. "Roo," she says to her. The dog doesn't respond.

In the kitchen, Araceli fills a pot with hot water. Above the sink, she looks out the window at Cuauhtémoc trying to cool the pickup. She wishes he'd come inside but she knows he needs to be alone sometimes, just in the way her husband needed to be alone. She wonders, occasionally, if her husband planned to get deported on purpose. But she always shuts those thoughts away almost as soon as they come.

She puts the pot of water to boil and opens the window to listen to the dark summer of Harlingen, Texas. The sound of cicadas.

In the air there's the smell of nosebleeds, which is to say the smell of fertilizer and pesticides. It all mingles with the burnt fetor that comes from the glowing coil stovetop, the crusting remnants of Araceli's past dishes pouring in spicy, humid waves from the screened windows of her trailer home parked in the creeping, darkness of the groves, the pesticide pouring into her home.

From just behind the window, she keeps an eye out for her husband in the twilight, in the distance, as if he might sprout up from that place the sun is going toward.

She looks again in that space on the horizon where the dirt is dry-clapped by the wind into the culvert off the highway before ricocheting up into the sky, setting the blackened night ablaze with neon, the dirty air holding the last striations of light long after the sun is gone. To Araceli, it's as if the earth is conspiring with her. The sky holding light like ransom before the dark completely snuffs it out. It's only then—when the sky goes completely black—that she stops waiting.

When the sun is gone, the wind shifts directions and curls in toward the house. There's a brief moment when the air goes static as if time has stopped for Araceli. Just the smell of the dusty sky and the smell, too, of the kitchen air pulled from the screened window by the negative pressure of the changing breeze. The smell of the hot coils, again, but also the smell of cake and melted ice cream. The smell of Uli's birthday, which she's trying so desperately to put together.

Uli is sixteen today, which more or less makes him a man in America, though there are no rites of passage for young brown men in this country. None that Araceli knows of anyway. None like the kind you read about in old books or like the kind Uli's friend, Craig, went through that made him a man at thirteen. She thinks *I could teach him to drive*. It wouldn't be the first time she'd taught her boys things she had to learn all by herself. But Araceli hasn't driven in years. She's not sure she could teach him the legal way, teach him the rules of the road in this country, though she knows the complexities of the gear boxes, fuse boxes, wiring and crankshaft. She knows how to keep the truck going.

Uli's father was supposed to teach him to drive before he was deported. She'd let Cuauhtémoc do it but she doesn't trust him—not the both of them together anyway.

She hopes Cuauhtémoc can get the truck running again. She decides that if he can't, then she will. The truck only appears to be overheated, but Araceli knows that you can never really tell with American vehicles. One visible problem might be the symptom of three other invisible ones.

All of a sudden, there's the tang of blood in her nose. She shuts the window to keep out the pesticides. She puts a dishrag to her face. A steady flow of bright red beading down from her sinuses.

As Araceli puts pressure to her nose, she feels sweat breaking from her pores, a rush of hot blood to the head. She knows what's coming next. She's become all too familiar with the spins the pesticides bring on. She holds onto the kitchen sink. She stares up at the ceiling to slow the blood.

In the center of the ceiling, the incandescent bulb paints everything in lacquered shades of gold. Everything pulses as the pressure builds up behind her eyes. She tries, so hard, to stare at a fixed point to keep her world from spinning. There are good objects and bad objects. Good objects stay still. Bad objects make you vomit.

Araceli's eyes shift toward the door. In the yellow light, the outline of boots stepping across the threshold. That's the last thing she sees right before her legs give out from under her, blood pouring steady from her head.

Araceli wakes to the rip of duct tape as Cuauhtémoc pulls long strips from the roll. He seals off the space between the bedroom door and the ground first and then the space between the door and the upper threshold before sealing the sides of the door. From the corner of her eye she sees Uli throwing a stack of bloody towels into a steaming PVC bucket of water. He's still in his track clothes. It's only June—track season hasn't even begun—but he's looking leaner already, the way Araceli remembers boys in the mountains of Guerrero used to look in the rainy season when the crickets multiplied by the thousands. Crickets were all any of those boys ate: dipped in chocolate, fried over a *comal*, eaten with a pinch of salt and lime and a swig of beer. All protein and brine. The smell of her own blood brings those memories back. The sight of her son too: sinewy muscles in his arms and legs, that close-cropped head of hair, that slightness of his frame as if a strong breeze could carry him away.

Uli flips on the window unit to suck out the rotten air from the room and filter in fresh air. In Uli, Araceli sees her own eyes looking back at her. Her husband's flat head. Her sister's wide mouth. She looks down at the puppy curled up at the foot of the bed, his mouth stained pink from lapping up Araceli's blood.

"She's awake," Uli says to Cuauhtémoc.

Araceli tilts her head back. She knows the drill.

"Did you turn off the stove?" she asks Uli.

"It's off. Everything's fine."

"How long was I out?" she asks.

"Just a little bit," says Uli.

A lie. She knows by the warmth of the sheets against her body. She hates her body for being weak, for breaking down, for ruining her son's birthday. She knows the groves did this to her. She dreams of the day she can finally leave.

"Crazy wind came in from the north. Shook all the pesticides from the trees," says Uli.

"Just washed that damn truck too," says Cuauhtémoc, looking out the window. "About an eighth-inch coat of dust on it now. I thought northern winds only came in the winter."

"There's a hurricane in the Gulf," says Uli.

"Probably some low pressure stuff," says Cuauhtémoc. "I wouldn't know nothing about that, 'cause I never graduated high school."

Uli ignores the comment. He puts his hands out in front of the window unit to make sure it's blowing in cool air. "Maybe some tape on the edges of the window," he says.

"No. The window is fine," says Cuauhtémoc.

"Just humor me," says Uli, wiping away the whitish buildup of pesticide along the accordion flap that seals the window unit against the pane.

"You act like it's your birthday or something," says Cuauhtémoc with a smile.

He rips a segment of tape with his teeth and lays it shoddily over the accordion flap.

The nausea hits Araceli again. *See-saw, see-saw* goes everything in the world. Araceli closes her eyes. The taste of cool water at her lips. In her right hand, she can feel Uli pushing a cigarette between her slender fingers. Nicotine to open up the capillaries.

Her blood runs cold in her veins. An explosion of geometrical shapes behind her eyelids—a migraine building, bright pain.

"Easy," goes Uli.

Araceli hears him take the cigarette from between her fingers and stick it in his mouth. He lights it to get it going before pushing the wet filter between Araceli's fingers again.

"Get the lights," she hears him say to Cuauhtémoc.

The bedroom lights go out. Just a single incandescent bulb shining from under the lampshade on her nightstand.

"Is he back?" says Araceli.

A pregnant silence. The air cooling between her sons and herself. Everyone pretends the question was never asked.

The wave of nausea passes. Araceli keeps her eyes closed for fear of crying. She wills herself not to do it.

Araceli alternates between taking sips of water and smoke. The taste of ash on her tongue. The smell of it in her hair too.

She looks out of the small sliver of glass above the window unit, her gaze fixed on the road outside. Nothing. *I'll find him,* she thinks. In her mind she goes over the cities she'd pass along the way. *Harlingen-Matamoros-Reynosa-Monterrey-Torreón-Delicias-San Miguel.* She can feel, in her muscles, the memory of how to drive. She closes her eyes. The darkness swirls like velvet.

꙳ ꙳ ꙳

Uli puts a damp, warm towel over Araceli's eyes to keep them from swelling. He waits until she's asleep, holding his new puppy with its mouth stained with his mother's blood. He sits at the foot of the bed and wipes the dog's mouth clean. He looks out the window. Cuauhtémoc taking a push broom to his father's old pickup, trying to wipe the pesticide dust away.

His mother snores. The puppy too. Uli leaves the puppy at the foot of the bed and eases out of the room, pulling the door tight to reseal the duct tape against the frame of the door, not that it's needed anymore. The pesticide winds have come and gone. There's a stillness in the air as Uli steps out onto the porch. It's still warm but the sweat in his Lycra tracksuit cools his skin so that he's shivering. He slips off his track shoes and feels his bare feet against the dry grass. Dark summer in Harlingen. The orange groves are abuzz with cicadas scarring the trees, their collective hum sharp in the night air like the razor edge of his mother's scissors. That Spanish steel she *slick-slacks* every now and then over a whetstone just to hear it, just to drown out the sounds of the groves at night.

Between his toes, Uli feels the heat gushing up from the earth. He hears all those insects going angry.

From the pocket of his tracksuit, the one his mother had sown in to carry a little square of satin for good luck, Uli pulls out one of his mother's cornhusk cigarettes—the kind she rolls herself with molasses soaked-tobacco that burns hot and spicy on the tongue. From the same pocket he produces the lighter his mother bought him last year from the Texaco. It says CUNT PUNISHER on it in neon pink letters. Last year, his mother asked for something masculine, so the cashier sold her this. A cruel joke. Neither son had the heart to tell her what it meant. Araceli can understand English, but she has trouble reading it.

Uli lights the cigarette with his cunt punisher Zippo and takes a deep drag, easing himself onto the porch steps. He keeps the Zippo lit and stares into the flame for a while before blowing it out. He makes a wish. *Sixteen*, he thinks. He takes the *Valley Morning Star* newspaper from the place on the step where his mother left it all marked up. Subjects circled in blue, predicates underlined in green.

Cuauhtémoc rounds the corner of the house with the push broom in his hand. He sees Uli with the newspaper and gets this grin across his face.

"Me first," he says, snatching the newspaper from Uli's grip. "Don't stand a goddamned chance."

"You're outclassed," says Uli to his older brother, laughing while trying to keep his voice down. He adjusts the Lycra strap over his shoulder.

"I've got a better brain than you. I've got a better ear too."

Since Uli can remember, they'd always done impressions of white people. They'd pick a headline from the newspaper— something about subprime mortgages, crop yields, Texas Longhorns football—and they'd riff from there. Their father would always be the judge whenever he was around. The winner got a can of beer.

"We playing for booze?" asks Uli, eager to be like his brother if only in small ways. His brother would bet on booze.

Cuauhtémoc cuts a smile before bending at the knee to reach his long arm between the porch steps. He pulls out an unopened bottle of Willet bourbon. The skinny neck of the bottle glows dark amber in the moonlight. Cuauhtémoc holds the bottle by the neck like he's holding a hammer. Uli's reminded, just then, that Cuauhtémoc has two sides to him. There's the Cuauhtémoc that he knows and then the other one rattling away inside those eyes when he's about to drink. That Cuauhtémoc scares Uli, if only by knowing that the same man inside Cuauhtémoc is inside Uli too—in his genes, anyway. All of them are cursed to be the same man.

Just then, overhead, a small plane banks hard over the groves. Both brothers look up into the sky. A Cessna 152, by the looks of it, but they can't be sure. It's dark and the plane's strobe lights are out.

The flaps are lowered. The plane creeps by in slow flight. From the pilot's window, a large gunnysack-like package drops. It lands with a thud somewhere in the groves. Almost as fast as it comes, it's gone again. Flaps up, engine at full throttle. The engine drones on until it's replaced by the angry noise of the cicadas.

"The fuck was that?" asks Uli.

"One of Ronnie's packages, I guess," says Cuauhtémoc.

"We should get it," says Uli.

"We should leave it. You don't want any part of that."

"What do you think's in it?"

"I know what's in it," says Cuauhtémoc.

"How would you know that?" asks Uli.

"Somebody has to translate for Ronnie."

"You're lying," says Uli.

"So, I'm lying. Give me a cigarette."

Uli reaches into his little Lycra pocket and hands one over. He puts the cigarette between his lips. Shoots Uli a look like *how-fucking-pathetic*.

"What's in it then?"

"Grass," says Cuauhtémoc, cutting the seal from the neck of the bottle of bourbon. He spits out some loose tobacco before popping the cap to the Willet. The sweet smell of whiskey in the air. Cinnamon and charcoal and molasses.

"You ever tried it?" asks Uli.

"The Willet?" says Cuauhtémoc. "Of course. I bought it for you."

Uli takes the bottle into his hands. He smells the mouth. The smell of their father's breath. It brings from the back of the mind other smells too. The briny, vinegary smell of his sweat. The smell of Chlorpyrifos pesticide in his hair. The smell of hot blood that would pour from his nose in thick, dark streams that covered his moustache and turned him green, that same shade they'd all turn in winter when the sun was weak and their blood was too. Cuauhtémoc remembers when his father used to get the spins. His face would bloat, his eyes would sink into his head. Every week he got the spins and every week there was a washcloth black and heavy with blood between his fingers. When Cuauhtémoc was little, it was his job to set the wash- cloth out on the porch until it turned brown under the white sun. Araceli hated this. The flies would come for the blood. She would set out jars of sugar-water with borax to kill the flies, and stray dogs would always lap it up in the heat. The dogs would shit for weeks, and then the flies would come for the shit. Flies find death like bees find honey.

The brothers each take a swig. Then a second. Then a third. Cuauhtémoc drops his cigarette and searches for it in a soggy patch of earth. When he finds it, it's damper on one side than the other. He puts it to his lips again and lights it. He's slow and deliberate with each movement, the way some drunks are.

He says to Uli, through squinted eyes, "Can't believe that fucker was dumb enough to fly at night. You never fly at night if you can help it—not by the Gulf. You ever flown a plane at night before?"

"You know the answer to that," says Uli, putting his lips to the bottle.

"I did one time. Over water when I was training."

"What's it like?"

"Scary," says Cuauhtémoc. "Can't tell what's a boat and what's a star. All the boats have lights, and the ocean, the Gulf, is pitch-black. I mean black-black. And when there isn't a cloud in the sky, who's to say the water isn't the sky? Ever heard of JFK Jr.?"

"No," says Uli

"Look him up," he says, sipping smoke from his cigarette.

Cuauhtémoc can feel his brother's jealousy growing brighter. He stokes it, goading him for no other reason than to goad him, though each word is laced with love and jest. Cuauhtémoc hurts his little brother in small ways. *I am the older and you are the younger.* He never lets Uli forget it. As long as

Uli exists, Cuauhtémoc will always be the older brother and Uli will be the younger. Their mutual existence is what keeps them brothers. And that natural order too.

"So, how do you not crash in the ocean?" asks Uli, breaking the long silence.

"You pitch down," he says, "and check the altimeter first. Then the artificial horizon. Then the climbing speed. That's how you don't crash. But flying over land is worse. Radio towers, birds, telephone poles. Did you know birds fly at night?"

"No way," says Uli.

"*Sí, güey.* They fly way up there. Ride the thermals in circles like buzzards, you know?"

"I'd kill to see that," says Uli.

At this, Cuauhtémoc looks out at the darkness of the groves. "You want to go up?" he asks Uli.

"Right now?"

"Tonight," says Cuauhtémoc.

Uli doesn't know what to say to that.

The grove boss is gone. Cuauhtémoc knows he can pull it off.

"I'll take you up," says Cuauhtémoc. "But if I do you've got to share some of this with me," he says, taking another swig of the whiskey. "Half and half. Split it down the middle."

Uli looks at Cuauhtémoc in the darkness. He knows already that for him there is no other way but to go into the sky with his brother.

Beside their trailer is the tool shed, and beside that is the hangar where the single engine Pawnee sleeps at night. Uli has only been inside it once before, but he knows all of the placards, the entire control panel by heart. Like Cuauhtémoc, he's read the pilot's operating handbook. He knows the last time the propeller's been replaced and the last time the oil's been changed. He knows where the pitot tube juts from the cowling, what Cuauhtémoc means when he tells him, "Take off the ram cover. Make sure the static vent is clear."

Cuauhtémoc checks the oil in the cowling, the fuel in the wings, the hydraulic fluid in the brakes, the fuel sump with a blue enamel cup, the elevators with an up-down motion that shakes the plane and kicks the yoke back and forth inside the cabin like a ghost.

"Pre-flight done," he says, then takes another swig from the bottle of Willett bourbon.

Uli takes a set of headphones from Cuauhtémoc's left hand, his right hand on the radio, dialing in the ATIS (the weather) coming out of Easterwood Field. The automated voice reads, "Harlingen Easterwood Field. Automated weather observation one zero five three zulu. Winds one six zero at three six. Visibility eight. Sky condition overcast one thousand seven hundred. Temperature three-three Celsius. Altimeter two seven five."

Cuauhtémoc turns down the ATIS and adjusts the altimeter to two hundred and seventy-five feet above sea level to match the broadcast. His voice comes in mellow to Uli through the yards of wire.

"Hell-lo, Hell-lo. Hear me?"

"Sure," says Uli. Cuauhtémoc hands him the bottle and gets ready for the call. It sounds like this: "Harlingen traffic, Pawnee five-four-zero-zero-Juliet with weather ready for taxi and take-off, departure toward the south east, Easterwood groves."

Cuauhtémoc says his location at the end of the broadcast so anyone in the sky knows where he'll be coming from. But tonight there's not a plane in sight, not in the sky and not on the radio. Just the night rolling on forever and the stars beyond that.

"You ready?" says Cuauhtémoc.

"I'm ready," says Uli.

"Clear!" Cuauhtémoc yells outside the window out of habit—no one is around.

Uli watches his brother's hands move swiftly about the dash as he flips on magneto one, then magneto two. Cuauhtémoc cranks the engine, and it sputters. He pumps the throttle three times with long strokes to push fuel into the engine. It's warm outside but the engine is cold, and there's no primer. The propeller catches and whirs fast so that it pulls the windows up and out on its hinges.

"Latch those down," Cuauhtémoc says to Uli.

Uli knows that rolling over the bumpy dirt could shatter the glass if not secured. A soft field runway is really a dirt field runway. The name is ironic, especially in the groves, because the earth is uneven, full of stones, full of potholes that dig the front wheel and strut into the ground so that it has to be pulled up into the air to keep it from slowing down on take-off, the full weight of the plane resting on the rear two struts so that the plane is popping a wheelie the entire length of the strip until it's airborne.

The soft field takeoff warrants fifteen degrees of flaps and a slight pull-back on the yoke until the front strut gets off the ground just long enough to build speed and ride the pocket of air between the plane and the earth—ground effect, it's called—until the air pushes up.

They ride that pocket of air until they reach 80 knots. The Pawnee gallops over the dirt as haughty and elegant as your average town drunk, rising and then falling back down to the earth with a thud on the main wheels and then a hop-skid-skip into the air again, a flutter of the ailerons to keep the plane steady and straight until Cuauhtémoc pulls back ever-so-gingerly on the yoke, nervous sweat dripping down the length of his arms. Uli feels his gullet tightening, a shiver up and down his spine that radiates outward to his fingertips. His hands go jittery. His brother's hands stay steady, keeping it together by pulling in a calm, labored motion as the plane builds just enough speed to clear the trees.

Looking from inside the windshield, the grove is inked out in the dark but it's heard in the scraping along the belly of the plane. The sound of loose, shaken oranges thudding to the ground. The rooty smell of chopped leaves like sweet grass freshly cut. And of course, the smell of pesticides too.

In the dim lights of the cabin, Uli sees Cuauhtémoc pull the bottle of Willett from between his legs. He takes a swig and passes it to Uli. The burn eases the tension in his gullet. Uli keeps taking pulls on the long neck of the bottle until everything outside the windshield is smaller, calmer, disappearing before their very eyes.

They don't talk as they drift upwards. For Uli, his first time in the sky is holy. And he thinks—just as Cuauhtémoc always thinks while flying—that none of this makes sense: this much metal floating up into the sky. Uli puts his faith in his brother, despite being completely terrorized by the nervous buzz beneath his skin, by the drunkenness which makes the stars seem too close and the ground too far as the plane pushes higher, faster. The black sky swallows them whole just over the juncture of Highway 77 and the railroad tracks that lead north toward Corpus Christi.

Uli sees the lake just a mile ahead at sixteen hundred feet. High enough to thin the air but low enough to see the headlights of the cars on the highway and some of the other roads too, the ones that wander back into Mexico where they become *rutas*, *calles*, little cities that form like phalanges on the other side of the border. They tow that line—the Río Bravo—just when the engine sputters and cuts.

The engine buffets inside the cowling until it wheezes for breath. The nose dips forward, the whiskey glugging from the long neck of the Willett bottle onto the floor between Uli's feet. And then not a word is said between the brothers—that silence that fills the space just before a car wreck. All you can do is wait for it. And that's what Uli does, every muscle tensing in his body as Cuauhtémoc pulls the lever to apply carb heat, waiting for ignition.

Uli watches for the idled propeller to spin, but it just stays there as they head toward the river below. Texas to the right, Mexico to the left. He's suddenly aware of his flesh, how soft he is compared to the metal around him and the earth below. He thinks about nothing else. Just his own softness as the plane dives to one thousand feet.

Cuauhtémoc hits the rudders and yaws toward the highway, toward Texas, careful not to use the aileron so as not to lose altitude faster. Uli knows if his brother can make the highway, they'll live, but if they hit the groves, they're finished. No one hits a tree and survives.

The wind whistles. Uli's heart beats so hard he hears the thud in his throat above the wind. It ticks like a clock, the seconds of his life numbered as he plunges to three hundred feet, low enough to see the faces of the drivers inside their cars on the highway. He thinks they look soft too, unworried and unaware about what's coming down above them. Uli's sweat sours at his collar. His stomach floats, his brain scrambles as the earth flattens itself outside the windshield and the sky halves itself. Uli would scream if he weren't out of breath. That silence again.

Twenty-five feet. And then just the thundering crack of flesh on metal.

THE FIVE SENSES OF HURT

SLEEP IS DELICIOUS. Uli doesn't ever want to wake up.

Tack-tack go the fox sparrows that hop along the engine cowling. They sing their cheerful morning song amidst the wreckage. Uli wakes to their dry wings flapping like a trilled breath or a hushed snore or something almost insect-like. They bounce between their perches on the plane's busted cowling and bent propeller.

Uli blinks his blurry eyes once, twice. Brown flecks of blood shining in the morning light over the crushed windshield glass. There's a pile of crystal-fine shards in his lap. He brushes it away with the tips of his fingers.

He moves to unbuckle himself. An electric pain in his right arm pins him back into place. All around him the birds sing and then more sparrows arrive. His pains ring out in unison, his mind shifting between them like channels on a television. Uli makes sense of these pains the way he makes sense of everything else in his life: by compartmentalizing them into tiny lists.

First he makes lists of severe pains:

His badly sprained wrist tender to the touch
His creaky big toenail on his right foot that stings when he pushes down
His broken little toe on his left foot
His ribs

The hot pain in his mouth like a thousand needles in his gums

Then of his moderate pains:

The friction burn where the seatbelt cinched his tracksuit and rubbed the skin over his abdomen raw
The mild sting of the wind brushing over his exposed wounds
The dull throb behind his eyes that keep the world moving in a blur

Then of everything that is okay:

He can breathe
He can move his extremities (not paralyzed)
He's not alone

Uli is swimming in his own topsy-turvy equilibrium. When he stretches his left arm out to reach for his brother, he finds nothing, no one beside him, just a bloody stain on the windshield in front of where his brother used to be. Uli feels adrenaline surge in his veins. A lump forms in his throat. He bargains with God until he compartmentalizes these feelings too.

Things that could have happened to Cuauhtémoc:

Flew through the windshield (least likely)
Was fine (not likely)
Was injured (not fine) but managed to get help (likely)

Being Uli, his mind dwells on the obvious worst-case scenario. *Did he go through the windshield?* Uli thinks about it. There would be blood on the propeller. Blood everywhere. And as far as he can see, there is little blood. The thought of his brother going through the propeller is enough to make his body pulse with phantom pains that rival his own very real ones. As long as Uli can remember, he'd always been that way with his older brother—cut from the same cloth, or so their mother had always said. Such was the strength of his empathy. Cuauhtémoc's pain was Uli's pain, but the reverse wasn't necessarily true.

Cuauhtémoc, having grown up close to his father, learned the masculine value of turning inward, though he felt deeply in other ways: in drink when his walls would gently crash down and he'd cry and cry and run out shirtless into the groves and everyone knew to leave him alone until he came back, which was always a day later, and who knew where he went? He could always be found in the enveloping warmth of a meal, or in the sad notes of his dinged up saxophone with the cork stops that he kept under his bed. Uli remembers that Cuauhtémoc would piece it together when he wanted to seem deep in some way. He'd try to play some fucked up version of Coltrane (or what he told Uli was Coltrane) and they'd both sit there at the end of his bed and go "whoa." Or they would listen to Jay-Z's "Black Album," which was the only record his brother ever owned.

When Cuauhtémoc ran track, he would blast the album through the rickety speakers of his father's pickup in the school parking lot, his before-workout ritual to get the juices flowing during his stretches. He'd cruise through the speedbumps in the parking lot for show, wreck the shocks in that truck so bad that their father would always beat him up for every repair the truck needed, beat him bloody until he was reduced to a puddle at the edge of the groves.

Nobody but Uli saw that part. In the parking lot, Cuauhté-moc was a sight to be seen, *el cabrón más poderoso*. A Mexican with a pickup, with the "Black Album" cranked, and a track star at that. Not that he was the greatest, but he was good. And there was a certain fascination with the way he trained in the middle of the blacktop. He would get to doing his stretches, the key still in the ignition, the Texas sun baking his already sweaty back, everyone looking on like *what's he going to do next?* Because even to his classmates he was a familiar stranger, and being a stranger, and a brown stranger at that, people always expected something violent of him. So they watched, waited. And he performed.

His big toe creaks as Uli pushes his foot against the floor to right himself back into his seat. There's a sharp, hot pain inside his mouth. There's a throbbing at the back of his eye. Everything is blurry. And then it's not. And then it is again.

His first thought: *I'm going blind.* His second thought: *That wouldn't be so bad if that's the worst of it. But if today is Tuesday, then tomorrow is Wednesday and the day after that is June 4th, the NBA Finals, and fuck—I'm blind. How am I going to watch it? Maybe it's just a concussion,* he thinks. *But then what if it's not?*

A second wave of panic washes over Uli. He rubs his eyes, moving his left arm to his face, but everything is blurry still. Everything hurts.

Whoosh go the birds as they sweep across the grass, startled by some noise in the distance. Uli hears it too but he's too sore to crane his neck to see what it is. Something is approaching. A tinnitus builds warm and steady in the hollow space between Uli's ears, a piercing, internal ringing. He concentrates on the buttery taste of his own blood. And then that sound again. Like the snapping of twigs under a heavy foot or like the rustling of a coyote across limestone.

As the world comes back into focus, he sees the birds lift into the sky in unison. Isn't it the most beautiful thing he's ever seen, all of them shifting in the air like that, like a grey-black cloud whooshing and then gliding to the shape of the breeze? *Come back,* he wants to say. *Don't leave me.*

From the corner of his eye, he spies one lonesome bird pecking at bits of glass in his lap.

He looks at the little thing flitting around the cabin, completely unafraid of him—this thing, impossibly delicate, impossibly light.

His eyes follow the bird as it perches on his left knuckle. Uli watches as it pecks out an impossibly tiny bug crawling in the slick of his own blood, an animal that's found its way into a surface wound on his wrist.

The approaching sound grows louder. Having captured its meal, the bird flits about the cabin briefly before darting out the opened cabin door. In the blur of his vision, Uli follows it as it glides over the scarred earth beneath the wing of the Pawnee.

In the mud, a pair of boot prints meander from the aircraft toward a place over the hill. Uli's adrenaline picks up. His head whips around despite the pain. And with his head turned, Uli sees a sheet of paper. He picks it up, pulls it close to his face.

WENT FOR HELP. DON'T LEAVE.

Before he can finish reading, the sound is already upon him. And then everything is black.

The air warms and cools but the heat stays in Uli's wounds. His skin goes furry with bugs soaking their translucent wings in his cuts. The sun beats down. And then the moon. And then that collective buzz that comes from everywhere, the angry hum of the cicadas that lull him to sleep.

That night, still in the plane, Uli dreams about Cuauhtémoc. When he sees him, he can smell him, dusty-sweet just like home. He wants to tell him that he loves him, but you can't say that you love your brother to his face. You can say you love your

mother or that you love chocolate, but you can't say you love
anything else. He needs to fall asleep. He wants to forget his
pain. He makes lists to think of anything else:

First of the people he loves:
Mamá
Cuauhtémoc
Papá
Frijol #1 the Armadillo (R.I.P)
Bill the farmhand

Then of the foods he loves:
Menudo
Domino's Pizza
The McGang-Bang (A McChicken sandwich, sandwiched
between the patties of a double cheeseburger)
Cabbage
Fideo

Then bands:
Hacienda (from San Anto)
Jimi Hendrix (after '69)
The Black Keys
Shakira
Molotov

Then girls:
Teresa
Marta, his childhood crush (with eyes like drops of cham-
pagne)
Priscilla, his babysitter (with big, deer eyes)
The Bus Lady (with old lady watery eyes)
Katie, the blonde girl from school (the Mexican dream!)

Kaylee, Katie's little sister (because she's the only pretty girl who talked to him).

He makes lists until that sinking feeling grabs hold of him and drags him downward into the part of sleep where you can't remember anything—pitch black.

Uli *knows* he's on the American side because he hears Hank Williams in his head. *Hey, good lookin'.* He feels a dumb, crooked grin pull across his face. His first thought: *I'm alive.* His second thought: *Water.*

Morphine numbness courses through his veins.

On his back he feels the cotton gown. The tightness of the covers tucked over his belly and into the mattress. His arms are clammy and cold inside two black casts. His ears are ringing. With his fuzzy vision, he can barely make out what looks to be a white, painted brick wall.

Hank Williams gives way to the sound of the ocean. Giant waves all around him. Uli dreams he can breathe underwater and then he dreams he's in the sky. He couldn't fall, even if he wanted to. There's a siren in the distance. He's read about those in Mrs. Hector's Pre-AP English class. Greek Mythology. You have to cover your ears with beeswax. In his morphine drowsiness, he doesn't have beeswax, so he just listens to the sirens. He thinks they sound like popcorn in his head. The staccato sound of Spanish. Then silence.

"Where were you born?" the too-trebly sirens ask.

Uli's eyes shoot open. He tries to knock the fog from his head. The vague, fuzzy outline of a man beside his bed.

"I don't know where I was born," he says after a while.

"Do you have family?" says the man. His voice hurts Uli's ears. Both high and loud.

"Yes."

"How many?"

"One family," he tells the siren before jumping back into the waves. *What a stupid question*, he thinks. *How many families—everybody knows you only have one family.*

He feels his lips part. He panics, tries to breathe. The acidic burn of orange juice lights up every hole in his head. He wants to spit it out but his thirst is insatiable. After a while, even those pains dull too.

Uli counts the pains in his mouth by the tip of his tongue: one, two, three, four, five teeth gone. He saves the sticky pain for last. He wonders how his smile looks.

Hey, good lookin'. Hank Williams' voice again.

How many days have passed? How many bones have healed? Uli knows the answer to neither. He only knows time has passed. A long sleep.

Uli opens his eyes after the burn has passed.

A man with emerald green eyes and a white coat appears beside Uli's bed.

"How old are you?" he says. The man's mouth doesn't seem to move.

Uli's mouth is dry, so he tries to show the numbers with his hands. He lifts his wrists. A little surge of adrenaline cuts the morphine.

He blinks his eyes once, twice. A woman behind the man is wearing a skirt that fits too snug. She writes something down. Her face is a blur.

"How old?" the doctor asks again.

The woman repeats it in English to Uli, which is peculiar, he thinks, if he's in Texas. He thinks about his immigration status, about his papers. *I'll say my mother has them*, he thinks. That'll buy some time.

"Sixteen," says Uli in his best English. He thinks if he speaks English, they'll believe him when he says he's American.

"Where is my brother?" he asks, but the woman speaks over him.

"What is your name? It's very important, this question. Who are you?" the woman asks in English again. Her mouth moves but her eyes are static.

"Uli," he manages to say with his mouth swollen. His tongue feels clumsy, numb inside his head. "Brother?" he tries to say. "Brother? My brother?"

Uli's bones hurt. The bright pain of healing. Uli balls his fist with his index finger slightly extended to show them the motion of handwriting. The woman looks at the man.

"That's enough," says the man.

The warm feeling floods Uli's veins again. He fights so hard to stay awake. And then he hears the ocean again.

That night, Uli reaches for a glass of water but only finds a bottle of Peñafiel beside his bed. He looks at the bottle briefly before unscrewing the cap and throwing it across the room. He instantly regrets it. He'll have to retrieve the cap eventually to keep the water fizzy.

Three glugs and he's not sure if he can finish the whole thing, but fifteen later he's pushing for the bottom. He stops himself just short of killing the bottle. His body craves what's left. The plastic is miraculously cool to the touch. The room is hot. Uli is hot too, full of the kind of heat that rests right under the chin and smells like sulfur. There are other smells too—the antiseptic of the hospital, the reek of bleach, the tang of urine. *Why is it that all hospitals smell like urine?*

Uli puts the bottle down on the nightstand beside his bed. He clangs the hard cast on his arm against the metal rail keeping him from falling out of the bed. He feels a tug in the crick of his arm. He looks for an IV. There isn't one.

When he lifts the cover from his lower body, he's surprised to find no casts on his legs, no splints either. Just a mess of swirled bruises, more like burns than anything else. The only way Uli can tell that they're not burns is by the absence of bandages, even on his feet and his toes that look more broken than bruised.

He swings his body around so that he's sitting at the edge of the bed, his feet dangling over. He closes his eyes before pressing his feet to the ground. A jolt of white hot pain. He lets out a breath, steadies himself by throwing out one hand to the nightstand. He rocks his weight back onto his heels. He waits for his nerves to stop jangling. With his hand still on the nightstand, he searches for a light but can't find one. Three feet ahead there's a window with a single pane of frosted glass. He thinks if he can open it, there might be a sliver of light that can help him find the bottle cap. He wonders if it's even worth it. *Fuck it—it's worth it.* He's craving a Coke, but the seltzer will do. Nothing worse than tasting bad seltzer. Maybe the only thing worse in Uli's mind is *A Prairie Home Companion*—fuck that show. His mind dwells on that, rests there for a while to distract him from the pain. The thought makes him laugh, but laughing hurts too.

He gingerly transfers the weight of his body back to his feet again, his right arm on the table and his left arm thrown out in front of him for balance. He moves slowly, carefully to the window's latch on the side opposite the hinges. The closer he gets he can hear the noises bleeding in from the other side. Behind the glass everything is a blurry collage of lights and shapes and shadows. He breathes heavy through his nose, trying to get the tang of urine out of his nostrils.

When Uli gets to the window, he unlatches it and throws it open. He's hit with a cacophony of car horns, a running faucet, the too-dry squeal of a fan belt turning over inside an engine compartment, a crack of thunder; the *clap-clap-clap* of a toddler playing with some trebly toy that cuts through all the racket of the night, dogs barking, a man scraping ice, a woman fighting with her husband in Spanish, the crunching transmission of a car in the far distance.

Uli pokes his head out the window to confirm the sounds. Mexico. *Fuck. Fuck fuck fuck.* He needs a phone, an internet connection, a nurse. He looks for those buttons you see on the TV shows. *Nurse!* Nothing. *Are you supposed to yell around here?* He tries to think of the Spanish word for nurse. He's never had to use that word before. *Fuck fuck fuck.* He looks back out into the street. Outside of his hospital window a man with scars covering his body. He's got a sign that reads CAMINO SOBRE VIDRIO 5 PESOS VER PARA CREER.

The glass walker steps into the intersection just outside the window, his belly swelling so that the scars dance in the gleaming traffic light as if they were slugs crawling over his skin.

He pulls his ropy muscles taut, stretching as the traffic light turns from green to yellow to red. He's flexible at the legs but bulky in the arms and chest. He unfurls his oil-soaked towel, filled with shards, on the oil-streaked pavement by his feet. The whole mess—broken beer bottles, jars and coins—glimmers in the streetlight.

As the onlookers watch, he takes a deep breath and dives into the glass shards with his hands outstretched as if he were diving into a pool. The man rolls the length of the towel with his back, planting his feet over a blood-spattered Victoria beer bottle at the end of the rag before letting his momentum pull him backwards into the glass, all of those shards eating up the soft flesh on his back so that they bleed this ungodly bright shade of red that glows neon in the streetlight. The man does a handstand after he's rolled out. He comes down on his head in the same spot. Bits of glass in his head. He walks across the shards with his feet, eager to continue the schtick. He pulls out all the stops to keep his audience's attention. He kneel-hops across the mat on his knees. And then he leaps on one leg, kicks into a backflip, and then comes down hard on his shoulder into the pavement. The grand finale. The light turns green and the cars drive by. Some people throw coins, some people don't.

Uli looks at the bleeding man, framed in his little hospital window, and tries to pull from memory what it was like to be Mexican at one time.

The man silently collects his earnings, bending ever so gingerly to reach down with his hands at the corners of the towel to peel it up off the street, blood sluicing down his back to his waist and then onto the pavement below.

The man is careful not to spill a shard or coin as he lifts his towel up from the ground. Uli watches as he puts the towel aside before pulling out a little brush from his back pocket to sweep away the stray bits of glass underfoot. Uli feels his own pain, like needles, in his feet as he observes the man, fascinated as much by his efficiency as by his concern for everyone else's well-being—anyone else who might step on a shard of glass passing by after him.

Who is this man with so little regard for his own body but with so much respect for everyone else's? Uli wonders if this isn't the first thing he must learn about his new home—this self-abnegation, this disregard for his own body amidst this larger machine. *Who am I here? Am I anybody? Am I nobody?*

He looks at his wrist for answers. Looks for a hospital bracelet, looks for a pulse. Nothing—no tag. Not even the sound of blood beating in his ears.

He listens hard, hears the street outside funneled in through that little hospital window. The scrape of an engine, the jangle of glass shards, the blare of a food-hawker's megaphone selling midnight meals. He feels like a blank slate, all of this new world projected onto him. He checks his wrists again and again. No tag, no pulse. It's then that his reality starts to sink in: if no one checked him into the hospital, then no one is waiting for him on this side of the border. It occurs to him that his mother is coming though. Of course, she's coming to find him, and he already knows where to meet her.

Where do I go now? he thinks. The quick answer is, *Back to bed.* He thinks he'll guzzle the last of the water and wait for another bottle in the morning. He wonders who is going to pay for all of this?

He thinks he'll find his clothes tomorrow. There's some money in his bloody tracksuit—birthday money. He looks about the room for it. No luck.

He limps back to the bed and slides himself under the covers. He stares at the ceiling and feels a swelling in his chest. Something like guilt over the idea that he's ruined his body. Guilt over the idea, too, that he's undone his family's life work. Of course, they're going to come look for him.

TRAITORS

LALO ONLY NEEDS ONE MORE SOUL. One more body from the streets of Matamoros to fill his quota. But it's June 4, Mule's Day, the feast of Corpus Christi, and nobody is out in the streets. *Anyone will do by now,* thinks Lalo. Then he remembers what his boss, El Jimmy, told him this morning: A kidnapped engineer or doctor would suffice, or someone who could fly a plane, with drugs, money, people. In short, someone who could speed up their departure. El Jimmy to his house in California, Lalo to anywhere in Texas where there are good schools for his daughter—the Woodlands maybe. He wonders if all of this isn't a pipe dream by now. Driving the streets of Matamoros, he's no longer looking for *the* body anymore, but rather *any* body. Any soul to fill his quota, to get Jimmy off his back.

Lalo steers his white painter's van just off downtown and smells the Tres Flores brilliantine on his upper lip from where El Jimmy grabbed him by the face with both hands as if to kiss him and said, "I know the end is tough. I know this is tough. We all want what's best for our families." More threat than comfort in his soft voice.

It reminded Lalo of his uncle who would always speak like that right before he would kiss him. He'd keep speaking in that way, soft like heather, as Lalo would pull his pants sagging around his ankles. Lalo remembers that one day he punched his uncle in the throat and the comic-tragedy of it all was that his uncle spoke that way for the rest of his life, his voice stuck in that wispy register so common among *viejos* and smokers and throat cancer survivors. Driving, Lalo smells the Tres Flores and remembers what that anger felt like. Remembers it felt good. But more than anything, he remembers the feel of his uncle's hands all over his body.

Lalo idles at an intersection and stares at his painted purple finger tips splayed over the top of the steering wheel, his hands unsure of which way to turn, left or right. He looks into the lacquered, glittery purple as if to consult them like one might consult a crystal ball. His daughter picked out the color. She said it went with his outfit, which was only partially true. It matched the purple boots that he bought after the divorce, which came like a lightning bolt into his life, splitting him into countless pieces, every piece a different version of himself. He thinks about that—how inside us there are nesting dolls of who we were five years ago, who we were five years before that. And coming undone, he thinks, is just confronting every self you've ever inhabited—father, husband, son, *puto*, killer. Emptying yourself like a shaggy *piñata*.

Idling at the intersection, he looks at his reflection in the rearview mirror. He thinks about how poorly he's aged now that he's nearing forty. He thinks about Darwin. Survival of the fittest. *So, this is the version of me that's won out?*

Every day he gets that feeling, like looking into the bathroom mirror on a bad morning. In his earlier days he looked like a dark Matthew McConaughey, his black curls greased back with pineapple-scented Moco de Gorila gel. High cheekbones. A long, lanky frame. Black eyes that smoldered like coals.

But now, looking in the mirror, his fat has rounded out his features. His hollow cheeks have filled. His skin is shiny, thinnere. The corners of his hairline have crept back so that his widow's peak grows more pronounced by the year. Below his chin, he's conscious that his chest has grown flabbier in recent months too. He tries to hide his breasts with brightly colored button-downs that distract from the shape of his body—fuchsias, bright reds, purples, yellows, greens. He always wears jeans and a button-up and, of course, those purple boots.

With no one in sight, he parks the van two blocks from Plaza Miguel Hidalgo and gets out on foot in search of candy to satisfy his sweet tooth. Even with no one out in the streets to see him, he feels uncomfortable in his own skin. He smells the Tres Flores as the breeze lets up. He thinks of his uncle. *Anything for my daughter. One more body,* he thinks, desperately trying to remember how to turn his self-hatred outward onto the world.

Lalo finds Cuauhtémoc collapsed on a bench in Plaza Miguel Hidalgo. A flat, black curly head of hair. A lean and lanky frame. Cuauhtémoc's shirt is sliced from the collar to right under the armpit of his sleeve. His hands are a mangled mess of blood, though the rest of him seems intact if only by shape. As far as Lalo is concerned, Cuauhtémoc's legs look like legs, his feet look like feet. But upon closer inspection, Lalo can see the bruises up and down the back of Cuauhtémoc's neck. They disappear into his shirt collar before emerging as road rash—or something resembling it—on his forearms. Lalo looks Cuauhtémoc in the face. Some burn marks where Cuauhtémoc's hairline meets his forehead. The reek of gasoline all over him.

Lalo figures that Cuauhtémoc could pass for his own brother if he were twenty years older or, perhaps, if Lalo was twenty years younger—what he wouldn't give to be that young again.

Lalo thinks the boy could be American, but he'd have to open his mouth to see for sure. Lalo knows, like everyone knows, that American teeth are instantly recognizable—healthy, straight, everything in place. *An American would be good,* Lalo thinks. *An American family would pay out good ransom at least.*

Lalo notices blood from Cuauhtémoc's pant leg dribbling onto the concrete. It's only when Cuauhtémoc adjusts himself that Lalo sees that the toes on his left foot have been crushed to a purple mess, his boot lost somewhere.

Could be a beat-up homeless person, Lalo thinks. *One of those kids who have ridden up from Guatemala and bottlenecked here once they found they couldn't cross into Texas. Or maybe one of those recently deported teenagers, the ones who always get jumped, the ones who file out of those gray buses in Brownsville and march across the international bridge, chain-gang style, until they're released halfway over, ghosts wandering into the streets of Matamoros.*

Lalo has taken his fair share of the latter. Teenagers are easy prey. They all want to belong to something bigger than themselves. They all have this cartoonish idea of what it means to be a man, what it means to be a *chingón*. That's what he wanted, anyway, when he was that age, eighteen, when his father lost everything after the floodgates of NAFTA opened and put their little farm out of business.

That little parcel of land just east of Torreón was his family's pride, but also their undoing. Lalo's grandfather obtained it after joining Villa's División del Norte as a teenage soldier in 1912, during the Mexican Revolution. Lalo remembers how his grandfather had said it was the silver of their spurs that made him want to join more than anything. He wanted to be a chingón. He wanted to belong to something outside of what he knew. But more than anything, he wanted boots like those, spurs like those.

It was only after his first battle in Celaya that his grandfather got those boots. Stole them off a soldier who died next to him. Lalo remembers how even as an old man his grandfather would still wear them in the fields, polished so bright that they stood apart from the dirt that put a patina over everything, even the cows that grazed on dirt but still produced milk, if only by the grace of God.

His grandfather was proud of those boots, but even prouder of his parcel of land that he got by petition along with a dozen other burnouts from the División del Norte. They made up an *ejido* after the war, a system of sharecroppers that repossessed the land east of Torreón that the rich abandoned for greener pastures in Texas, California, New Mexico—away from the battlefields of the Revolution, away from the land that had given them so much.

Maybe it was because Lalo's grandfather had fought, or maybe it was because he couldn't stand the idea of waste, or maybe it was because he couldn't stand the idea of cutting and running that he came to resent those people who owned the land before him, who had enough money to leave forever. It was in this way that he came to teach his sons (and by extension, Lalo) that only the weak left the land. Every Mexican who went north, who left Mexico for a better life, was a traitor. Because the land gave you everything—food, water, shelter, dignity. It was the great irony of Lalo's grandfather's life that the day after he died, the farm stopped giving.

NAFTA happened. And it wasn't long before subsidized American milk flooded the Mexican market to undercut what little their cows could produce. The land around them got bought up. The milk spoiled in the containers. And still Lalo and his father refused to leave the land. Lalo came to hate everyone who went north. More than that, though, he came to hate the Mexicans who somehow made it, against all odds, *en el Norte*.

Lalo remembers wondering if there was anything left for him here. Of course, he thought about going north. Making some easy money to send back home. At one time he thought he might save the farm, might save his aging father who was dying of heart failure. And it wasn't until a silver truck rolled up at the ranch gates one day that he saw a glimmer of hope in the boots of a man who stepped down onto the dirt of their field. A man who promised Lalo anything if he was only willing to carry a gun.

Looking down at Cuauhtémoc's blood, Lalo thinks about those boots coming out of that truck. He knows what's going to happen to Cuauhtémoc if they can't ransom him. Lalo knows it won't be a quick death, but a body is a body and he needs one. One more for the day. One more, and put this boy out of his misery.

Just then, Lalo thinks of his daughter. Thinks about that thing his grandfather used to tell him: *the descendants of traitors are still traitors*. He hears those words as he kneels down to put his face close to Cuauhtémoc's before prying his jaw open with his fingers to examine his teeth.

Cuauhtémoc wakes to the sound of the road in his head, his temple pressed to the van's gritty floor. His first thought: *I want to go home*. His second thought: *I'm dying of thirst*.

There's tape over his mouth. He couldn't drink even if he tried, but that doesn't stop him from thinking about water passing through his body, ice cold streams of it falling down into his belly.

He'd panic if his adrenaline weren't shot already—too much of it in his system from the pain. He's almost numb now. Just the sound of road in his skull again and his own thirst that occupies his mind and lets him know he's still live.

He tries to scratch an itch on his nose. In this way, he finds that his hands are zip-tied behind his back. Cuauhtémoc rolls onto his belly, starts to panic now. A metallic taste coming from his gums. His thirst is replaced by a tightening at the top of his wind pipe. A small, hyperventilating hiss is all the noise he can muster, like that remarkable noise cattle make once they know they're being led to slaughter. Cuauhtémoc remembers that noise from the summers of his childhood—this in the time before his family left for Texas—on that farm of his uncle's just outside of San Miguel in Chihuahua. Within the sound of his own bleating voice he can see, against the dark of his eyelids, his father as a young man, ankle-high in rivulets of blood that stained his skin so deep it became a kind of rust he could never wash off. In those days, when his father and his uncle slaughtered cattle, Cuauhtémoc remembers that his father could do nothing but talk of Texas, daydream about that new life as if the mere soil of the United States would wash the bloody rust from his skin, make him a shade lighter with that indoor job he so coveted. Within that sound of his own voice, Cuauhtémoc can see his father at the end of those killing days, his bloody fingertips tapping out the rhythm over the arms of a wooden chair to those jazz records—John Coltrane, Chet Baker, Thelonius Monk. American sounds falling on his ears like news long delayed to a prodigal son out there wandering but always wondering about home. Cuauhtémoc thinks that's how his father saw himself—as an American first, an undocumented immigrant second. And at this he thinks back to the crash, feels the pain in his bones. *How did I end up here?* He wonders and feels his own skin rusting with dried blood. He thinks about his father. He thinks about his brother. He thinks about that shame and fear resonating now in the hiss at the top of his throat.

At the far side of the van's bed, he sees dusty light piercing its way in through the cracks of the doors. At least it's still daylight. *Some hours have passed,* he thinks. Not too long. *Don't fight it.* He drifts in and out of consciousness. He succumbs to the burn of his thirst and lets his soul lie in that place for a while, his skin thirsty for air.

They drive for hours until they reach a town called Potrero. Midnight wind brings sound in on its breeze. From this dusty little town's one good juncture, the trickling noise of sulfur springs bubbling black at the spillway under the town's one rusty bridge. Under the awning of the rodeo corral, just beyond the town cantina, there's the sound of whistling laughter that breaks from the wet lips of the men and women inside. Then comes the sound that silences the cantina: the grinding pull of the diesel engines revving down the road, past the juncture, past the cantina, across the town's one rusted bridge, into the swinging gates of the rodeo corral, into that place the locals call the killing field.

The white van stops short of the far gate by the awning, where the rodeo spectators might sit, and Lalo hops out and opens the back door. An old man, blindfolded and gagged, steps from the passenger side of the van. A teenaged boy hangs the canvas strap of a little league baseball bag around the old man's neck and leads him hobbling toward the center of the corral. Once there, Lalo unzips the bag and takes out a rusted chain and a machete.

"This one first," says Lalo.

All eyes are on the old man.

At Lalo's direction, the teenaged boy pulls the tape from Cuauhtémoc's mouth with his skinny, sticky fingers. Cuauhté-moc's face is bloated. Every tooth throbs inside his head. There's blood in his mouth but he's too dry to spit, his lips stuck together, his whole mouth shut closed. He runs his tongue across the inside of his cheek. Rough and raw inside. The metallic taste of blood. He lets his tongue roll into the groove where his molar used to be. He gathers enough moisture to spit, but it comes out too aspirated, too thin. A sliver of tooth dribbles onto his chin.

The boy hoists Cuauhtémoc up by the shoulders and cuts the zip tie around his wrists. The feeling comes flooding back to his fingertips, as tingly and numb as they may be, and he can barely stand the pin pricks in his skin, first slow, and then wild like a swarm of ants. He feels his knees crick, the blood pouring back down into his legs. His heart quickens. Everything is bright. A shot of cortisol to the heart. He thinks about running, but he doesn't trust his legs.

The old man is staring at the machete stuck upright in the ground.

Of all things Cuauhtémoc thinks about just then, he remembers when he and Uli were little and how they would stave off boredom in the groves with this one question: What is the worst way to kill someone? Cuauhtémoc remembers he would always come up with the worst ones, the ones that were scarier than ghost stories, the ones that made him wonder about himself—if he was sane or not.

There's one time that he told Uli that the worst way to kill someone was by lowering them into a pile of ants. Another time he told him it was by dropping him off a highway bridge. How many times had they talked about this over a cool glass of Coke at odd hours of the night when neither of them could sleep?

The old man opposite Cuauhtémoc goes for the machete. Cuauhtémoc can faintly make out the tattoo on the back of his bald head. A she-devil holding a rifle. The old man lifts his machete and touches the sharp edge with the tip of his finger. He moves toward Cuauhtémoc and lifts it.

For Cuauhtémoc, everything is a blur after this. He remembers a tremor, a thin line of red and then shock turned to rage turned to action. Cuauhtémoc looks down to his arm flayed just above the elbow. And here comes the pain, finally, as he's been expecting it all along. A surgical kind of pain, cold and precise.

The old man swings again. This time Cuauhtémoc tumbles out of his way toward the ground, and the swing misses. There's a percussive racket between his ears and then the burning squeal of the machete blade slicing the air. Cuauhtémoc catches the small of the blade close to the handle mid-flight with the palm of his hand. The blade slides across Cuauhtémoc's tendon. White heat in his nerves. He grips the machete with a bloody, clenched fist. The old man's knuckles go white around the handle. Their muscles tense but neither of them move.

At this point, the old man knows he's going to die because though he's uninjured, his energy is fading. And when he finally loses grip of the machete, he runs. He jumps a giant puddle of stagnant water and trips on his forward momentum when he lands. For Cuauhtémoc, that image is burned into his memory forever—a dying man jumping a puddle just to keep his feet dry. And then Cuauhtémoc is upon him.

There are no reservations for Cuauhtémoc, at least none that he might remember. If he remembers anything, it's the look on Lalo's face as he unzips the old man's skin with the edge of the blade, the man's flesh pouring out into the open air, expanding from under his skin like so many saturated sheets of dyed, wet cotton. There's an ashen look in Lalo's eyes as the natural order of his life comes undone, the very unraveling of it an omen as dark as his own shame.

In that moment, Cuauhtémoc watches Lalo moved by the old man's death. He watches Lalo shudder as the old man's voice ricochets from the one good hill in town, though the rattle of his throat carries on much further than that.

BAD NEWS FRIEND

THE NIGHT OF THE CRASH, Araceli dreams she's a fish. She can breathe underwater. She can look up to the silvery surface where the air meets the waves. She can see stars. Beyond that, darkness.

She's jolted from sleep by five raps on her trailer door. Araceli thinks three knocks are friendly, but five knocks mean business.

Each knock is measured, equally spaced apart. Before she can shake the sleep from her head, she knows there's a cop at the door.

She's not dizzy anymore, but her head aches. There's dried blood on her upper lip. She looks at the duct tape over her bedroom door. She remembers the pesticides made their way into the house last night. She only vaguely remembers everything that came after she fainted.

The knocks come again, only this time they don't stop.

Araceli bolts from her bed to the bedroom door. She rips the tape off, pulls the door open. She goes to the bathroom window that looks out to the front of the trailer. She spots a police cruiser parked beside the pickup. Her suspicions are confirmed.

On the porch steps, the shadow of a man wearing a Stetson hat.

"Fuck," she says to herself. *Fuck* is her favorite English word—she knows every grammatical usage of it. She knows you say it when the cops come. Cops are never good. Cops deported her husband. She thinks of a way out of this. She looks behind her.

"Uli!" she hisses between her teeth, her voice splattering against the bathroom tile and then out into the hallway. She knows Uli speaks better English than his older brother, whom she brought to Texas too old. She knows the cop won't suspect Uli of being undocumented—nobody does. He can explain his way. She calls his name again. Nothing.

"Cuauhtémoc!" she hisses. No response.

Five knocks again. Then the sound of her own blood beating hard in her ear.

"Sheriff's Department," shouts a man on the other side of the door.

Araceli freezes in the bathroom hallway. And before the Sheriff can knock again she's at the kitchen window, her right foot hobbling behind as she stutter-steps across the floor.

"Fucking Cuauhtémoc!" she hisses. "Uli—fucking Uli."

That usually gets their attention. She waits. No response from either of them. She swings around on her bad foot to square herself with the window above the sink before unlatching the heavy pane.

She clacks the window up and climbs onto the counter, looking out into the orange groves. *I can make it*, she thinks. If she can't, then she'll get caught, which wouldn't be so bad. She feels a little pang of shame at the excitement of possibly being deported. She would miss her sons but she would be able to live her life the way it used to be—before she met her husband, before she made a family for no other reason than it was the thing to do. To leave the trailer would mean a new life beyond the milk jug in the road. A life of no fear, no hiding. *Deportation wouldn't be so bad,* Araceli thinks.

"Fuck it," she says to herself.

She gets her arms out first and then her torso before the sheriff rounds the corner of the house, the heels of his boots clomping up chunks of wet earth. Araceli feels his eyes on her.

"Ma'am, that's about an eight-foot drop, head first. I'd say if you're resigned to break every bone in your arms you can go for it. Otherwise you can climb back in the window and open the door. Either way, we're gonna talk. Not to alarm you or nothing. I just need to talk with you."

Araceli sizes up the sheriff from way up in the window. He's a small man for his booming voice, although he's big around the waist. Ashy brown hair, brown eyes. His leather belt squeaks under his paunch as he shifts his weight from one foot to the other.

"*No hablo inglés,*" she says to him, her torso hanging out the window.

"*Será bien,*" says the sheriff.

Fuck, she thinks.

It's only a few moments before she pulls herself in from the window to open the door. She pours a cup of dehydrated coffee from the percolator that's timed to go off at 8:00 every morning. It's 9:20 on the coffee maker's clock. She figures a cup of coffee will smooth things over. "Common misunderstanding," she practices in English under her breath. She's heard the grove boss say that before. She sets both feet on the ground and starts for the door. She unlocks it, shoves it open just as the sheriff rounds the house again and makes his way up the ramp.

"Some coffee?" she says in broken English. "Common misunderstanding. You know?" she says confidently.

She smiles too big. She feels embarrassed of her teeth. She thinks that it'll be her first time being deported. Not bad for almost fifteen years here. She knows people who have had it worse. Deported the first day on the job or deported right after a child was born.

The sheriff takes his hat off before entering Araceli's home. He sets himself down in front of Araceli's own cup, which she sets out every night on the Formica table before going to bed. Araceli pours the cup in her hand into the one in front of him. The sheriff smiles a little and then nods.

He hangs his hat on his knee, the underside of the table scarring the felt around the Stetson crown as he rocks his boots back and forth over the blue carpet, his leather belt squeaking.

The sheriff is quiet. Araceli wonders what business he has here. Maybe something about Eugenio, her husband, she thinks. That has to be it. The thought of it makes her sweat. She thinks if he were going to deport her and her sons, he'd have come with more people. So, it must be Eugenio.

"Some milk?" she says, breaking the silence.

"Just black, thank you," says the sheriff, grasping Araceli's cup now between his fingers.

"Sugar?"

"No, thank you."

Araceli sits in suspense at the other end of the Formica table.

"I'm going to speak slowly," says the sheriff, "so you can understand. Understand?"

"Yes, I understand," says Araceli.

"Just a few questions first."

"Okay," says Araceli. "Few questions. Okay."

"First things first: Do you know where the grove boss might be? According to my notes, it's a man by the name of Sampson?"

"Sampson gone."

"Where to? How long?"

"Two week. Vacation. I no know where."

"Is that his hangar out back?"

"I no know hangar."

"Airplane. *Avioncito.*"

"Yes. Airplane."

"When was the last time you saw your sons?"

"I no understand," she says, struggling with the English.

"*Hijos,*" says the sheriff.

"Two *hijos,*" says Araceli.

"Where?" says the sheriff. "*¿Dónde?*"

"Here," she says. "Birthday *anoche.*"

"Whose birthday?"

"Little son. Uli."

"Last night?"

"*Anoche,*" she says to him. A sinking feeling creeps into her belly. "Is there wrong?" she asks him.

Araceli doesn't hear much after that. Just words. *Plane. Crash. Night. Not Found.* She collapses into her seat at the Formica table, the sheriff across from her. The puppy jumps up on his lap, licking at his fleshy hands. Araceli stares at the veins on the back of his hand. She looks at the dog's blood-stained mouth. She feels her own dried blood still on her upper lip from her nose-bleed the night before. She wipes the blood away with the back of her hand.

"Not found," Araceli says, "not same as lost."

The sheriff nods, which gives Araceli some hope.

In his broken Spanish, he explains the plane's emergency location transmitter had been bleeping on the mayday frequency through the night. The NTSB couldn't tell where it'd crashed, on which side of the border, that gray zone made up of dried riverbed and ranches—all private property.

"*Bien difícil para encontrar.* Really complicated to get to, you understand?" says the sheriff to Araceli.

Araceli nods that she does.

"Have you heard from them?" he asks her, switching back into English, speaking slowly.

"No," she says.

The sheriff takes his hat from his knee and puts it back on his head. She thinks he's going to go, but he stays in place at the table, nursing his coffee with one hand and rubbing the puppy with his other, his big leathery palm over the crown of the dog's head.

The sheriff stares out of the kitchen window as if looking for something in the highway. Araceli feels a certain anger toward him just then. For all of the trouble he's gone through to get here, he doesn't seem as concerned all of a sudden. Araceli is angered at his presence, at the fact that he's still here, at the way he anchors himself like he belongs here, at the fact that he does. His country, not hers.

Araceli wonders what he's searching for if not her boys. Or her husband. She wonders if he's trying to comfort her but can't find the words. She keeps sitting at the table with him because it's rude to let someone sit alone. But she wishes he'd leave. She needs to act. She needs to do something *right now*. Go find her boys, go fix the truck.

She takes out the little square of satin from her side satchel and rubs it with her hand the way the sheriff is rubbing the crown of the dog's head.

The sheriff breaks his gaze, looks down. He asks her, "What's that?"

"Satin," she says in English, reaching over the table for the puppy. The sheriff takes the puppy from his lap and hands it over to Araceli who places it in her lap. She takes a safety pin from her dress and pushes the sharp end through the middle of the cloth before pushing it once more through the fabric of the puppy's collar so that the square hangs off the puppy like another one of his tags.

"What are you doing?" he asks.

Araceli knows that to tell the truth to the sheriff would make her seem foolish, simple. She's superstitious. *So what?* Everyone knows you use dogs to find people. They find everyone eventually.

Outside of her home, Araceli says to the sheriff, "It's just satin," without explaining anything further. She puts the puppy's feet in the dirt and lets it wander out into the groves. She feels the intense stare of the sheriff's eyes on the nape of her neck. She knows he's wondering, *What crazy woman is this?* Which is how she knows she's alone in her search. She knows, already, that she's going back to Mexico. She's going to find her family. She already knows where they are.

That night, Araceli hobbles down from her trailer to the truck parked next to it. She hops into the cabin to release the creaky pull-lever that sets the hood groaning, the rusted spring-loaded hinges pushing against the pull of the hood clasp just behind the grill. At the sound, she feels a pang of anger well up in her chest at the thought of having to explain all of this to Sampson. Of course, the plane would be their first concern. Her family would come second. *But this is not going to happen,* she thinks. *I'll be gone long before that.*

At this, her disparate angers and fears and hopes fuse into a single knot in her throat as she looks into the smoke-blackened engine compartment, that chemical smell—either from the truck or the trees—wafting up into the air again. She knows she'll have to work fast. She's resigned to it: she'll work through the night.

The skies are dark. There's a purple tint to the air. A flock of the tiniest birds she's ever seen glide in the shape of the wind. They blot out the moonlight.

From the hangar, Araceli borrows a funnel, a can of belt dressing, a gallon of distilled water, a bottle of DOT 5 brake fluid, a bottle of steering fluid, a bottle of 5W-20 engine oil and something called Magical Mystery Oil which says on the red bottle that it can fix anything. Araceli carries it all to the rusty Ford Lobo in a plastic grocery bag, except for the bottle of Magic Mystery Oil which she carries in her arm like a baby, like something precious that can't be trusted to the inferior carrying capabilities of plastic.

She places it all, including the mystery oil, on the ground just under the driver's side fender.

Araceli takes the key, hidden under the driver's side mat, and sticks it in the ignition. She kicks the emergency brake pedal on the floor before trying to turn the engine over. She gives it a little gas. Just a series of clicks. Nothing. Araceli hops from the truck and rounds the fender.

In front of Araceli, just a mangled mess of rust and dust, the complexities of the engine compartment like the map of a foreign land she barely remembers.

She's worked on engines before—when she was younger and her slender fingers made her an asset to her father's farm—but her memory is hazy. She stopped working on cars the day she didn't have to anymore, which is to say the day she married Eugenio, although he barely knew his elbow from his asshole, let alone a wrench from a socket.

Araceli never let on that she knew how to fix his mistakes. Partly to shield his own fragile male ego, but also because she held out hope, however slim, that he might throw in the towel and buy them a new truck someday.

She looks at the engine and tries to remember everything she learned from girlhood, tries to remember how to unfuck up her husband's handiwork.

Araceli starts with the radiator right in front of her. She takes off the service cap and pours in half the gallon of distilled water. She takes the funnel and pours the quart of oil into the engine next. She takes the same funnel and moves to the separate compartments of cylindrical steering fluid and brake fluid. She unscrews the bottle of Magical Mystery Oil with the hem of her dress and throws the cap to the ground. With the fabric, she stops up the mouth of the bottle, turning it upside down to soak into the fabric. She smells the oil—synthetic like gasoline but also fragrant like laundry detergent. She pauses for a second, a kind of reverence she gives the moment, before taking the hem and cleaning the spark plugs under the disconnected leads of the distributor. She lets the oil dissolve the carbon deposits one by one, taking her time until the plugs shine like silver in the morning light. She blows on the leads, connects them. She pulls them away, douses them with Magical Mystery Oil before reconnecting them again. She lets the bottle sit at the corner of the engine compartment and, with belt dressing in hand, she observes her handiwork. She rounds the fender again, cranks the ignition.

The engine turns once, twice before it catches and purrs to life, the dried, stiff fan belt letting out a high squeal as it flaps along in its serpentine pattern. Araceli hops out of the truck to spray it with the belt dressing until the noise dies away.

She pulls the bottle of Magical Mystery oil from the engine compartment and kisses it. She takes it and splashes a healthy sluice over the vibrating engine that's moving so fast it's all a blur. Araceli watches the red beads of oil hit the engine before rippling into a splash with the vibration, exploding outwards into a fine mist that colors the air an aspirated shade of pink. The air in front of her turns iridescent. She loves the chemical smell. She splashes the oil over the engine again and again like a priest splashing holy water over a congregation. The pistons sing. *Proof,* Araceli thinks, *that anything can be brought back from the dead.* Even her sons, her husband, her entire world if she's patient enough.

ᘏᕒ ᘏᕒ ᘏᕒ

On slow mornings like this—most mornings are slow these days—Iván sometimes stands in front of the vanity and wonders if he isn't the only thing that's aged in Hotel Luna. He stands in front of the mirror this morning and checks for any new gray hairs, any new wrinkles that have appeared overnight. He's only 60 but he thinks he might look a decade older. His photographer's hunch has made him a full inch shorter than his former 5'5" frame. He's narrow in the shoulders. He has a little belly. He wears square bifocals whose temples have broken off long ago and have since been replaced with green twine that he's attached at the hinges and looped behind his ear to keep them on. Though he doesn't know it, his clothes belong to that time-capsule as well. He wears the same green sweater that he bought with his first check as a photographer for a magazine called *Extremo* in the mid-eighties. The brown buttons on his beige shirt and brown pants have either chipped or fallen away. He makes up for that slouchy, sloppy way his clothes hang on him by ironing the creases of his pants and shirt to death. Everything about him suggests he's clean but washed out, completely dried up in every way.

He sits down behind the faux marble counter of the hotel to read the day's news. But as soon as he does, Iván glances up from his paper and stares at the plague of grackles perched along the streetlamps and powerlines and frayed banner string that cut up the sky of Matamoros. He hates those birds for the noise they make, but he hates them more for being untethered. He lays his paper down and gets up off his own perch behind the counter in his five-bedroom hotel and steps outside to feel the heat rising up from the pavement into the soles of his cheap Tres Hermanos brand sneakers. He throws his hands together into a single palmy clap, the sound of which ricochets from the concrete squat single-stories across the street and trebles out with a long, electric *waaaaang* that sets the birds up from their perch, all of them in unison. They take off into the sky like a long, black cloud overhead. Just the flapping of their wings. And then that sound that Iván so much longs for—silence, if only for a little while.

He soaks in the quiet the way he does every morning. He closes his tired eyes and exhales and then, as if resigned to his own fate, he walks back into Hotel Luna—that hotel which he never wanted in the first place, which he inherited from his mother immediately following her death ten years ago and holds him every day like a rat in a cage.

To Iván, everything around him is a time capsule of when his mother was still alive: the counter; the too-large, mahogany vanity that takes up the short wall perpendicular to the counter that gives the tiny foyer the optical illusion of being bigger than it really is; the pale, green doors that seal off each bedroom; the digital cash register from the 80s that just won't die; the brass hooks screwed into the wall behind the counter with four-sided Enfield keys hanging from each one except the last one, which has Iván's old plastic Diana camera hanging from a leather strap.

He'd stopped shooting right after his mother died but made it a point to keep that camera around, if only to remind him of who he is or, rather, who he *was* at one time in his life: a photographer with a beat and a budget and a plastic lens which distorted everything but through which he saw the world that his mother tried her entire life to keep him from.

As a boy, Iván had spent three quarters of his childhood behind that faux marble counter. His mother had her various reasons.

At first it was sun-exposure (too much of it). And as he grew into a teenager, it was the gang violence she saw on TV. And as he grew older still, it was the general violence of Matamoros, which could be escaped but couldn't be denied—the images were on every newsstand around their hotel. And it was in this way—when Iván went to buy a Coke for his mother, say, or when (often) he'd sneak out to buy a *Playboy* for himself— he also came to know these images, love them even, because along with the violence came stories and details about the world around him.

He'd buy one copy of every crime magazine he could get his hands on. His favorite, by far, was *Extremo*. He loved it not because the stories were particularly good or the violence more or less graphic than in any other magazine, but because each issue came with a sensuous centerfold that he'd quickly rip from the stapling, fold into an impossibly tiny square, and stick behind his driver's license in his wallet. Instead of buying *Extremo* and *Playboy*, he could get two for one. There was a new woman every week to masturbate to in his room above the hotel, hating himself for finding any pleasure at all in the women that had been chosen for him by some crusty editor whose taste was 70s Americana. Aqua Net hair spray, Lycra everything, bad eyeshadow that came in all colors of pastels.

It was during one of Iván's typical mid-morning masturbation sessions that the reality of his situation dawned on him. He was in his early 30s, unmarried, childless, careerless and still under his mother's thumb. Something had to change.

It was in that desperate moment, with his pants around his ankles and this faux french maid with blue eyeshadow looking up at him from the glossy page, that he flipped over the image and found, to his great surprise, a classified ad on the back. *Extremo* was in need of a photographer. And Iván decided, then and there, that he would be their man. Never mind the fact that he'd never owned a camera. Never mind the fact that he'd rarely left his block. Never mind that he would finally, probably, have to meet the man who chose these centerfolds and shake his crusty little hand. He was going to do it. And so that day he borrowed the teal Diana from his cousin, Erica, she'd won it at a carnival in Dallas and accidentally kept it in nearly pristine condition due to the fact that it was the worst camera she'd ever owned and had thrown it in a shoebox under her bed and forgotten about it until the day Iván called and didn't so much ask to borrow it as demand it from her.

She warned him in advance. Everything about the Diana was plastic. The casing around the camera was made from two molds that clicked together and so it suffered light leaks that would expose the film. The plastic lens distorted everything in front of it, and even when you got the right angle, the edges of the photograph would blur. She told him that he would waste more film than any money he could possibly earn, but this was assuaged by the simple fact that the Diana Erica handed over came with three rolls of 35mm film previously unused, along with a black, narrow strap that seemed to hug Iván's shoulder as if it were custom made.

Because the Diana was a horrible camera, no amount of skill could enhance the outcome of any one photograph. But for Iván, the entire exercise came as natural to him as if he were a seasoned photographer. At the very least, the result was the same: plastic, dream-like photographs whose blurry edges gave the impression that each subject wasn't already dead but in the process of dying. While other photographers' cameras professionally snapped and whirred alongside him at any given scene, a simple plastic *click* sounded from Iván's camera. Often, it would happen that the flash of another camera or the intensity of the street light above or the headlights of a passing car would leak into the casing, exposing the film inside. Streaks of orange would cloud the photograph, occasionally appearing just above the body. These were the ones *Extremo* loved the most. They always wrote about how their photographer could capture souls right as they were departing the body, that orange haze (always consistently there) proof enough. And it was in this way that Iván made a name for himself in crime reporting, his photography always maintaining that impressionist quality that became the style of his era.

He was fearless—or stupid as some in the industry said—in that he was willing to photograph any corpse in any part of the city at any time of the night. No questions asked. Such was his loyalty to *Extremo* for ripping him from the Hotel Luna that had imprisoned him for the better part of his life. He never made much money, but it was enough for him to live on as long as he had the free room above the Hotel Luna, where he slept only when he had to.

To this day, he does not know which published photograph set someone off on the dark path of revenge. He does know, however, which one ended his career. Truth be told, he'd never thought of photographing murder as particularly humiliating to the corpse or to the corpse's living family, for that matter. He only saw those murders for what they were: murders and nothing more, nothing less. In his heart, he knew there was no art to what he was doing. No redeeming quality or skill to those photographs. Just reporting. Just a cheap camera. Just a way to get out of the Hotel Luna.

It should have come as no surprise, after having worked in the industry for more than ten years that eventually the gore would find its way to the other side of his lens and grip him as it had so many other photojournalists in Matamoros.

He remembers that it was his mother's body that ruined his career. He remembers the smell more than anything. That familiar iron rot that permeated so many murder scenes he'd photographed before. That dampness tinged with the sweet smell of his mother's perfume, like lilacs in the air. That same smell by his bedside of so many nights of his childhood. That same sweet lilac that was always thickest behind his mother's perch behind the faux marble counter of Hotel Luna. He put his camera down that night and crawled into the bed beside her, 70 open knife wounds in her flesh, and put his opened palm over every single one as if to try to stop the blood that was already congealing on her skin. He whispered something to her that he no longer remembers. If anything, he remembers heat of camera flashes on his skin once his colleagues arrived. The slick of the blood on the side of his face.

From inside Hotel Luna, Iván watches a hawk boy no older than ten—the street eyes of the Zeta cartel or the Gulf cartel or the Juárez cartel, he can't tell which one anymore—snap pictures of something with a cheap HTC One phone camera. Iván knows the boy well or, rather, he's seen the boy countless times over the last few years. He's seen the boy age day by day, seen him go about his morning routine: photograph the street, then photograph the cars on the street, then photograph the license plates of the cars parked on the street, then photograph anything worth seeing on that given day—a busted water pipe, a traffic accident, a fist-fight in the Soriana grocery parking lot three blocks down, limes rolling everywhere—and uploads it all to the cloud for someone to see.

☙ ☙ ☙ ☙

Araceli doesn't know it yet when she returns to Mexico looking for her sons, but everyone on that side of the border wants a piece of what they did. It's in every paper on both sides of the border. Depending on which newspaper editor has which gun pointed to his head, every paper writes a different version of the same story. Some papers say it was the Zetas who shot down a Sinaloa cartel aircraft. Other papers say it was the Juárez cartel reviving their trade routes with rookie pilots. The Mexican government claims to own the official, historical truth about what happened, which is that their military shot down an unnamed cartel's plane about to enter American airspace—let it be a warning to those that might try to undermine the Mexican state.

Nearly every article concludes by saying that one pilot is at large and the other is at a Matamoros area hospital, under surveillance of the Mexican authorities. In one newspaper, there's a grainy border surveillance photograph of Cuauhtémoc scrambling from the aircraft just after it crashed. In another newspaper, there's a picture of the wreckage. As Mexican news goes, everyone believes what they need to hear. And because of this, everyone in Mexico seems to be looking for Araceli's sons too. Their mother knows none of this because she's kept the pickup's radio off to save the battery.

Araceli gets to north Matamoros when a plume of smoke breaks from under the edges of the rusted pickup hood. The smell of gasoline pours in from the A/C vents as she skids along the curb toward the Hotel Luna.

Across the street, an elementary school. So many faces pressed to the window looking down on her. At the corner, another boy with a Nextel phone snapping pictures.

Araceli hops from the pickup, coughing up smoke. A trickle of blood streams from her nose. She wipes it away, hobbles toward the pickup bed on her bad foot. She reaches over and pulls out her little duffel bag filled with clothes.

Iván appears in the threshold of the Hotel Luna. He waddles toward the truck with a heavy bucket of water he carries with both arms between his legs. He shouts over the street noise in Spanish, "Step away, lady."

Araceli bristles at that—*lady*. She can tell by the way Iván carries himself, by his soft hands even, that he's the kind of man that doesn't know what he's doing, but she stands back anyway.

He runs around to the driver's side door, releases the lever to pop the hood. Flames leap up into the diesel-blackened air. He throws the bucket of water over the flames. There's a giant explosion at first, a fireball into the sky, and then a darker, jet-black cloud of smoke that escapes from the spot where the carburetor caught fire, so much gasoline leaking out into the street.

"Line's busted," says Iván proudly to Araceli.

Araceli stands in the threshold of the Hotel Luna door, screening her eyes from the smoke.

"Easy fix," he says. "You're lucky your battery didn't explode. A lot of heat under that hood. But it's an easy fix— the carburetor, I mean, which is melted, I mean. You spray some sealant on the line. Take the carburetor out. I could do it for you."

Araceli hates the man already. She thinks he's an idiot.

She shifts back and forth between her good foot and her bad one. It occurs to her then that she's back in her mother country, but she doesn't feel that yet. It's been years since she's seen a Mexican flag waving from any kind of building. And now she's shadowed by one hanging above the entrance to the school across the way. She knows that she should feel something, but she feels resentful more than anything. Resentful she has to be here, resentful of her sons she might never see again. Resentful of her husband and the life he gave her. Resentful that of all people she has to meet, it's Iván that is the first to welcome her home, although what is *home* anymore? If she's honest with herself, she's never felt home anywhere in her life.

She feels Iván's eyes scanning her head to toe. She watches him look at the Texas plates on her truck. She takes a blunt from her pocket and lights it.

"I can fix it myself, thank you very much," she says.

"Mind if I ask where you're from?" says Iván, desperate for small talk.

Araceli curses her luck. To be stranded is one thing, but to be stranded with a talker is a whole other thing. "Says right there on the plate," she says to him, wiping her nose of blood. She feels the spins coming on.

"But where are you *really* from?" he asks.

"Does it matter?" says Araceli, surveying the engine damage herself. She knows he's wrong about the line. Maybe a small leak but it's the carburetor that caught fire. She can smell that much, even through the blood in her nose.

"Lady, you're bleeding," Iván says to her.

Araceli dabs her hand over the spot just under her nose. She wipes away the blood, then puts her wet hand into her dress pocket. A wad of cash in there—everything she's saved, everything she's brought with her.

"You need to lie down," he says.

"I know what I need and don't need," says Araceli. She feels a fresh wave of nausea take hold of her.

"Come," he says, holding out his arm.

Araceli hesitates before grabbing hold of it.

"Your truck is fine right there. I own this place. *Casa de huéspedes*. Used to be a hotel, now it's a guest house. It's my house, but I rent out rooms. I can show you the cleanest if you want."

"You get a lot of business?"

"Mostly migrants coming through. They stay with me until they cross," he says.

At this Araceli begins to feel a slight pang in the pit of her gut. *What have I done?*

She feels the wad of bills in her pocket and calculates how long she can stay at the Hotel Luna. She's guessing twenty bucks a night (twenty-five maybe) by the looks of the place.

"Here," says Iván, taking her bag. "You don't even have to climb the stairs. It's on the first floor. Right here. I reserve this one for my lady customers," he says with a wink. He produces a damp cleaning rag from his back pocket and puts it in her hand. "For the blood," he says and points to his own nose.

He places Araceli's bag just inside the threshold of her room.

"Can I get you a drink of water, lady?"

"I'm Araceli," she says. "Yes."

"I'm Iván. Where you driving from?" he asks before heading for a glass water tank just inside the living room.

"Harlingen," says Araceli.

"Not too far from here," he shouts from the water tank by the counter. "About thirty minutes."

"Less," says Araceli softly.

"You didn't get too far did you?" says Iván, nearing Araceli's room again with her glass of water. He places it in her trembling hand.

She downs it in three big gulps.

"Another?" says Iván.

"Please," say Araceli.

Iván is on his heels to the living room again. "Where are you going?"

"Here," she says.

"Well, you made it. Family visit? I don't like to stay with my own either. Not to pry or anything."

"My sons," she says taking the glass again into her hands. Again she downs it. "They're here, I think," she says looking out the window.

There's still smoke in the air from the pickup's engine. That boy with the Nextel phone stands framed in front of Araceli's window, looking at the license plate on the bumper of her truck. She can't hear anything, but she makes out the shape of his lips calling in the plate to somebody. She wonders who could possibly be on the other end of that line.

"How many?"

"What's that?" she asks Iván.

"Sons," he says pulling up a stool to the doorway.

Araceli feels suddenly trapped. She'd panic if it weren't for the rheumy, dumb look in Iván's eyes to show he's harmless. A grandfather maybe. *He's about old enough*, she thinks.

"They crashed a plane outside the city," she says matter-of-factly.

Iván's face hardens. "A plane?" he says. "A small one?"

"A Pawnee. If you know what that is."

"Look, lady—"

"Araceli."

"Araceli. Sorry, look. I run a really good business here. Family business. And it's really no business of mine, but if your sons are *narcos*—"

"They're from Texas," she says to him. "My oldest is an agricultural pilot."

"Cropduster?" he says, his face changing again. Less dark, more shock.

"Yes," she says, looking into her bag now. Something missing. *My medicines*, she thinks, downing what's left of her water. Her thirst is ignited by her diabetes. *Fucking medicines.*

"That plane that crashed by the river?"

"That's the plane," says Araceli, putting her glass down on the nightstand by the bed.

"It's been in the papers, if you haven't seen," says Iván. "I've got a few of them here in the living room."

"Did they find bodies?"

"Said one was at the hospital," says Iván.

"Do you know where that's at?" says Araceli excitedly.

"Not too far from here," he says. He goes to the counter and gathers up his papers for Araceli to see.

That night, Araceli makes the short walk to the hospital on foot. It's only four blocks, but it might as well be four miles. She hobbles along the pavement, her feet swollen in her shoes, the arch of her bad foot smarting with too much pressure on the small toes.

As she moves, Araceli thinks about how she belongs to this place but it doesn't own her. She owns nothing in it except for her husband and her sons and that house they'd abandoned in San Miguel. Though, if she's honest with herself, she sometimes wonders if she ever owned her husband at all. As she walks she sees his eyes, his mannerisms, his slouchy gait in everyone that moves past her. She sees Cuauhtémoc too. She sees Uli.

A block goes by, and then a second one, and then a third one and all she can see is her husband looking back at her—smiling eyes, sad eyes, eyes that haven't slept, eyes too sick to see. And it's as if her family has been broken into a million different people, two million pairs of eyes. That's what Araceli thinks it will take to find them again: two million pairs of eyes.

Well, I've only got two, she thinks. Which is some small chance out of two million but it's all the chance she needs about now—enough to keep moving. She'll start with the hospital.

Araceli is both relieved and horrified to find that Uli has been cared for in a public hospital, where the staph infections almost always outdo the free medical care. Araceli has been in these hospitals herself too many times than she cares to remember. She's got the scars to prove it—Chikungunya shots, measles shots, rabies shots. The hospital, being a government facility, is like all the other public hospitals across Mexico. A two-story building painted white with rectangular windows that makes it look more like a Catholic school than a hospital.

There are sets of green, double doors on each end of the building. Araceli knows the left door is for the medical personnel and staff. The right door is for everyone else. She walks into the right door.

She's immediately blasted with the tang of urine. She covers her nose and instinctively moves to the left where there's a triage nurse waiting beside a burnt-out EKG machine still plugged into the wall, spitting out what sounds like Morse code.

Araceli takes in the nurse—a fifteen-year-old girl—behind the desk, possibly the only link between Uli and herself. The nurse is texting someone on her phone.

Araceli stands there for a long time catching her breath, but the nurse does not look up. Araceli coughs to make her presence known. "I have a question," says Araceli politely.

"Doesn't everyone?" says the nurse back to her, that piece of shit canned answer rolling off her tongue with a syrupy confidence only attained through daily practice.

Araceli resents this most about her countrymen and women. This shell they've built around themselves. It's exhausting to penetrate.

Araceli begins her journey with a simple declaration: "My son is here."

"And who did you hear that from?" says the nurse, looking up from her screen now.

"The news," says Araceli. "My sons crashed a plane from Texas. Landed here. I was told one of them was at this hospital."

At this the nurse puts down her phone. Without moving a muscle in her face, something shifts in her eyes.

"You're his mother?" the nurse asks.

"Is he here?" asks Araceli, conscious of not answering the question. She knows the policing of her country. She knows that this will become a long nightmare if she doesn't undo the mistake that's already been made.

"He *was* here," says the nurse, picking up a landline phone.

"What do you mean, he *was* here? Who is *he?*"

"Are you his mother?" the nurse asks again, more firmly this time.

"We couldn't be talking about the same person," says Araceli, trying to backpedal now.

"Your son was here," says the nurse, trying to appeal to Araceli's motherhood.

Araceli hates the woman for trying to confirm, trying to put into words what has yet to come out of Araceli's mouth.

"We had him. There were police everywhere. He escaped in the middle of the night. Slid out the window. Why do you think he would run?" the nurse asks her. "Who do you think is after him?"

"Goodbye," says Araceli.

"There are some police that want to talk to you," the nurse says, her tone formal now, full of distance.

Araceli can feel them behind her before they can even announce themselves. Jackals in the wings hungry for the only scrap of knowledge they can hope for now: not where her sons are, but where they will be.

EL ATÓMICO

THE ONLY THING ULI KEEPS from his old life is the birthday money inside his tracksuit: 80 bucks which he converts to a little over 1,000 pesos at a Santander bank at the world's shittiest conversion rate. The first thing he buys is a pair of knock-off Nike's from the market on Avenida del Niño. After that, a pair of Levi's 514s and a San Antonio Spurs shirt that fits too tight around the collar and too loose around the arms. He pockets what's left of his cash and wanders the aisles of the market searching for a meal, his body craving something oily, briny, filled with heat.

He wanders past the men's clothes, past the used Xbox 360 videogame dealers, past the fat man with a muscly arm scraping a giant block of ice with an aluminum scoop to make *raspados*, past the cricket salesmen, past the flimsy baby clothes filtering sun through their cheap fabric, past the *raicilla* liquor dealers bottling their product in empty plastic Coke bottles, past the glass cases full of *gelatina*, until he finds himself in the middle of the *comida corrida puestos*, where clay pots boil under open butane flames and *comales* hiss their blue smoke up into the air, everything grey and rustic and reeking of charcoal and sweet diesel. He stands there in the center of it all, temporarily stunned by the choices in front of him. The wad of cash burns in his pocket.

He saunters off toward the smokiest stand, the one crowded by a group of men, young and old alike, jockeying for plastic stools to park up at the white bar that's littered with red and green salsas, salt shakers shaped like tomatoes, tin bowls of too-dry limes, used napkins balled up and rolling around in the wind and greasy plates.

At the far side of the taco stand, there's a vat of boiling grease filled with *longaniza* and *suadero*. Next to that, a steam tray with organ meats: cow's tongue, cow intestines, graying eyeballs, hacked ox-tail—all of it covered with saran wrap.

The man in charge is, of course, the man with the biggest knife. He hacks and scrapes meat over a wooden tree stump impregnated with hot fat and moist wood shavings that roll around in the grease so that the stump looks furry where the knife has scraped. The *taquero* collects money, gives change, hacks meat and takes orders all at the same time in rapid-fire fashion.

When the taquero's gaze falls on Uli, he shouts, "Güero, güero, ¿qué quieres, güero? What do you want?"

"Three *campechanos*," says Uli.

"Just three?"

"And a Coke," says Uli.

"More like it," he says with a smile.

Uli smiles back, almost cries because that's the first smile he's seen in days. How long has he been here? He can't say.

He watches the taquero slice his blade into the vat of meat with a shallow angle to pull up a sliver of popping grease, which he promptly throws down onto the edges of a pile of corn tortillas to keep them from burning on the comal. With the same angle and speed, the taquero pulls out a link of longaniza and a hunk of suadero meat at the same time, slicing the link open with an elegant drag of the blade before placing both meats under the heel of his knife and moving, with rapid efficiency, back and forth over the furry stump to mix them together.

Uli stares into the glistening blade under the taco stand's one incandescent bulb. His eyes move from that blade to the taquero and then to everyone around him, working their jaws over the food. Everybody stares straight ahead, avoiding each other's eyes. Uli wonders how many of these men belong here in Matamoros and how many are just passing through. How many of them are going to Texas tomorrow? How many are going much further than that?

It's then that the weight of it all sinks in for Uli. He might never go back to Texas. He knows, however, where to go if he has a shot at getting back: northwest, toward San Miguel, where his father built a house with horse-racing money. Where he was born, where Cuauhtémoc was born, where everyone will end up eventually (he hopes), on the only patch of land his family owns in this world.

As he walks off into the night, the world is both fast and slow like a dream. He feels the burn of money in his pocket. He decides that tomorrow he'll buy that bus ticket to San Miguel, to the northeastern part of Chihuahua, to the desert, to where he comes from, to where his blood belongs (if that's even true anymore).

In the parking lot of the bus station there's a man crying inside a gun metal Mercedes C-class coupe. Uli looks at the car, then at the man behind the windshield. He wonders if he'll ever be able to afford luxury sadness. *Maybe,* he thinks. Though he'd buy a Land Rover instead. That way he could have an all-terrain cry instead of a parking-lot cry, which seems less dignified somehow.

The man wails so loud that he's audible through the rolled-up windows, his face warped into a bandy patchwork of wrinkles. Everyone observes him as they file into the Estrella Roja station to buy their tickets to the only bus left going to Chihuahua.

Uli buys his ticket and boards the bus, a Coke and a bag of chips in his hand as he walks up the steps. He sits in the very back row, closes his eyes and presses the cool Coke to his forehead. By the time he opens his eyes, the crying man is onboard too. He holds a clipboard in his hand as he goes up and down the rows talking to the passengers, ticking off names from a list, his little frame swimming inside his oversized uniform—a green and yellow patch on his arm, a white nametag on his shirt. When he gets to Uli, he's all manic smiles and alcohol. His eyes are too sad to look at. Uli stares into his teeth instead. They need work.

"Which city are you headed to?"

"San Miguel," says Uli. "Are you the driver?"

"I am," says the man.

Uli closes his eyes and waits to be there already. He's weary but like all teenaged boys he feels invincible. Having survived the plane crash only confirms his hunch that he can never really die. Death happens to other people but not to him, not to Cuauhtémoc either. In his boy's heart he knows that everyone is still alive because they have to be.

He half-sleeps the entire way, his head pressed up against the rattling window pane, and tries to remember the San Miguel of his boyhood. He remembers his father's Fender reverb amp, his father's record collection, his home with the L-shaped floor plan. He remembers his best friend, Ernesto, who lived next door. He remembers the street named Ocotepec that stretched on and on forever, all those houses and their gleaming glass in the desert. It was the perfect life. He wonders, sometimes, why they ever left it at all.

When he opens his eyes, they're too dry. Everything is a blur. That's his first impression of San Miguel—an impressionist painting. One color bleeding into the next bleeding into the next. The bus is empty except for Uli and an older woman sitting across the aisle from him, back by the engine compartment. She snores so soft and shallow that for a second Uli thinks she might be dead. He thinks to shake her but decides against it.

He collects himself and walks, sleep-drunk, toward the front of the bus.

In the rearview mirror over the driver's seat, the driver's shiny temples pulse in the morning sunlight, his jaws working over a piece of gum. "*Suerte*," he says to Uli as he descends the stairs onto the asphalt of the bus station. *Luck.*

In the bus station, the ceiling buzzes with fluorescent lights and fans. There's no one else to be seen but the bored ticket vendors and teenagers working their concession stands. They all blend in with the white walls and laminate counters and concrete floors.

There's a Carl's Jr. at the far end of the station with a red neon sign and an eating area off to the right. Scuffed yellow chairs are bolted to the ground. There's a Pepsi machine and a Paletas Solera stand. There's an arcade next to that with a coin-operated Ninja Turtles game and a horse that goes *up-down-stop, up-down-stop*. There's a bike chained to the horse, and the chain rattles against the horse's fiberglass body when it moves. The sound echoes across the tiles of the bus station, but nobody seems to mind. Ticket counter after ticket counter, there are clerks dressed in beige sweaters and cheap, light blue-collared shirts, their lapels starched straight and stiff and dry. The clerks stare idly into their glowing screens, their eyes unmoving as if spacing out. Not one word read. Not a shred of work being done. Everything an act.

The taxi dispatch is on the opposite side of the bus station. There's a girl in a cheap blue uniform sitting in the dispatch booth. She's reading a book and sucking on a red lollipop. She lays the lollipop on the laminate counter in front of her as Uli approaches. She smiles at him in a way that makes it seem as if it hurts her to smile, her eyes like upside down crescents, her candy-stained lips curled over her puffy gums that make her teeth look too small.

"*Buenas*," she says with the smallest voice.

"*Buenas*," Uli says.

"Twenty pesos for the regular taxi. Fifty pesos for the Radio Taxi," she says, launching into her spiel.

"What's the difference?" Uli asks, cutting her short.

"The Radio Taxi will get you there," she says matter-of-factly.

"The regular taxi won't?"

The girl pretends she doesn't hear the question. She lifts the lollipop from the laminate and puts it in her mouth, leaving a red dot of spit behind.

"Luggage?" she says.

"Just me," says Uli.

"No luggage?" she says.

"No."

She sighs and prints out a ticket. She slaps it on the counter, right next to the red dot, and says, "Take this outside to the taxi in the front of the line. The driver will know what to do."

On Calle Ocotepec, the houses are all close to each other. They all look the same. Block after block of beige single-story boxes with square concrete façades and haloed arches above the doors like miniature Spanish missions. Adobe, cement, plaster and wrought iron. There's splayed rebar where the concrete's been knocked away from a shifty foundation. Everything is overgrown with weeds and unruly magnolia trees never meant to have grown that large. Everyone is missing. The roads are full of sand and concrete barricades and boulders that look like they were dug up from the guts of the earth.

The boulders are strewn pell-mell in the road so that the taxi has to expertly navigate around them, the Nissan's suspension creaking and buckling at every turn. A wheezing noise oozes from the air conditioner. A blast of Freon-cooled air fills the cabin. It smells like cigarette smoke and floral air freshener.

The driver scrapes his fender on a boulder as he moves between it and another boulder. The frame of his car shakes as his tires slip over the sandy road. The engine idles and then dies. He shoves the clutch in and starts the car again.

"What's with the rocks?" asks Uli.

The driver says nothing. He knows, like everyone in San Miguel knows, that the boulders were put there on purpose. The west end of San Miguel is, after all, nothing but a small grouping of cartel safe houses. Immediately after the cartel arrived, everyone else left. Everything was abandoned. But the boulders stayed. The boulders kept the police out of the neighborhood. And then the *autodefensas* after that.

The taxi driver pulls over on the corner of Juárez and Valle de Palmas, five blocks from his father's home.

"We must be in the wrong neighborhood," he tells the cab driver.

The cab driver is not hearing it. "This is the only Calle Ocotepec in San Miguel. You're in Colonia Rivera del Bravo. This is it, *compa*."

Uli looks out the window again. An endless horizon of homes crumbling in the wind.

"This can't be," he says.

"It's the only Ocotepec I know," says the driver before hitting the clutch again and shifting the car into neutral as if to settle the issue. "This is going to sound shitty, but are you sure you're in the right San Miguel? There are seven of them in Mexico—cities I mean."

That thought had never occurred to Uli before. He simply went to the Estrella Roja ticket counter and said, "San Miguel." Thirty-eight dollars on the nose.

The driver looks at his watch. "That'll be fifty, *compa*," he says.

Uli reaches into his pocket to produce a handful of ten peso coins. "You can't drop me off at the door?" Uli asks, a quiver in his voice.

"You think this is 'Back to the Future,' compa? Flying car? Fly over all these boulders? No way, compa. Five blocks. Fifty pesos."

Uli hands over his fistful of coins and hops out of the car.

"Be careful," says the driver, counting the coins in his palm.

Before Uli can put the remaining coins back in his pocket, the white Nissan turns the corner on Juárez. Gone.

Above all other sounds in Rivera del Bravo, there is no sound louder than the dogs, because they are everywhere. Their paws scrape asphalt louder than litter in the wind, louder than the plastic bags caught up in the barbed wire, razor wire and telephone wire lines that cut up the sky. The barks come from everywhere. First one dog and then the call and response of a dozen others nearby.

He walks down the dusty road, his broken, painful gait shaking the coins in his hand. He closes his fist around them to keep them from jangling, stuffs them, one at a time, into his jeans pocket like he's feeding them into a machine. He counts forty-three pesos at his fingertips. A buzzing, bright pain beneath his nails as he scrapes them along the ridges of the coins. Since his casts were removed at the hospital, everything feels too heavy, too sensitive in his fingertips, his nerves bright and hot with blood. It took two weeks for his sprain to heal. No compound fractures. It was the week they took the cast off that he escaped from the hospital. He guesses he's been here three weeks total, give or take some days.

In the near-distance, he sees a house resembling the one he used to live in. A small, adobe structure—like all the others—but with a black door (not a brown one) and a heavily pruned tree not unlike the lusher orange tree from his childhood. He remembers the large branches stronger than he sees them now. He recalls him and his friend Ernesto used to climb that tree and throw citrus at passing cars. One day a car stopped. A man came out and pulled Ernesto by the leg and hit him so hard in the head that his eyes wouldn't stop shaking. Uli passes the tree and looks at how faded it's become. His eyes fall to the scarred trunk where that same man tried to shake Uli from the branches by ramming his car into the tree. That was Uli's first encounter with insanity. Uli hung on for hours. He survived that day. He'll survive this, he thinks. He looks for fruit on the remaining branches, but finds nothing—just a withered version of what once was.

From the outside, the house looks mostly intact. He remembers his father left it in impeccable shape. The house had never been cleaner than the day his family left it eight years ago. As if preparing for his eventual deportation and return to Mexico, his father had covered the furniture in plastic to be clean for when they'd need it again. He'd left a change of cotton sheets in the bedroom closet, a bottle of dish soap next to the kitchen sink and a bottle of aspirin and a razor in the bathroom. In his bedroom, he left his jazz records, his fender amplifier and a snare drum that he never learned to play among other things. His father was the only one in the family who took nothing with him to Texas. He remembers that before he left, his father rigged the home's utility box to connect with the street lamp outside so as to keep the refrigerator running, fully stocked with Coke. A kind of peace offering to anyone who'd break in and steal his possessions. *Take the Coke, not my stuff.* He knocks with two dry rasps on the wooden door, his busted knuckles stinging. The pain swells and before it subsides he's knocking again, ready to be let in, ready to drink the tallest glass of water in the world.

He waits. He waits. Nothing.

"Apá!" he shouts into the door. He peers out to the side, looks in the window. "Apá!" he shouts again. Silence.

He tries for the doorknob but it doesn't turn so much as it jiggles off its socket. The door swings open. Inside, the air is spiced with the smell of sulfur and mold and creosote. The ceiling is speckled, dull and yellow. The tiled floor is covered in sand.

At the back of the house, the wind pushes through a broken window. Uli shuts the door behind him. A low whistle as the air passes through the saw hole where the knob has fallen off. The dusty curtains by the window flow out and drop inside the pane. He rips them from the curtain rod to plug up the saw hole and make the whistling stop.

On the walls, there's a varnished piece of wood with a picture of George Strait glazed into it. From the door, Uli is maybe two steps from the living room and fifteen steps to the kitchen beyond. There's a bedroom just off the side of the kitchen and a backyard too, out the door by the stove.

Uli makes his way to the fridge, hoping for a drink of water. But inside he finds a half used bottle of Valentina, a stack of congealed, processed meat, a quarter of an onion and about forty bottles of Coke, the bottles completely pristine, untouched.

He quickly pulls a Coke from the shelf and slams the edge of the cap down on the corner of the sink. A carbonated spray shoots from the glassy neck and, before it can even clear, Uli tilts his head back and drinks, trading breath for Coke. His blood goes chill, his head goes numb, the carbonation working its way through his sinuses. His teeth ache from the sugar and cold.

He walks to the living room, light headed, and eases into the greasy maroon sofa, locking eyes with George Strait on the wall. *Amarillo by morning*, he sings to himself. Uli will take any part of Texas by now, even Amarillo, which is officially the worst part outside of Dallas (which is actually officially the worst).

He feels a breeze coming in from the busted window to the right of his face. He looks out into the backyard filled with shit: emptied sun-bleached bottles of dot 3 steering fluid; cellophane bags half-opened and filled with trapped and condensed rain water; discarded shoes (none of them matching); a red Chicago

Bulls jersey, number 23, *Pérez* written in sharpie across the back; dusty Lala brand milkboxes crumpled and bloated with desert rain; shredded cigarette butts browning with oil and spit and dust. The filters all shimmer in the sun like so many tiny slivers of unspooled fiberglass. There's a pile of fluorescent tubes busted and dusting in the wind. Next to that there's a stack of computer monitors. Next to that there's a stack of televisions. Next to that there's a stack of radios with their speakers ripped out and their soldered wires splayed wild in the air. Tied to an oak tree is a single, barking dog. Uli assumes it's a girl because of its puffy teats.

There are scars all over the dog's face and ears and neck. The fresh ones are bright red. The old ones are blistery gray, puckered and pale. For every new blister there are twelve old ones. They bulge up and then fade back into the dog's jet-black fur. Her eyes glow a deep, dark brown. Her tongue is blood red. It hangs sloppy from her watery jowls, jutting in and out of her head between sharp, filed, yellow teeth that are exposed as the dog picks up on her haunches and lets out a fierce bark. It's almost as if she does it out of duty more than anything, a habitual kind of vigilance. Tensing her back, she summons another bark, lazy but fierce to show Uli she means business.

Uli pulls two Cokes from the fridge and snaps their tops off on the counter. He pours one out into a plastic container, his peace offering, and carries it outside with the heavy reverence of a priest, inching slowly toward the dog.

She jumps up on all fours and bolts forward at the sight of him. The rope that holds her to the tree snaps taut with a dry rasp that sends powdered dust smoking into the air.

It's an eternity before Uli builds up enough guts to place the Coke in front of her. Now that he's closer, he pegs her for a Lab-mix. Maybe some Rottweiler in there.

The dog sniffs at the container. She looks up at Uli. Down at the Coke. Up at Uli again. Her red tongue pours from her head. She laps slowly at first, then wildly, insatiably like she hasn't drunk anything in days.

"There you go," Uli whispers to her and tilts the pale, green bottle to his own lips. Uli keeps his own Coke bottle between his legs as he sits down in the dirt. A sip for him, a sip for her.

As he tilts his green bottle over the container to keep it full she lunges at him. He waits for the bite but it never comes. Something else instead. A lick, her sloppy tongue over his salty hands, full of sweat. The meaty scar tissue of her face gently brushes along the hairs on the back of Uli's hands. He grows suddenly aware of his own scars.

She stretches the rope so that it grinds along the serrated, wooden groove rubbed into the base of the tree. Underfoot, the cloying smell of dried shit strewn about the radius. The closer Uli gets to the tree, the stronger the smell of urine grows. He decides he'll let her off for a while. He'll give her a bath tonight. For all he knows it's his father's dog. He decides then that he'll treat her like his own.

Uli wobbles around to the base of the tree where he unties the small knots of vinyl rope. Before he knows it, the rope zips hot in his palms, his skin on fire. He lets go as the dog's eyes go wild with aggression, the whites rolling and rolling, anxious for a prison break.

Uli can only watch her as she darts through a curled hole in the bottom of the backyard's chain-link fence. The dog slaps her paws against the pavement at the front of the house and then keeps slapping them until the *tic-tack-tic* of her claws pounding concrete are swallowed up in the sound of the wind.

He waits and she never comes back. But he hears her everywhere, those paws still slapping and that dry, haunting bark all around him.

At first, Uli hates himself for losing the dog. But then he wonders if he hates himself for loving the dog too much in the first place. Of course, he had to love the dog—it was a piece of his father. He gets to thinking about hate, which is to say he gets to thinking about the way hate is always tied to one anxiety or another.

In his mind, he goes through his list of hates: He hates that he's alone. He hates that he's destroyed his family over a plane ride that was never worth it to begin with. His hates the ache he carries for his mother. He imagines her waking up to no one. The plane gone. Sampson, the grove boss, yet to come back. Of course, she's on the run right now. There's no other way for her to be. Uli would call her if he could get hold of her, but no telling where she is now. Not in the groves, not anywhere he'd know. She has no e-mail. She has no Mexican cell phone. He hates that she's always been unreachable. He hates that he knows she's coming here to San Miguel. Nobody should be coming here to San Miguel. He thinks, if he's honest with himself that this place could be easy to hate, and he barely knows it yet. San Miguel, he feels, is the end of the world. The last place on earth he wants to be. *But she's coming here*, Uli thinks. That's the only place she'd be—on the road to here. This house. This desperate patch of broken land, which is the only thing in the world that his family owns. He hates that simple fact, though he also banks on it. *This is where she's coming. This is where you need to be.*

From there he starts thinking about things he misses. Like Blue Bell ice cream (vanilla). And the humid heat of Harlingen. And the sound of English—God, what he'd give to speak English to anyone about now, to read something in English, write anything in English to anybody who also speaks English. A love letter. A hate letter.

He misses Whataburger (the A1 thick and hearty burger with a small Coke which is always a liter). And he misses school. And he misses his brother. He misses the flat of his head. That crooked smile that only comes out when he's drunk or eating his favorite breakfast. Bacon and eggs with Tony's seasoning on top. Uli imagines his brother right here in front of him. A big heaping plate of bacon and eggs and Tony's with a steaming cup of coffee. He misses the fleeting memory of that cheap, crooked grin. He hates that this image doesn't even feel like a real memory anymore, but rather just some hope of a possibility constructed from the fabric of a former life that he's trying so desperately to reconstruct. Uli hates that he feels like he's losing his mind. He hates that he imagines his brother and himself right now, right here among their father's other cast off things. He hates his father for having left their family. *This is his fault, really*, he thinks. He hates that he thinks that. He hates this busted house, which he's still figuring out how to live in. More than anything, he hates the fact that the dog left him like everything else has left him. He hates the dog for shattering his world twice. And it's in this vein of thought that Uli gets to wondering if he might salvage just the tiniest bit of dignity if he doesn't find that dog. That thought gives him some hope. That task gives him a job. A mission. *It's worth a try*, he thinks. Isn't that really just life? A series of tiny missions? Tiny tasks? One foot in front of the other?

It's in this spirit that Uli heads out into the neighborhood armed with only a Coke and a slice of gelatinous lunchmeat with which to lure the dog back. He sets off east, toward the sounds of the city, walking between boulders and burnt out cars and abandoned homes feeling like the only survivor of this place he's never known.

He walks five blocks toward the highway. At the end of the street, right before the turnoff to the *periférico*, there's a Pemex gas station. Standing at the corner, by the pumps, a kid dressed like an angel with a Bible at his feet. He's standing on a wooden crate protesting something.

His face is painted with glitter and white powder. He's draped in a white tunic that has wings attached at the back. His lips are unbelievably thin, and as Uli approaches, he can hear that the kid is praying. In front of him a cardboard sign reads: *END THE LOTTERY.*

Uli looks at the boy and the boy looks back. Uli nods to acknowledge him but picks up the pace a little, walking hard toward the bridge that feeds the periférico. Minutes later, he sees another stray angel with the same sign, the same ghostly look in his eye. And then another. And then a group of them in front of a mass of people crowded around a building that looks like any other building on this strip but a little more official perhaps, which is to say it's in the same shape but made of brick, not cement or adobe. It stands among a string of storefronts and offices. A post-office at the far corner.

Uli guesses there are about three hundred people in all, milling about with strips of papers in their hands.

There are families, construction workers, policemen and women dressed as house maids. From where he's standing, Uli can see all of them move about the periphery of something in the middle of the crowd, trying hard to gain an advantage on one another. A tiny man is climbing up a ladder. His lean arms flex and pull as he reaches for a crossbeam hanging over the sidewalk where the sign of an establishment might go. Uli watches the man produce what looks to be copper screws from his pocket and carefully place them between his browning teeth. The man grinds the copper screws into the cross bar with the blunt scrape of a hammer. Sparks fly out against the angle he strikes. He does it all without so much as blinking his cataract eyes, his full concentration on the next silvery blow of steel on copper.

Uli watches the tiny man as he works with a steady efficiency. He produces two wooden plaques from the painter's satchel on his side.

The first one reads: *For Those Who Didn't Believe.*

The second one reads: *For Those Who Continue to Disbelieve.*

On the first plaque, ten or twelve names are branded into the wood with red paint crossed through them. Every name begins with a title: *Colonel, Captain, Lieutenant, Mayor.* There are only two names that don't have titles, who could be anyone. The second plaque is full of those kinds of people. The nobodies.

The people review the names before scrawling something furiously onto the strips of paper. And then the tiny man comes by with a bucket. Everyone pays him five pesos before putting their strip in. Old hands, young hands, baby hands with their parent's hands wrapped around them put their strips over the lip of the bucket, one-by-one, as if they were putting their dreams at the feet of a saint. Under the noise of the crowd, the perpetual hum of the praying angels. And under the noise of the angels, the piercing bark of dogs.

Uli cranes his neck toward the sound coming from an alley just adjacent to the crowd. At first, he thinks there's one dog until he realizes there are many, their barks squealing to a snuff, one by one. As he leaves the crowd their sound grows louder. The scraping of paws. The panting of tongues.

When he reaches the alley, he finds nothing. A lonesome, grey industrial door at the end. A meowing cat with pink whiskers, wet paws fishing in a bucket of blood next to the door. More barks come from inside that building. Then the sound of a plunger, a bolt entering flesh. And then the echoing sound of the drain beneath Uli's feet.

Uli returns home defeated, that quivering cold meat still in his hand. No dog, no father, no family. He lets the facts sink in.

Why can't he be at home with his mother? Why can't he be back in school already? Tomorrow morning, the track team will be doing sprints. And he won't be there to beat everyone and get to the shower first (like he always does) after the Gatorade bath that he always pours on himself if only to mock his other teammates (*Look, I beat you*). Why, he wonders, does he have to go further into Mexico to get back to Texas? *I was right there*, he thinks. And then keeps thinking, wondering about his brother before letting that thought, like the million others coursing through his brain at any given moment, fade out into the detritus of his brain.

His mind floats between what he saw that day—the crowd, the building and then that grey industrial door with the bucket of blood. *The fuck was that place?* And the magazines in front of him. A thick stack of his father's old copies of *Extremo*.

Uli leaves the meat on the kitchen counter and picks up the magazines, holds them to his face. They smell like his father. The sweet reek of nicotine and cheap cologne. On the cover of one magazine, there are two men lifting a man in a grey, blood-soaked shirt from a car. The cover is vertically divided so that next to the man there's a picture of a sexy lady in a blue swimsuit. Carrie Prejean. At the bottom left corner it says *Junio* 2012. Uli thinks about that man on the cover, how he's been dead two years now.

He thumbs the corners of the magazine, flipping the pages quickly to see the little animated drawings his father would make at the corners. A stick woman undressing. Circle boobs at the end. The very existence of the drawing is enough to make Uli blush.

Every page drips with red ink. The most heavily marked sections are the pages that include love letters. Cuban beauties looking for love in Mexico (and beyond).

There's one woman who dots her i's with hearts. She's into fat men with or without mustaches, as long as they have steady work. There's another woman who has children (but no scars). She says only young men need reply and Uli thinks beggars can't be choosers. She includes a dark picture of herself printed on the next page. Her hair is sloppy, her eyes the saddest things you've ever seen. On the next page there are stories of ghosts, demons, shadow figures and strange things in general. Red ink is all over that page too, which includes a story with a picture of a dog, his eyes growing green like deer eyes in the headlights. The magazine says that the dog wasn't even present when the *Extremo* photographer took the picture, but there he was. The dog, *Extremo* says, is a legend of photographers. Folk healers call the dog a psychopomp—a medium between this world and the next—that brings the souls of the dead to the afterlife. Another *curandero* says it's pure evil in the guise of a dog. The story ends by saying the photographer died three months later.

Uli puts the magazine down between his legs and remembers his father told him that story once. Now he knows where it came from, which makes it less magical somehow.

Uli thinks of the house, of the dirt inside the house, of all of this stuff still left behind. And then he hears the silence of his own breath.

He takes the magazines to a bedroom and puts them on the head of a busted snare drum that acts as a nightstand beside the bed. He puts the burnt out digital clock on the stack of magazines.

In the corner of the room, by the window looking out into the street, there's a chest of drawers flecked in gold leaf and lacquer. In the top drawer, there are stray brown and beige buttons scattered everywhere, a packet of Alka-Seltzer, a pair of brass scissors and a polaroid of his brother when he was little and riddled with chicken pox, sitting naked with pink calamine rubbed all over him. In the drawer beneath that one there are some pencils and an emptied Docker's wallet with a single five-peso coin in it. In the drawer beneath that is a ratty Bible bulging at the spine, a fat rose pressed perfectly between the pages of Revelations.

From the window you can hear the dogs. The cicadas too, screeching loud because their death is coming. *It'll be winter before long.*

Like the dogs, the cicadas blare from everywhere and nowhere at once. Filtered through the glass of the window, they sound like the hum of an engine.

॰ॐ ॰ॐ ॰ॐ

When the bloody girl arrives, she brings the black dog in her arms. The dog brings the flies that ride the dog's stench. *Zizz-zazz* go their wings that jolt Uli from sleep before the girl can even notice he's in her bed.

From the corner of her eye she sees movement. She lowers the bloodied dog to the floor, pulls a pistol from the small of her back and points it at Uli's head.

"Don't move. Not even a breath," she says, backing out into the hallway.

Uli does exactly as she says. She watches his hands. They're planted flat on the mattress.

Her eyes are adjusting. In the hallway, she flips the light switch so the hall light shines behind her. She can see him clear as day, but he can only see her silhouette. She learned that squatter's trick from her old crew who all slept with their backs to the east side of every wall. *Always keep your back to the sun.* The light would buy you a second or two. Enough time to slip out and run.

She thinks about running—every squatter's number comes up, every squatter moves on—but she looks at her dog bleeding on the ground, barely able to move. That wet look in his eye that says, *Don't leave me.*

"Get down on the floor. Hands where I can see them," she says.

Uli does as she says, sliding from the bed to the floor. His scars shine in the light. The bloody girl sees how gingerly he moves, how painfully slow each joint bends and flexes to get him down to where he needs to be. He lays there prostrate on the ground, pathetic. Every movement is labored, every breath is too deep. She keeps the gun on him. She knows he's not a threat, although he's got to be the one who cut her dog loose. *He's already done some damage, and that makes him dangerous.*

"Where do I know you from?" she asks him, only the profile of his face visible now that his eyes are on the ground. "Don't be shy, friend. Answer me."

"This is my house," says Uli.

"First time I've seen you in it," says the bloody girl.

"My father's house. He lived here."

"Past tense—*lived*. I don't see him anymore. These are my things," says the bloody girl pointing around the room with her pistol. "My bed. My sheets. My dog. Which, by the way, you cut loose."

"I thought he might have been my father's."

"Well, you thought wrong. And now you owe me. You talk funny. Where are you from?" says the bloody girl, the pistol still aimed at his head.

"Texas."

"Explains your father's bad taste in décor. Should have gotten rid of that George Strait a long time ago," she says, lowering the gun. A long silence between them. "You can go on and get up," she says.

But Uli just lays right there.

A moment or two passes. Neither of them knows what the other is going to do.

"Go on, get up. I'm not going to shoot you. I know where I've seen you," she says. "That picture up in the living room. Family picture. You're older now."

"No shit."

"Which one are you? Uli or Cuauhtémoc?"

"Uli."

"I'm June," she says. "Why do you move so slow? What's wrong with your body?"

"What happened to the dog?" says Uli.

"Butcher got him," she says.

She looks at Uli's face, his eyebrows working like he's trying to shake himself from a dream. She explains, "Butcher takes any animal. He doesn't discriminate. You see any cows around here? Pigs? Chickens? Well, how many dogs do you see?"

"I see the floor," says Uli.

"Well, how many do you hear then? Huh?"

"A lot."

"A hell of a lot," says June. "We're in the desert. You let that dog go and he's meat the next day. You cut lose all I've got in this world, understand? I've got good reason to shoot you dead tonight, but I won't. You know why? Because I'm compassionate. And because you're a cripple. I can tell you're injured by the way you're lying there. Can't even wipe your own ass."

"I can wipe my own ass," says Uli, visibly agitated, wide awake now.

"I'd say prove it, but looks like getting up off that floor would make it a good day for you."

"How long are you going to stay?" asks Uli.

"This is my home too—squatter laws."

"I don't know what you're talking about."

"You just need to know I'm staying here. The dog couldn't make the trip anyway. I caught the butcher right as he made his first slice. Had to sew him up on the table right there. You believe that? Didn't catch the artery, thank God. But fucking bastard made me pay for the meat. You believe that?"

"I'll pay you back," says Uli. "I have some money. If you don't shoot me, I can pay you what she's worth."

"*He* is worth more than you can afford, friend. He's a prize-fighter."

"I thought he was a girl. What's his name?"

"Atómico," says June. "His equipment is small but it's there."

"Atómico."

"He's radioactive," she says with a straight face.

The next morning, they lay out on the driveway with Atómico between them to let the sun cure his wounds. June stares up at the sky along with Uli, her eyes peeking out from a fleshy mask of scars.

Her face is a patchwork of pink and white and gray. The left side of her face is like a sheet of rice paper, a shiny blister that's never healed. She's missing part of her nose and part of her ear too. She's got wrinkles around her eyes. She's about Uli's age, maybe a little younger. An emo haircut, bangs plastered to the side of her face to cover the scars. Around her neck a chain and padlock. She wears a beige Sex Pistol's shirt covered in dog's blood. *God Save the Queen.* Skinny black jeans, red Chuck Taylors, too many bracelets on both wrists. She looks like she hasn't eaten in days. She looks like her name isn't really June, but that's what she calls herself.

Over the skies of San Miguel, an endless stream of aircraft crisscross the sky. Some of them are jets but most of them are propeller planes, their flam-blast engines cutting the air. They sound closer than they look.

"Where do you think they're going?" asks Uli.

"Texas." She leans over to shoo away the flies around Atómico's wounds. "Army's coming. Gonna wipe all those motherfuckers out. They're trying to get it while they can."

"Get what?"

"Their money," says June.

"Would you believe it if I told you I crashed in a plane, and that's why I'm here?"

"I wouldn't believe anything you say," says June. "But that would explain a lot. You've got enough scars to make the left side of my face jealous."

"What happened to you?"

"Well, what the hell didn't happen?" she says, avoiding the question. She takes a bottle of water and pours it over Atómico's blood red tongue. He's got these sad eyes that look up at June, who looks back up into the sky again. All those planes moving so slowly, she wonders if she could reach out and pluck one out of thin air.

"You were that boy in the papers, weren't you?" June asks.

"I don't know what you're talking about," says Uli.

"Couple of brothers crashed a few weeks back. A lot of people took a lot of credit for it."

"I don't know anything about that," says Uli.

"Papers said one of the brothers was a narco."

"That doesn't make any sense," says Uli.

"Are you sure that wasn't you? You said you crashed a plane, didn't you?"

"I don't fly planes," says Uli.

"So, your brother then. He was the pilot," says June.

"I don't know where my brother is at," says Uli, looking from the sky to June.

"Told you so," says June, a little smirk across her face that makes her scar jut out a little.

"He's coming back," says Uli. "This is where we're supposed to meet."

"Is that a plan?" asks June.

"That's the only plan I know of."

June mulls this over in her mind a while. She can't decide whether she hates him or feels sorry for him. She wonders how long he'll wait. She could use the help. The gears start whirring behind her eyes.

"I need to go into town," she says, peeling herself up from the dusty driveway. The padlock and chain thud against her collar bone as she brushes herself off. "We need some medical supplies for the dog. Can't let those wounds get infected."

"Some antibiotics?"

"Something like that," she says. "You said you had some money?" She bends down, steadies her back as she prepares to lift the dog back up to her chest.

"Just enough money to not get my head blown off last night."

"Sounds like enough for me," says June. "You'll get it back." Uli peels himself up from the ground, a pale look to his face. June grabs him by the shoulder. "I promise you you'll get it back. Hey, look at me. Do you trust me?"

She puts her face up in front of his, holds his gaze for a second or two. On the ground, the dog strains his neck to see what's happening. He lets out a little growl, something low and guttural at the back of his throat. She knows she shouldn't move him too much.

"You have to eat, man. You have to exist while you're waiting. And I know this city better than anyone you're going to meet. I'll get you your money back. You owe it to me in the first place too, remember that. You trust me?"

"Doesn't seem like I've got much of a choice," says Uli.

"You do," says June, her eyes going sad now. "I wouldn't ask if I didn't need it. But seeing that I didn't blow your head off— and that you got my dog sliced up—I think you owe it to me. Think of it as seed money: Give me what you have now and I'll get you double that. Maybe triple."

Uli spits in the dirt, watches the sand absorb it as soon as it hits the ground.

They set off east toward the sounds of downtown San Miguel. There's the low rumble of a highway nearby, the sounds of car horns and street vendors too. The noise of life happening. Along the way, June points out every home she's ever squatted in. They walk into some of the homes. Others they just pass by.

In one home, there's a room full of flies swarming over a molded dinner left out on placemats over a plastic table. In another, there's the static blue of a television never turned off. In another, there are sheets of paper spread out over a kitchen counter. Some kid's homework, someone's bills. All of the homes are stripped clean of the copper pipes and wires in the walls. There's adobe and plaster all over the ground. And that's the first thing June teaches Uli: money is all around them. In pipes, in wiring, in car parts, in sink faucets—anything that can be scrapped or pulled or gouged from the walls.

June says the whole city used to be a factory town, a *maquila* town. There were expendable jobs, expendable labor, expendable people before the drugs came in and San Miguel's militia started fighting back. The autodefensas took everything over. Then the cartels took everything over. Then the autodefensas again. It went back and forth, back and forth like that until everyone left—the maquilas too. There were three maquilas in all: one that built American televisions, one that built Chevy transmission parts and one that built toaster ovens for cents on the dollar. Newly deported and recently arrived people in the town needed jobs, and for those jobs to keep going, the factories needed scrap: rubber, copper, steel and aluminum. The scrapping was good for a while, but the factories relocated closer to Juárez. June says there's only one scrapyard still open, and that's where Uli and June fit into the equation.

"Scrapyard still needs the metal, and we give it to them. Simple as that."

"How well does it pay?" asks Uli, hobbling along on his bad feet. His arches are tight. There's a throbbing in his right big toe.

"Enough," says June.

They walk in the road, between boulders and burnt-out cars, until they come across the aftermath of a car bomb which stops them in their tracks.

A jeep filled bumper to brim with barbed nail shanks and fertilizer. The smell of the bomb still hangs peppery and damp in the air. Every breath is like inhaling mud.

They can smell the fertilizer from fifty yards out. The barbed nail shanks are strewn much further. The nails twinkle in the morning light, a silvery constellation against the oil-streaked pavement.

Uli bends down, ever so gingerly, and picks up one of the nails. He holds it in his hand, imagines the way it might have sounded. All that metal striking pavement at once.

The further they walk, the denser the nails are scattered. Uli walks tiptoe to keep them from puncturing the soles of his cheap shoes. His arches tense, his right big toe throbbing.

Beside the Jeep there are two greasy, charred bodies shimmering in the morning light, the silvery nails riddling the length and width of them. The skin of their palms are fused together so that the bodies look like they're holding hands. One of them has a golden wedding ring. The other one has a platinum band that's somehow maintained its luster through the blast. Their legs are matte, covered in debris and flies that crawl about the slivers of blistered tissue puckered beneath their burnt and shredded clothes. The flesh of the man's ears has melted into his shoulders. He is wearing a plaid shirt. She is wearing a navy blue dress. The clothes are the only way you can tell them apart, where one body starts and the other begins.

By Uli's foot, there's a warped prosthetic. No telling who it belonged to—the man or the woman.

Uli touches his busted foot to the prosthetic foot. He looks up to June, her eyes peering out from inside her fleshy mask of scars.

"Cartels and autodefensas," says June, picking up the prosthetic by the ankle and swiping it in long arcs in front of her to displace the nails scattered on the ground.

"Which ones you think they were?" asks Uli.

"Probably narcos. Or a narco and his lady friend."

Uli looks at the bodies and tries to guess who they were, who they might have been. Husband and wife married fifty years. Boyfriend and girlfriend. Man and mistress. No telling. Uli looks to where the man's head is supposed to be.

Beneath a puckered blister of flesh, a set of gleaming white teeth barely visible in the charred skin of the corpse. Just then he sees June nearing the body, the collar of her shirt pulled up over her nose.

"What are you doing?" he says.

"The rings," says June.

"You can't be serious," he says.

"Just trust me," says June, laying her hand over the man's ring to find the best angle to pinch at it, drag it off without touching the corpse. She does this for maybe ten, fifteen seconds, before deciding that there's no elegant way to do it. She pulls at it. The flesh builds up behind the platinum band as June tugs. She shakes the flesh to the ground. Then starts in on the woman's body, the golden ring.

Uli falls to his knees and feels the arches in his feet burn. He hurls. He feels his diaphragm rattle between his ribs. It's as if all of the wind is pulled out of him and then pushed back into him again.

NIGHT FLIGHT

THE HACIENDA DE SAN SEBASTIÁN is a desert ranch of twelve thousand hectares situated halfway between Ciudad Juárez to the east and San Miguel to the west. The northern outposts of the property are made up of a chain of low hills that cut highway 45 in half just south of Samalayuca in the Mexican state of Chihuahua. The southern outskirts of the property make up part of the Área Natural Protegida de Medanes de Samalayuca, a federal nature reserve. As a nature reserve, it's the last thing to be guarded by any one of the cost-cutting (money-embezzling) Mexican federal entities and, thus, the perfect place to put a Juárez cartel airstrip.

It's accessed by a desert road so straight and smoothed by sand that you can't even tell you're moving if not for the sound of the engine pulling you along, the dirt gliding underneath like an endless ribbon. Big sky. Low horizon. Lalo always dreads coming here. He has to bring his daughter every time. Boss' wishes. The daughter's too, though she only comes for the ponies that seem immune to heat stroke.

Lalo drives up past the stables and wonders what kind of evil shit bred those ponies—white feet, short necks, all shriveled up like they're about to die but they never do. The devil couldn't have thought up something uglier.

"Ponies!" Lalo's daughter shouts on cue. Her tiny, sloppily lacquered fingernails curl around the door handle as Lalo eases the truck past the gates.

"Goddamnit, Carla! What'd I tell you about opening the door when the car's still moving?"

"I saw him do it, so I did it," she says.

Lalo looks into the rearview to get a look at Cuauhtémoc. Cuauhtémoc's entire weight is shifted to one side, his hands on the door like he's about to make an escape.

"Mr. Cuauhtémoc is a little simple in the head," says Lalo to his daughter. "You're smarter than that. Don't be like him."

"Is that why he likes to ride in the back?" she sneers, all sugar and brine in that way only twelve-year-old girls can be.

"Mr. Cuauhtémoc just gets sick up front is all," he says.

"What happened to his arm?" she asks.

"Mr. Cuauhtémoc had an accident, but Mr. Jimmy is going to make him all better now, isn't that right, Cuauhtémoc?"

"That's right, sir," says Cuauhtémoc sheepishly, easing up on the door now.

"You're not too good in the kitchen, huh?" says Carla to Cuauhtémoc, pointing at the slash along his arm.

"You can open your door now," says Lalo, breaking her line of questions. "Go pick out a pony to ride while me and Mr. Jimmy try to help our friend, Mr. Cuauhtémoc. Don't run out from my sight, okay?"

"Okay!" she says, jumping from the front seat of Lalo's pick-up. Her feet thud against pavement, a little spray of dust carried off into the wind. Her entire body pulls at the door to swing it closed. Lalo turns from his daughter to Cuauhtémoc, the half-smile still plastered across his face.

"What the fuck, man?"

"You'd do it too," says Cuauhtémoc.

"You were going to make me shoot you in front of my daughter."

"You wouldn't have shot me," says Cuauhtémoc.

"Like hell I wouldn't have. How far did you think you were going to get? Like, really fucking tell me."

"I don't know," says Cuauhtémoc.

"Like, man, I'm trying to save your life here, and you're about to pull some shit. On my boss' property. With my daughter in the front seat. Are you fucking simple?"

"You told your daughter I was simple."

"Was right then," says Lalo. He steps out and opens Cuauhtémoc's door, grabs him by the arm and says, "Don't try any dumb shit anymore. I'm your only friend now, right? So don't fuck this up for me."

"I didn't ask for this," says Cuauhtémoc.

"Neither did I. I wish I could tell you that enough, brother."

"I'm not your brother."

"Then I'm your God, understand? I'll end you. Or we could make this pleasant."

"Let's get on with it then," says Cuauhtémoc and plants a foot on the ground and then the other.

They both walk gingerly, in sync, leaning on one another to keep Cuauhtémoc from falling. The distance between the pickup and the ranch house feels like a mile that Lalo would drive if it weren't for El Jimmy's peculiarities about tread patterns in the sand outside. His boss likes the earth outside his house clean, trackless, the way nature intended for it to be. Lalo limps along and looks toward the airstrip behind the ranch house, the airplane grave yard just a few hundred feet past that. Seventy or eighty aircraft, big and small, burning out there in the desert. Most of them are caked with dust on one side, the static vents and pitot tubes clogged. Some of them are riddled with bullets. Most have been scrapped for parts. The biggest one is a DC-3 that looks like the next hard breeze could blow it all apart. On the ground, there are black and red puddles of steering and hydraulic fluid, oil and gasoline.

Past the planes, on the north end of the property, there's a stampede of ponies—eighteen or twenty—pushing dust through the air like a great fog coming down from the hills. Behind them, one of Jimmy's vaqueros is hauling ass, trying his best to corral them. Lalo imagines all of those wild things cutting loose toward him. He imagines the sound of all that flesh, galloping in and out between the wings and bodies and struts of the aircraft in the graveyard. Hooves and flesh and metal. An endless rumble and jangle, like what the earth might sound like were it to open and swallow them whole.

"Why are you staring out that way?" says Cuauhtémoc.

"Just picking out a horse for my daughter," says Lalo, ducking into the shade of the awning. The front door of the ranch house opens before they can even knock.

Before them stands Lalo's boss, El Jimmy. He's looking fatter these days though much more like his younger self, like the man who recruited Lalo.

Lalo feels like it's been twenty years or so since he's seen Jimmy smile like that, even if those teeth are someone else's. Perfectly straight veneers. His green contacts that make his eyes look manic. An old man's faux hawk haircut, like all the Euro soccer players wore in the early 2000s. He looks taller than what Lalo remembers, or is it the heels of his boots?

"Come, come!" says Jimmy backing into the living room of his house now.

There's track lighting everywhere. Steel and concrete too. The modern aesthetic of it shocks Lalo once again—from the outside, a ranch house; from the inside, a sterile loft of sorts that could have been ripped out of the late 90s.

Along the walls are oversized and overstuffed pale beige leather sofas, like the kind you might find in the waiting room of a dialysis clinic or at a discount furniture store. In the middle of the floor, where a coffee table might go, there's a giant, two hundred gallon cast-iron pot, like the kind used to melt sugar cane pulp down into molasses and then into sugar bricks. It's filled with coins and bills: the preparations Jimmy likes to talk so much about.

The first thing Jimmy asks for is Cuauhtémoc's wallet, which Lalo produces. Jimmy splits it open and takes all of eight dollars from inside and tosses it into the pot.

"Small price to pay for your life," he says to Cuauhtémoc and invites him to sit on the couch in front of a seventy-inch wall-mounted TV that makes everything glow in blue and white hues. El Jimmy connects his laptop via Chromecast to the television. On the screen, in front of Cuauhtémoc, is a picture of him taken by a security camera from the Mexican side of the border. That same picture is the one being used as propaganda by the Mexican government, the one that's been plastered all over the papers in recent days.

"New clothes, same face," says Jimmy with a smile now, looking between the screen and Cuauhtémoc. "Tell me that's you, boy."

"That's me," says Cuauhtémoc.

"Were you the only one in that aircraft?"

Cuauhtémoc looks to Lalo. Lalo nods for him to respond. "I was," says Cuauhtémoc.

"So, you flew the plane."

"I can fly anything," says Cuauhtémoc.

At this, Jimmy smiles. "I didn't ask that, son. I asked if you flew *that* plane."

"I'm sorry. I'm a little thirsty. I'm not thinking right," says Cuauhtémoc. "Yes. I flew that plane."

"How rude of me," says Jimmy. "I didn't offer either of you anything to drink. I don't do alcohol myself. Some water?"

"Please," says Cuauhtémoc, eyeing the glass tank in the corner next to the television.

El Jimmy moves slowly across the room. He picks up a clay mug, blows into it to dust it out. He looks as if he's about to say something but decides against it. The sound of water in the mug is like liquid silver in the air to Cuauhtémoc. As soon as Cuauhtémoc's handed the mug, he downs the water with two fierce gulps. Water dribbles down his chin and into the collar of his shirt.

"Another glass, please," he says to El Jimmy.

At this Lalo puts his hand over his face. A look of surprise comes over Lalo's face as El Jimmy gets up almost as soon as he's seated again and takes the clay mug back and forth between Cuauhtémoc and the glass tank, buying Cuauhtémoc's loyalty one glug at a time.

Later that afternoon, Cuauhtémoc finds himself sitting at the end of a stained red oak table in Jimmy's kitchen. There's an elderly woman in a simple, cotton skirt and blouse stoking a fire inside an old-timey kitchen range made out of enough cast-iron to crack the tiles it's resting on. Cuauhtémoc guesses the range is original to the property. It looks completely out of place in the modern aesthetic of it all.

"¿Un cafecito?" she asks him.

"Sí, por fa," says Cuauhtémoc to the woman.

She smiles in this suppressed way, her lips drawn wide, as if to suggest that she's not supposed to talk to Cuauhtémoc more than she's allowed. She turns her back to him and pulls out a top-crank German coffee grinder from a cabinet above her head. She measures out the coffee by the palmful, her hand going wrist-deep, back and forth, into this burlap sack of whole beans. Cuauhtémoc looks out the kitchen window just over her shoulder to see Lalo leading a pony by the reigns, his daughter proudly in the saddle with his oversized Stetson dominating her head. Their shadows run long on the ground, the hottest part of the day already over. A ring of sweat drapes Lalo's shoulders. Every once in a while, the pony starts licking at the salt on the back of his neck which makes Cuauhtémoc chuckle to himself. Cuauhtémoc notices the graveyard of planes in the close distance. He's momentarily startled by the loudness of the grinder sawing away at the beans. Jimmy's boots pound over the tiles behind him. He slaps Cuauhtémoc on the back with the flat of his palm as he moves to the other end of the oak table and says, "Dolores, *café, por favor.*"

"*Casi listo,*" the old woman says from behind him with that same flat smile. From his vest pocket he pulls out a matchbook and silver cigarette case filled with Gauloises.

"Cigarette?" he says to Cuauhtémoc.

"Just the coffee."

"We can speak in English. I want to hear your English. Have you eaten?"

"Lalo took me out for some *chilaquiles* this morning."

"Tst—chilaquiles. I have some Pan de Muerto. It's out of season but I always have some on hand. Dolores makes them with fresh eggs."

"I'm good. Just the coffee, please."

"Suit yourself," he says.

Dolores puts the percolator on the range. The smell of coffee and ash fills the air. "You take cream with your coffee?"

"Just black," says Cuauhtémoc.

At this El Jimmy smiles. "*Tan americano.* You said you were from Texas?"

"South Texas," says Cuauhtémoc.

"Whereabouts?"

"Harlingen."

"I know Harlingen," says Jimmy taking a slow drag from his cigarette. "We used to have a supply house off Highway 83. A little town called Weslaco just to the west of Harlingen proper.

It was a ranch out there—some private property impossible to get a search warrant for. We rigged it that way. We used to drop loads out there in the pasture and then circle back, get more product, drop again. Day and night. That was before the Zetas and the Sinaloa war and Calderón and all that. We flew everywhere. We were like Pan Am," Jimmy says with a smile. "And that was just my cell. This one."

"And then what happened?" says Cuauhtémoc.

"Well, what the fuck didn't happen?" he says with a heavy, pensive kind of exasperation. "The short of it is that the air routes have all but stopped. Our turf has shrunk. What's that expression you Americans say—writing on the wall? We're fucked. We're just business people, most of us. We didn't ask for the war to come to us. But now that it's here, we have to look at our options. So, here's the hard truth: this cell is not part of the Juárez cartel anymore, understand? Officially it is, but it isn't. It's all going to implode. The game is this: we need capital. To get that we need to move product. To do that we need an American pilot."

"Why an American pilot?"

"Because we need an American accent. You get where I'm going with this?" says Jimmy.

"You want me to talk on the radios."

"Exactly."

"You want to fly analog: an American pilot with an American accent taking American vectors from a class C American airport with an American transponder and radio frequency flying Mexican product."

"You're sharper than you look," says Jimmy, that little bitch cackle of his ringing out at the top of his smoker's cough. His eyes are visibly excited now.

He leans forward in his chair just as Dolores places the coffee in front of him. He ignores it. All he can see is Cuauhtémoc now.

"Do you have an American plane?" asks Cuauhtémoc. "None of that would work without an American tail number."

"We have a few," says Jimmy, a little too over eager. "I noticed from the photograph that you were flying a Pawnee."

"I can a fly high-wing or low-wing. Doesn't matter."

"We used to have a lot of Cessna 172s with American tail numbers. Brand new ones, but all of those got scrapped. We used to fly into small municipal airports, class D or E. Didn't matter so long as they didn't have towers or security. We'd unload right there on the tarmac, leave the planes. We could afford to buy ten more the next day."

Just then Cuauhtémoc remembers those rows of planes at Harlingen field, the airport where he trained with Sampson's son. He remembers a row of Cessnas parked back by the fence, all of them plastered with orange stickers layered over the windshields—tickets for each day their parking fee hadn't been paid. Cuauhtémoc remembers that the planes were parked there so long that the flight base operator called the sheriff out, asked what he should do. "Soon as these folks come back for what they left I'll be collecting some major income," the operator told the sheriff. Nobody had the heart to tell the man that nobody was coming back for those planes. Back then, Cuauhtémoc could only guess at what he saw, which is that they were scrap planes. Everyone treated them as such.

"I'm glad you were able to see our doctor," says El Jimmy. "I heard your arm took a slice."

At this Cuauhtémoc lifts up the sleeve of his shirt to show Jimmy the damage. Eighteen stitches to his bicep. Another eleven on the heel of his palm.

"Did the doctor give you a timeframe for recovery?"

"A month or two. The good thing is that they were clean slices with a sharp blade. Not too deep. No tearing."

"You should have never been out there in the gladiator fights. Between us chickens: Lalo is a little bit desperate. For his daughter, understand? He's stressed, which makes him a bit of an idiot sometimes. He didn't know you were a pilot. You should have told him."

"He didn't ask," says Cuauhtémoc.

"Of course, he didn't. Can you still fly? I need you to fly," says Jimmy.

"What do you want me to fly?" says Cuauhtémoc.

"I thought you said you can fly anything. Prove it then."

"When?"

"Right now. Tonight. You fly for me and you'll get out of this alive. I promise you."

He pounds his palms on the table, grabbing hold of the corners of it. His cigarette falls from between his fingers, embers and ash fanning out across the cold tile. The cigarette rolls in circles around the filter's axis.

Jimmy locks eyes with Cuauhtémoc. "Hey, look at me. Look right here: I promise you. I'll get you out of this alive."

The contract is remarkably simple: Cuauhtémoc flies product for El Jimmy's cell and so becomes a salaried underling of his. Because they've spared his life, Cuauhtémoc agrees to throw half of what he's paid into Jimmy's pot for preparations. If a brick goes missing, Cuauhtémoc dies. If a plane goes missing, Cuauhtémoc dies. If Cuauhtémoc goes missing, they find Cuauhtémoc (wherever he's at in the world) and Cuauhtémoc dies. They promise him that if they can't find him, they'll take next of kin, which Jimmy emphasizes by giving Cuauhtémoc a jailbroken iPhone loaded with dozens of pictures of his mother: in the streets of Matamoros, cranking something under the hood of his father's busted and smoking truck, talking to a strange man with her oversized bags in his hand, smoking a cigarette on a bed as she stares at the ceiling of some room Cuauhtémoc doesn't know.

Cuauhtémoc doesn't ask El Jimmy how he found her. All he knows is that they haven't found Uli yet, and there's some hope in that.

He wonders about this new life. What it entails, how long he has to do it. *However long*, he guesses. There's no real choice here. No way out. The main thing is to stay alive. Cuauhtémoc knows he can't find his brother if he's dead. He can't keep his mother alive if he runs. He's trapped. And knowing that he's trapped, a silent rage boils deep inside him not unlike that same rage he felt that night in the killing fields or that same rage he feels toward Lalo now for bringing him into this in the first place.

That night, Cuauhtémoc makes a promise to himself: if they kill his mother, he'll kill Lalo's daughter. He stokes that rage, lets it bloom, keeps it glowing as he prepares for the flight that will save his life. His mother's and his brother's too.

In the bathroom of Jimmy's home, he stands under the hot pour of the showerhead until his skin feels like rubber. His pink sutures sing with pain as blood fills his wounds.

When he's done, there's cold water that he splashes from the faucet onto his face. There's electricity and heat and gas. He gets to thinking about how strange it is to him—all of these things that could bring a house down to its foundation, and we invite it all into our homes. Cuauhtémoc soaps up, thinks of a million ways to kill Lalo's daughter.

Over the toilet seat rest his new things: a plain white cotton T-shirt, some black Wrangler's jeans too stiff at the crotch, a pair of white socks, a pair of dark brown boots.

Once he's dressed, he steps into the dark of the house. He follows that darkness to the open door just off the kitchen, where his eyes adjust to the desert night, which is darker than dark. Like stepping into nothing.

He puts his hand out in front of him, and he can't even see that. His feet only know where to walk by the silver arc of pickup headlights that spray across the ground. He imagines disappearing into the darkness, running off into the desert. They'd never find him.

As he walks, out in the far distance Cuauhtémoc sees a floating city. Which one? He couldn't say. He squints. Just in front of that, the silhouette of something very big. The stars too bright now, silver pins in a purple, plush cushion.

It's midnight by the Big Dipper's position in the sky. Cuauhtémoc blinks. Looks at the silhouette again. A very large plane appears, right in front of him, against the night like a ghost out of thin air, like some kind of David Copperfield trick. The plane is bigger than anything he's ever flown before.

El Jimmy's sour, ashy voice rings out from behind Cuauhtémoc's ear. "Can you fly it?" he says.

The sound jolts Cuauhtémoc from his thoughts. "I don't know," says Cuauhtémoc, which is, of course, the wrong answer.

"You must fly it," demands Jimmy, suddenly severe. "You said you could fly it."

Cuauhtémoc looks back, but there's nothing there. Just darkness and the voice ringing out, "Show me you can fly it. Show me. Show me right now."

From the darkness, a hand takes hold of Cuauhtémoc, leading him by the shoulder with a soft tug. The tips of Jimmy's fingers gingerly pull along the seams of Cuauhtémoc's sutures.

Cuauhtémoc follows his pain into the darkness. Just under the wing of the colossal plane, he can already tell that he'd be lucky to get it off the ground. At the wheels, a red puddle of hydraulic fluid dripping from the impact cylinder to the tread of the tires and then into the dirt. At the connecting joints between the wing and ailerons, there's a lot of gleaming, painted rust. On the leading edge of the right propeller, there are so many nicks and dings from the desert sand and stone that have flown up behind the propellers and shredded the plane to pieces.

Jimmy's voice softens when he asks Cuauhtémoc, "Do you think it will fly?"

Cuauhtémoc, surprised by the question, says to Jimmy, "It hasn't flown before?"

"We've never seen it fly," says Jimmy.

"Where did you find it then?"

A long silence between Cuauhtémoc's question and Jimmy's response. "Bought it."

"From?" says Cuauhtémoc, emboldened now by his aviation expertise. They trust him, which gives him a little courage.

"The *ejército*."

"The army?"

"Well, yes, a former general in the army," says Jimmy in this guttural tone, slightly embarrassed at the fact. Cuauhtémoc wonders how a cartel buys a plane from the very army they're fighting against.

"What kind is it?" asks Jimmy

"A Beechcraft King Air," says Cuauhtémoc. He points at the tail. "If it weren't painted, it'd say it right there. I'm sure there's a pilot's operating handbook somewhere inside that'll prove me right."

"It's old?"

"Very old," says Cuauhtémoc.

"If we steal an American tail number and repaint it could you fly it into Texas?"

Cuauhtémoc doesn't answer just yet. He works his way around the aircraft, Jimmy close behind. Beyond the port side wing, a dozen pickups filled with men watching his every move.

"Mechanically, I think it will fly. But not to Texas. Not yet," says Cuauhtémoc.

"Cuauhtémoc, I trust you. You are honest, I can tell. But can you fly this tonight?"

"I can try," says Cuauhtémoc as he makes his way around the plane once again, Texas on his mind. He opens the door to the cabin.

The pre-flight ritual for Cuauhtémoc comes flooding back from memory. At the rodeo corral he never thought in a million years he'd live to do this again. His broken body tries to recreate, from muscle memory, every part of the pre-flight check.

He slips the steel elevator lock from the yoke shaft, tucking it into the back seat pocket behind him. He knows he's supposed to keep loose things latched down lest they become flying projectiles on impact. Sampson's son taught him that. He never forgets that one.

Cuauhtémoc swings his body into the cockpit, eases the cotton shirt on his back into the pleather seat cushion. The cushion lets out a little wheeze of air under his weight. He lays his toes into the hydraulic brakes over the rudder pedals. He tests their pressure.

"Needs more red," shouts Cuauhtémoc to Jimmy in English, a momentary lapse of memory. His body is in Mexico but, behind the yoke, his mind is in Texas.

"More red?" says Jimmy back to Cuauhtémoc in English, a slight tone of embarrassment at the sound of his accented voice.

Cuauhtémoc is impressed with how comfortable he feels behind the dials and knobs and switches. He knows where everything is. The fuel mixture rod is still red and the throttle rod is still black. Most everything else he can guess at.

He sets the fuel mixture rich by pushing in the red rod. He throttles to neutral by pulling out the black rod. He flips on the master switch to listen to the whirring magnetos swimming in perfect sync behind the faux wooden panels. He rounds the DG to the nearest tenth by the whiskey compass on the windshield. He cranks the engines with a turn of the key. Both propellers wheeze. They let out black smoke that looks orange in the headlights of the trucks surrounding the plane as if the smoke were on fire. Cuauhtémoc thinks the engines on each wing are rough, but they work. Beneath the radio deck, he flips on the landing light and then the strobes, which are burnt out but flickering on the port side wing. The light makes the propellers dance and warp as if he were looking at them underwater. The port side engine coughs hard, and Cuauhtémoc instinctively leans the mixture, pushes the throttle with his toes spread out over the tops of the rudder pedals to burn off the carbon deposits. And like a charm, it works. The engines roar to life. The engines sing now, and in the dancing strobe light of the wings Cuauhtémoc can see a few dozen bodies jumping out from inside their truck cabins to watch the spectacle, all hopes placed on him. Weirdly enough, his anger dissipates, if only for a moment. He looks at those bodies piling out to watch him and feels, for maybe the first time in his life, a certain value to himself, to this newfound position of importance. *Everything rides on this*, he thinks. He feels proud. Eager to please.

With all the engine gremlins coughed out, the air gusts hard over the desert sand. There's a deafening *whoosh* that vibrates the length of the airframe, right up to the yoke where Cuauhté- moc imagines those grains of sand gritting under his fingernails.

He flips on the avionics switch and there's a squelching noise blaring from the headphones lying next to him. He looks out the windshield once again. All of the men out of their trucks now, the whites of their eyes flashing in the strobe. Cuauhtémoc looks from them to that city on the horizon. Beyond that, the border lights of Texas.

On the ground, he aligns the plane to zero degrees on the whiskey compass and digs his toes into the rudder. And without giving so much as two thoughts to the whole process—about how to take off on a sand strip or how to coerce an aging plane into the sky—he shoves the throttle in full to the chrome gilding and pops the yoke back into his chest to keep the front wheel from digging into the earth. The plane eases from its idled position. It goes fast, faster. Cuauhtémoc rides that pocket of air until the plane violently shakes. It's only when he's reached seventy knots that he shifts the plane's lumbering weight from the ground to the wings and lifts the main wheels off the ground to hover in that pocket-bubble called ground effect until eighty knots, ninety-five knots, and the wind shakes the tips of the wings, and you can see the turbulence spiraling down by the patterns made in the sand. *Whap-whap-whap* go the blades cutting air. And then silence. That split second when everything swims in sync and the thing is airborne, ready to stall and yet still climbing skyward, another silver pin among the stars.

In the air, the engines groan as Cuauhtémoc pushes toward cruising speed. He looks down toward the earth, and there they are still. All those men waiting like idiots. A fellow thief, for all they know, flying their plane, and all of them standing around hopelessly looking, watching, waiting for him to land.

There's a hubris that overwhelms Cuauhtémoc when he sees Texas. *I could go*, he thinks. But who knows if he'd even make it? Who knows if there's even enough fuel in the wings?

For the first time in his life he feels truly powerful. He's in control of his body again, of this machine. He leans the mixture till the engines gurgle, too little fuel. He puts some mixture back in to keep the engines running clean. He cuts the throttle back, the tailwind doing all the work now, and he whispers to the plane, convincing it to stay cool if only for just a little longer. *That's fine*, he says to her, *right there. Right like this. That's fine.*

A thousand feet up, and he kicks the left rudder crosswind to land. At the turn again he feels the winds shake the plane, and the lift spreads goosy over the wings, the plane dropping suddenly as if the landing gear has been knocked out beneath him. The wings buckle on a pocket of invisible wind that rattles the airframe before setting him right again on a downward slope to land. A lump in Cuauhtémoc's throat now. A nauseous rocking in his stomach like it's a fishbowl filled with water, the only thing keeping him upright, and the plane drops again. He aims the nose at those silver arcs cutting the desert. All of those men standing in and around the headlights. And then he watches those arcs grow bigger and brighter, the plane descending toward the earth.

He sees Texas out in front of him again, rising in the windshield. He thinks to himself, *Last chance—do it, do it!*

Out of the windshield, everything is falling apart before his very eyes. He notices a loose rivet bobbing at the nose of the plane, just in front of the datum. That gives him all the excuse he needs not to go to Texas. The plane groans again.

Cuauhtémoc dumps in ten degrees of flaps, then fifteen, then twenty until he's falling steady at seventy knots. He listens for the squeal of the stall horn. He pushes the throttle, checks his rate of descent. Carburetor out, gas switch set to both engines, undercarriage down, fuel mixture rich, primer switch locked, seatbelts and switches on.

His hands are so tight on the yoke that his sutures bead bright with blood, little speckled dots appearing on his white cotton shirt.

As the plane slows, there's the ripping sound of air. The northern winds dumping over the wings that push him firm to the earth like an ant crushed under foot into the ground—the entire sky is above him. He rolls along the ground, set to plow right into those silver arcs cutting the desert air. And he thinks about it—he thinks about killing all of them. One swipe of the propeller, and it'd be done. He imagines those trucks shredded like tin cans. He imagines Lalo's daughter resting in the bed of one of them. He imagines how that might feel before his feet crush the brakes, and he can feel his body pressing hard against the seatbelt. All of the blood rushes to the front of his body. It leaks out from every open wound in his skin.

GIG

ARACELI WAKES UP THIS MORNING the way she wakes up every morning: by the burn of her thirst. She clutches her throat with an open palm. She swears that *this* will be the day she finally gets her diabetes medication.

There's a black market she knows of at the back of an arcade nearby. She has the money to buy her medicines, but wonders how much the drugs will set her back. She needs a bottle of Glyset, a bottle of Amaryl and a bottle of Amitriptyline.

This morning, she thinks back to those pills she left behind. She knows exactly where she put them.

She uncaps a bottle of Topo Chico mineral water on her night stand by pulling her wedding band under the cap and rolling her palm forward to peel it off. She lets the carbonation fizz drift up the neck of the bottle and then drinks it all in one go.

She lines the empty bottle up against the baseboard opposite her bed like she's done with all the other bottles she's downed. She counts her days by the number of empties along the wall, all of them filled with her cornhusk cigarettes. This morning she starts on bottle eighty-five, which makes three weeks drinking four bottles a day since she's been in Matamoros. Three weeks that her truck's been broken down. Three weeks since she's last seen her sons.

She lights a cigarette, her three hundred and thirty-seventh by her calculations, and parts the curtains to the window that looks out onto her blue pickup parked in the street. She checks the clock on the nightstand. Five in the morning, which makes it one hour until the food stands open, which makes another two hours before the boy that Iván's hired comes by with his little rag of shitty tools to work on the truck.

Araceli has a good mind to go out and fix the damn thing herself. She'd do it if her nerve pain weren't killing her. She thinks about her sons, thinks about her medications. She knows exactly where her sons are going to be. That thought calms her a little. No rush. They're grown now—they know how to get to San Miguel.

On Calle Ejido, Araceli walks into the first arcade she sees. There's a cashier at the entrance, a Chinese man lighting a Faro cigarette with the blue flame of a votive candle, the Virgen de Guadalupe. There's the rich spice of smoke and cologne in the air.

The cashier lowers the candle from his face, nods for Araceli to come in. He knows she's here for the black market, the entrance of which is located by the pinball machines via a staircase that leads down into the market itself.

Araceli follows the rattle and clang of the pinball machine toward the back of the arcade. A pair of brothers, the only patrons of the arcade, bang their tiny fists against the Plexiglass of the single working pinball machine by the stairs. Araceli can see their hopes pinned on the sway of a steel ball that curves along a lit sprung peg that jolts up and down inside the glass— no telling which way the ball will roll. *What a life.*

Araceli descends the stairs at the back of the arcade that lead to the black market, the *fayuca*, which is all fluorescent and bleached concrete, an endless maze of counterfeit clothing, counterfeit shoes, leather goods, DVDs, home appliances, tables filled with knives, rotting meat unchilled and bleeding in the open air behind glass cases full of *gelatina* and melting wedding cakes. It's like night and day—the arcade and the fayuca. There is everything here, and everything is abundant. Araceli feels her chest swell with hope. She looks for her medicines.

She weaves in and out of booths of fortunetellers, Freon vendors, rosary makers and blaring televisions. At the end of a row, there's a Jensen speaker blasting Hank Williams from inside a cracked Fender amplifier, the bass turned up so loud it pushes air all the way into the black particle-wood dens. Araceli feels the noise in her sternum as she walks by. At the end of another row, a neon yellow cardboard sign dances from the air pushed by an electric fan. The sign says *Viajes a Texas. Cowboy Cuntry. Viajes a Virgenia también. Más barato, bien barato.* Next to the sign is a small, dingy operation with a simple wooden sign: *Medicinas.*

In the medicine booth, there's a woman sitting behind a cheap desk, the kind you might find in a mechanic's shop or a church office. There's a phone on the desk that's disconnected, its line coiled tight into a roll beside it. There's a stapler, a receipt book and a box of unsharpened pencils. A sham consultation office or doctor's office or whatever it's supposed to be.

Araceli fixes her hair before she approaches the woman who has the phone receiver winched between her head and her neck.

"Hello," says Araceli to the woman.

The woman looks up at Araceli, staring daggers. Then she points to the phone as if motioning, *Can't you see I'm in the middle of something?*

Araceli looks down beside the phone, the cord still tightly coiled. Disconnected.

"Uh-huh," says the woman into the receiver. "Uh-huh. Perfect. I'll call you right back," she says.

"Hello," says Araceli again.

"Get to the point. We're very busy here at *Medicinas*."

Araceli looks around as if to confirm where she's at. The black market? Yes. She's in the black market.

"Very busy?" asks Araceli.

"Yes," says the woman in this mock-professional tone. "We have everything you need. Blood thinners, steroids, antibiotics," she says, launching into her spiel.

"I get it," says Araceli cutting her off.

A slight look of embarrassment comes over the woman's face now.

"I need Amitriptyline. Do you have it?"

"We have everything," says the woman behind the desk, staring daggers once more as if Araceli is intentionally trying to stump her.

"How much?" asks Araceli.

"Depends on your dosage," says the woman, looking smug now.

"Five hundred milligrams."

Hesitation. "Just a second," says the woman trying her best to discretely connect the phone now to a line that runs into the concrete floor.

From the receiver, a clicking sound and then a dial tone. The woman punches some numbers. Araceli can hear the distinct, buzzy sound of a man's voice picking up on the other end of the line.

"Amitriptyline," says the woman into the phone. "Five hundred," she says. "Yes. That'll do."

Araceli reaches for the bills in her pocket but decides against taking her money out in public. Instead she reaches for the cornhusk cigarette resting in the far corner of her pocket. Her last. She takes it out and puts it to her lips.

"Do you have a match?" Araceli asks the woman.

"Is that a cigarette?" the woman asks her, a look of mild disgust on her face.

"Yes," says Araceli sheepishly.

"Tobacco?"

"Yes," says Araceli again. "What else would it be?"

Just then a motorcycle roars up to the back entrance of the medicine stand. A brief flash of daylight as the back door opens into the stall. Some steps just inside the little gut-alley behind the stall leading up to the street.

An older man appears behind the desk, his gray head of sweaty hair lays plastered to his scalp. He rests his helmet on the cheap desk.

"Five hundred," he says to Araceli, walking toward her with a case of Amitriptyline under his arm. Farmacia Benavides brand.

The woman takes Araceli's cornhusk cigarette from her mouth to examine it closer. "Look," she says to the motorcycle man. "Like a baby tamal."

The woman looks to the man. A knowing glance between them.

"Can you make these?" says the woman to Araceli. "Do you need a job?"

Araceli thinks for a while before plucking the cigarette back from the woman's hand. "Yes," she says, plucking her box of drugs from the man's arms too. "In fact I do."

Araceli wishes her sons back as much as she wishes for her husband back. She thinks if she had to choose, she'd choose her husband to die. If she had to choose herself over everyone, she'd choose herself. She feels deep down in her gut that she might be given the choice, which keeps her in Matamoros working steady out of indecision, going nowhere for fear of the wrong choice, a bad move, a single fatal error.

It happens, every morning, that she wakes up at five and runs toward the bus station. No food in her belly. Just two ten-peso coins in her pocket jingle-jangling in the dead of darkness. Nobody sees her this early except that hawk boy always on the corner talking into his phone, reporting what he sees. Always there.

He watches Araceli sweat, her unsteady foot landing on the pavement so closely in time to her good foot that the pair of them together sound like the slowed down syncopated clop of a horse's hooves.

She'll sit in the terminal of the Estrella Roja station for five or seven minutes, staring up at the departures list, before a look comes over her face. Araceli reasoning with herself. She'll count her coins, and the morning bus will leave. And she'll hobble back toward the hotel, the hawk boy's eyes trained on her all the while.

She'll sit in her truck and cry till daylight. She'll pop the hood when the sun turns orange and take a look, shake her head. Nothing to be done. Everything burnt inside.

She'll count her money again, over and over, until the sun bursts bright in the chemical air of dawn. Exhaust smoke, kitchen smoke, factory smoke piling high as the cars build up on the bridge. She'll count her coins again and go to work. A skipped meal here, another there—*It all adds up*, she thinks. Her hunger makes her proud. With every step she thinks, *Today will be the day I find my sons.* She'll believe it too.

She'll think, in these long mornings, that for all she knows they're still in the city. Although, deep down she believes they must be in San Miguel. She knows it—and so she'll work another day.

Araceli will go to the black market to work where she gets her medicines. The woman at the desk will always say to Araceli, "new stack," pointing toward an empty pallet behind her. On the pallet a cardboard box. Two sacks to the left and right of a chair positioned in front of a picnic table. Araceli will simply say, "Good," before she gets to work, ready to be rid of the woman, ready to work in silence for the rest of the day. She'll position herself, legs straddled, behind the picnic table with the remnants of yesterday's work: a marijuana grinder—a clipping machine used to cinch the ends of a blunt—and a razor blade used to scrape the leftover marijuana into new piles to be used in the next batch, and then the next.

She'll start by taking a handful from each sack beside her. A palmful of marijuana buds to her left, a stack of dried corn husks to her right. She'll put both piles at opposite ends of the table, the cinching machine in the middle. She'll listen to Hank Williams playing in the next stall over and grind the marijuana bud to the music, grind it to a fine dust that she'll segment into lines with the razor. She'll take the cornhusks and strip them lengthwise, taking the razor once again and cutting long strips in halves, then quarters. She'll take the razor and scrape it beneath the marijuana dust and dump it into a segment of corn-husk and roll it between her middle fingers and thumbs until packed tight. She'll lick it to make it hold and then take a nico-tine adhesive that she'll paint over the length of the seam to make it stick. She'll put the blunt into the cinching machine to crush the ends together until they fuse under the pressure. And with the razor she'll lob off the crushed ends to make a perfectly round blunt, the ends of the cornhusk thrown back into the palm grinder to cut the marijuana even further. She'll earn fif-teen to twenty pesos more—a peso a blunt—if she stretches the marijuana this way. So, she'll do it often.

Each day she'll work steadily, efficiently. Until one day she slips, taking her eyes off her work when she sees a man bring in a carburetor just like hers into the stall across from *medicinas*.

The salesman, a skinny, coal-eyed boy, shakes his head of curly hair at the sight of the part and talks with the customer a while. Araceli watches him produce a milk carton from under the table with a hole in the side of it, a bottle of glue funneled toward the bottom near the red pop-off cap. She watches the salesman put a silver pipe into the side of the milk carton. That's about the time she presses her left index finger beneath the blunt cincher.

Blood boils hot beneath her nail bed. It spills in a steady stream onto the table in front of her.

Araceli applies pressure around her finger with the grip of her fist. She backs up out of her seat in shock. *No*, she thinks, *sit down. Calm down. Slow your heart rate.*

There's nicotine glue in the palm of Araceli's hand and by squeezing the wound with her fist, she makes it sting something fierce. Araceli's first thought goes to infection. *Hydrogen peroxide*, she thinks. She fumbles with her slick hands inside the various cabinets that make up the back room of the medicine stall. She goes through the system quickly in her mind: top row for medicines, middle row for herbs, bottom row for surgical supplies.

In the bottom right cabinet, she finds a small packet of cotton gauze, a roll of surgical tape, a pair of scissors. *Where the fuck is the hydrogen peroxide?*

She opens all the corners first and then starts in the middle of the cabinet grid and works her way out. Bottles of pills, bottles of crushed leaves, band-aids, wooden tongue depressors, ointments and creams, until finally she finds the brown bottle of hydrogen peroxide behind a giant brick of marijuana.

Araceli pulls both the brick and the hydrogen peroxide from the cabinet. She thinks about it for a minute. *No*, she says to herself, *that'd be stealing. And what would you do with it any-*

way? The sight of it almost takes her mind away from the pain. If it weren't for the steady drip onto the ground, she could have admired that brick all day.

She cracks the bottle of hydrogen peroxide and douses it over her hand. The whole mess roars to a fizz, that silvery smell in the air. Over her bloody nail, she rolls a piece of gauze that blooms red under the pressure of the surgical tape. Three rolls in a spiral fashion from the knuckle to the nail. Three rolls back the other way to keep it snug. One more layer of gauze. Two more spirals of tape.

She hobbles on her bad foot around the table, her shoes making prints in the blood on the concrete. *No matter,* she thinks and picks up the brick once again. It must be ten pounds. Eleven maybe. Split the right way that brick could be worth its weight in gold.

Under the hood of her pickup, Araceli cuts the crown off the hydrogen peroxide bottle with surgical scissors. She punches three close holes in the screw-on cap and one large hole in the side of the plastic crown by grinding the tip of the scissors into the plastic and turning the finger slots one over the other. She takes her materials and lays them to the right of the engine compartment: her new make-shift carburetor, a roll of surgical tape, the scissors and the tiny jar of nicotine adhesive. She tears out the old carburetor with a hammer and her weight, the sound of groaning metal flexing along the tensile points. The plastic rivets squeak. Araceli hammers and pulls, hammers and pulls again only half-sure that she's pulling at the right part. Her bloody, greased hands burrow into the maze of fan belts and fuse boxes, her knuckles scraped raw by the cast-iron V6. When the carburetor finally gives, there's the stinking, sweet smell of fuel in the air.

The circular hunk of metal lands with a crash on the sidewalk behind Araceli. The hawk boy cuts her a glance. She cuts him one right back. The boy backpedals on his haunches, his phone click-clacking onto the pavement. The sound is satisfying to Araceli. She turns back to her work and straightens out the bent fuel line.

She pushes the aluminum fuel line into the side hole of the bottle's crown, her blood pouring in driblets from her finger to the fan belt below. She takes the roll of surgical tape and makes an air tight seal between the gaps in the plastic and the aluminum, lacquering the tape with the nicotine adhesive. She rolls another strip of tape over the lacquer. She makes a debris screen by stretching the surgical tape into a grid pattern over the top of the opened crown. She makes a seal, too, in the same manner between the bottle cap and the V6 engine.

"Iván!" she yells, waving her bloody finger at him through the glass. "Come crank the engine."

Iván comes out to turn the key and black, chemical smoke pours from the starter clicking into gear. There's the sound of the spark plugs lighting, the leads firing in staggered sync with the fuse box then a clicking rattle like the sound of a ticking clock.

"Give it gas," she yells to Iván.

He pushes the pedal down, and the fluid from the aluminum fuel line drips into the crown of the bottle. He cranks again as the fuel filters down into the screw-on cap, pours through the holes and makes its way into the engine. Combustion. A tiny flame leaps from the taped seal, melting it around the bottle cap.

"More gas!" yells Araceli, blood trickling down her arm now. "More. Give it! Keep the pedal down!"

Another chemical blast of smoke and the engine roars to life, the pistons jumping up and down inside their aluminum cage. The engine warms, the fan belt turns, the lights blast their weak light over the ruddy pavement as the hawk boy watches and speaks into his little phone.

THE BURNING MARE

ULI STANDS AT THE BATHROOM SINK with his hands under the faucet trying to wash the greasy smell of the death from his fingers. There's hot water in the bathroom, thanks to June who has installed atop the roof a gravity-fed Rotoplas rain collector. She's also installed a cheap boiler that burns through a tank of gas a week. Uli says there's a leak in the line, but June says his showers are too long and that's the problem. He reasons to himself that they can afford it now. They fetched a couple thousand dollars between them from the rings. Enough money to eat, buy the dog his medicines, shower however long he wants. He gave June her cut of the money. He should enjoy the return on his investment. He turns the faucet hotter.

Uli doesn't know what he wants to do with his money yet. He's thinking about saving up to cross over into Texas from Ciudad Juárez. His father used to cross there. It'd be one way to get home. For now, he puts his chunk of money in the back of a Bible he found under his father's bed—the last place June would look. June keeps her money somewhere too. Uli doesn't know where yet. She says she's saving up for a car. Something Chinese, something cheap.

At the sink, Uli feels the water on his skin. He needs his shower like he needs his morning bottle of Coke. He loves the waste of it—a shower in the desert—but mostly he loves the feel of the heat in his muscles, his pain melting into his heated flesh.

He watches a blister form over his right knuckle under the scalding faucet. He takes his hands out of the water and opens the medicine cabinet over the sink. He looks for a cream, but only finds a pack of condoms, a brown glass bottle of vitamins and a Swedish steel straight-razor with a stain of dried blood.

He takes the packet of condoms out from behind the mirror and shakes it. Chuckles to himself. He puts the condoms back before downing two vitamins from the brown, glass bottle and taking the straight razor with him into the shower to shave.

The little mirror that hangs from the showerhead fogs up as Uli takes the razor and holds the blade up to his face. He watches the little dot of blood wash away from the steel as the water glides over it.

Of all things to think about just then, he remembers a story his father used to tell him about the first beating he had ever taken.

"One time I met Holy Death in my dreams," he'd start.

He said he prayed to her daily, to Santa Muerte, and when she finally came to him, she was cutting silver strings with a wet scythe. She grazed his cheek with the back of her wet finger. She talked to him in a language he never knew but understood. He asked if he was going to die that night, and she said, "Worse than death is dying. But not to worry—you will have a good death."

His father was so scared, he went to confession the next day. He asked the priest, "Is it wrong to pray to her?"

His entire life, Uli's grandmother would sit her son down in front of Santa Muerte's image, an intricately painted ceramic statue with smoky, velvety eyes and a long, blue cape. She'd push his father's hands together so that he could pray for the return of his own father from the North where he worked. Uli's father prayed to her every night without fail.

"What is she?" he asked the priest. "Is it wrong to pray to her?"

"Yes," said the priest, "yes, you satanic, idol-worshipping fool. You've prayed to a demon in the guise of a saint. You've forsaken the Holy Spirit and put a curse on your family, which can never be undone."

Uli remembers that his father had said he was sorry, that he'd never do it again and then he said his penance.

"Wait," said the priest as his father stood to leave the confessional. "I want you to go home and prepare a dish. I want you to take it to the people who live in the fields across the railroad tracks on Calle Tres Cruces. As charity. And I want you to come back in the morning and tell me what happened."

So, his father did. He prepared the only thing he knew how to make, chicken with *mole* sauce from a jar, hungry the whole time because of the fasting that comes with penance. It wasn't until he reached the edge of the lot that he smelled the makeshift village: the soggy, wet fumes of burning cardboard, the smell of vinyl tarps, the propane tanks on full blast.

A dozen bodies appeared. They walked quickly toward him, dark, naked and dirty.

"And then what happened?" said the priest.

"They beat me," said his father. "They beat me, and the dish I cooked fell to the ground."

"And then?"

"And then they beat each other. They fought over the food. They ripped the flesh from the bones of the chicken like dogs. They licked the *mole* from the dirt. And then they beat me for my money."

"And did you give it to them?"

"Yes," his father said.

"And what did they say to you?"

"Your money or your life," his father said.

"And how did you feel?" the priest asked.

"All alone."

"And *that*," said the priest, "is Santa Muerte."

By the moonlight in the window, Uli puts the tip of the straight razor to the back of his blistered knuckles and presses down. Pus and blood stream pink down the drain. Just then, an incandescent bulb pierces the creeping darkness outside. His blood glistens in the glow.

He looks out the shower window. A porch light across the street. A man in the driveway with purple boots and a Stetson hat.

He's parked his burnt-orange Ford Lobo in front of their house. He's talking with another man who's behind a screened window. Uli turns off the shower and creeps down so just his eyes are peeking above the tile. A woman appears in the threshold of the door. She takes the hand of the man in the driveway and leads him into her home. Even from that distance Uli can tell she's the most gorgeous woman he's ever seen.

"Forget about her," says June to Uli the next day in the backyard. "Only thing you have to know about her is that she's your neighbor. That's it."

June rolls Parvo pills up into little balls of processed cheese in the kitchen and feeds it to Atómico, whose tongue smacks dry against the roof of his mouth as he tries to swallow his medicine. June pours him a bottle of Coke and pushes the container toward his snout. Atómico lazily cranes his neck toward the Coke and makes a mess lapping it up, the liquid splashing everywhere around his face.

While he's distracted, June redresses his bandages, applying a topical antibiotic to his sutured wounds so they don't get infected.

"He gonna be all right?" asks Uli, petting the dogs legs with his own busted foot.

"He's already all right," says June.

"You ever met her?" asks Uli, shifting the subject back to the lady.

"I know of her," says June, cutting a length of gauze with her teeth and tearing along the seam. "Tape," she says, nodding toward a band of vinyl electrical tape by Uli's foot.

Uli hands it over.

"What is she? A witch?" says Uli, jokingly.

"Something like that," says June. She takes a long stretch of tape and pulls it around the dog's neck like a collar. "She keeps this part of the city safe, anyway. Neutral turf, if you catch my drift."

"I don't."

"She keeps a lot of dangerous men happy, and they're all interested in her keeping on as she's keeping on."

"Does she make you happy?" Uli says to June, a smile creeping across his face now.

"Money makes me happy."

"That's because you've got a hole in your heart," says Uli. "Always trying to fill it."

"You're gonna have a hole in your face if you don't let it go."

"What's that?"

"You know. Let it go or you'll find out," says June, looking at him, serious all of a sudden.

She takes another fistful of processed cheese balls filled with melatonin supplements and throws it at Atómico for him to lap up while they're gone. Too much movement isn't good for a recovering dog, or so June says. Melatonin will keep him calm, keep him knocked out.

"Why do we even have to work today?" says Uli.

"We work every day. Right now it's easy, but soon you'll see—it'll get *lean*. Leaner than lean. You'll reach for that kilo of tortillas, and it'll be gone. And then you reach for your money and only half as much is there than you last remembered. And then you wish you would have saved, wish you would have kept working. You work in the lean, and you work in the fat. *Especially* the fat."

"Are we fat right now?"

"We're about to get fatter," says June, throwing her arm into a backpack strap.

"Where are we going?"

"To get some copper," says June, handing him the handle to a wagon full of smelting equipment: a butane torch, some gloves, a rubber hammer and rope.

June watches the military jets in the sky as she walks. She makes a game of spotting them before they come. At first, they appear as tiny glints of gleaming metal before quickly ripping the sky apart at its seams. She loves the feel of the noise in her heart. She marvels at the way something so relatively small can make a tear in the sky so loud as to drown out the sounds of a city itself. Even the dogs shut up for a second as jets pass overhead, and she loves that too. She thinks sometimes that's the way she'd like to be. Here and gone. A blast of noise in her wake.

Just then, she thinks about the car bomb, the charred stink of it still on her clothes. She wonders if charred skin isn't just scar tissue and if so, was anything still breathing in that mass of flesh? *Could they have survived?* she wonders. A certain heaviness falls upon her heart. *Don't be dumb. They were dead,* she reassures herself. Though just thinking on it, she can't help but think back to her own scar that formed over the charred skin of her face.

She lugs the wagon filled with scrapping supplies between the boulders in the street, Uli is close behind and remembers how it felt to be left for dead at one time. Sometimes, June wishes she would have died that night. Or any other night really. Maybe she wishes she would have died sooner, like her older sister who was found by a priest down by where she worked.

June's sister, Gloria, built transmissions in the *maquila* by the river. They'd moved to the border from Michoacán along with their mother who made and sold *licuados* and *aguas* at the gate of the maquilas.

Like most every other migrant soul in San Miguel, they'd been bottlenecked here by accident. So close to the border.

June's mother said they'd wait, they'd work, until their luck came along and they could cross over. San Miguel killed each of them except for June

Gloria was killed for no reason other than the fact that she was a woman. Like all the other women who'd been killed in San Miguel, she was killed in the early morning on her way to work. Her body had been cut from pubic bone to sternum in one single rip. No motive, nothing taken from her.

It was a priest who found her on her side. When the police came, it was said the priest, who was red from his fingers to his waist, had tried for hours to make Gloria whole again. He told the medics, when they finally arrived, that he didn't want to move her because he knew if you moved a patient, you might hurt them worse. And the medics looked at each other. They didn't know what to make of that.

If the priest seemed touched at the scene, he was quickly forgiven by the medics, the police, the *ejército*, the maquila boss too, all who came to see the scene more out of rage than grief. Because it should be said that Gloria, like her sister June, was one of the most beautiful women in San Miguel. And it wasn't long after her death that the whole city took a keen interest in her murder, despite countless other women from the maquila having been killed before. *But this one mattered*, everyone said. The papers even declared it in bold print.

An autopsy was done at the request of the mayor, who wanted confirmation that she hadn't been raped before she'd been murdered.

Over time, Gloria's virginity became sacred to San Miguel (and by extension its reputation), and there was a sigh of relief when illustrations of the autopsy were published in the newspapers (a vertical incision that cut her open twice, running parallel to the wound that actually killed her) revealing that she did, indeed, die a virgin.

Parties were held in the streets, *tesoritos* were stamped with her name on them and they were hung in churches. One man even wrote to the Pope for her to be canonized. But all of this was too much for June and her mother, who felt the burden of public fascination too much.

Her mother stopped eating and grew ill. And neither of them could handle the priest who'd found Gloria. He stopped by at all hours of the day with his rusty, brown hands. He refused to wash them of Gloria's virgin blood, *possibly saint blood*, he'd say. He would stay for hours on end, begging forgiveness from Gloria's mother for finding her too late.

The smell of his hands made June's mother sick, but she always accepted him for no other reason than that he was a priest. When the dried blood finally faded, rubbed away with time and the shock of Gloria's death, June took to disappearing for days on end if only to escape the priest. And, of course, her mother, too, who could not be consoled.

June wandered the city night and day—by bus, by foot, by taxi whenever she got lost, which was often. At first, she walked only the triangle between Galeana, Mejia and Lerdo streets, where the prostitutes sashayed and the arcades were full. It wasn't long before she discovered the diesel *pesero* buses with their rambling engines that purred something smoky toward the back, where you could lean your head up against the cool, scratched glass, close your eyes and let sleep fall over you with a heaviness that can only be undone by time.

It was in this way that June came to know the entire city of San Miguel, wandering from bus to bus, station to station, for days on end. And it was in this way, too, that the entire city came to know her. Not only as Gloria's sister but as a different being altogether.

Over time, June's clothes wore themselves ragged. She took to cutting her hair short. Her skin hung heavy and grey on her face. She barely ate, and her days all blended together. Chapped lips, sunken eyes, she looked like she'd been dead for weeks.

The city took to calling her *the sleeping girl* or *the druggy girl*. But the people who rode the pesero buses built their own mythology around her, and it wasn't long before her image became synonymous with Gloria's spirit: ragged, cut and dead.

To those who had read the newspapers in the days following Gloria's death—to those who'd read every gory detail alongside Gloria's picture—June was the spitting image of her sister. And soon it was out all over town that the devil himself had brought the murdered girl back to life.

The papers caught the story and published a picture of June sleeping in her Sex Pistols T-shirt. From then on, everyone who rode the peceros crossed themselves in her presence. Old men would ask her for favors. They would try to get June to contact their friends in the afterlife, as if she was some kind of human Ouija board. Children would wake her up just so she could tell them the exact date and time of their deaths and whether or not it would hurt. All of this was too confusing for June, who just wanted to sleep, who'd missed the entire spectacle surrounding her existence. So she ignored both the men and women. She would answer every child's question with, "Ants. Sixty years old. Noon."

Just a few days after the story was published, a street gang came to June believing that if she could never die, then she would be an asset to their group. They'd make her their own Santa Muerte, their own virgin to ward off evil.

June, growing lonesome in those days, was all too willing to fall in with any group that would have her. And so, when the gang took her in—those boys and girls who called themselves the F.U. Mordida—she didn't fight back. She became the ghost everyone needed her to be.

One day, a boy from the F.U. Mordida boarded June's pesero bus. His head was shaved and he was dressed in black. He spotted June sleeping in the very last seat in the very back of the bus—exactly where the papers said she'd be.

The boy called out June's sister's name, Gloria. "Gloria!" he kept shouting. "Gloria, is that you? Gloria?" Silence. The crowd watched on.

When the bus stopped, June woke up and stared at the boy calling her sister's name. She acknowledged him with the slightest of nods before standing up to stretch, though to everyone else it looked like she was standing to answer his call.

A collective gasp could be heard throughout the bus as June stood. Even the driver looked back in his rearview mirror.

June exited the bus, ushered on by F.U. Mordida, and wandered back with them into the guts of the city. It didn't even take a day for the rumor to be confirmed: the devil himself had, indeed, brought Gloria back from the dead. And suddenly everyone feared the F.U. Mordida because, it was also rumored, that evil could not die. F.U. Mordida became invincible, if only in the eyes of their enemies. Everyone feared the gang, even the police, who had it printed in all the papers that no one from that gang was to be arrested, not even for dog fighting, which was how certain gangs made their money in San Miguel and how June became an expert dog fighter in the first place.

Dog fights kept peace among the gangs of San Miguel. The dogs were mainly street dogs, which kept the playing field level. Before the *ejército* came, the fights themselves were meant to be a lottery of sorts, a pack of dogs rounded up and a single coin tossed to see which gang got which dog and which fought first.

Every gang put in their five hundred peso buy-in, and this one particular night, weeks after June had been taken in by the F.U. Mordida, all eyes were on June who, rumor had it, could never lose.

The night of her first fight, all eyes were on her—the spitting image of her dead sister—until they shifted their attention to one dog in particular. This big, sloppy mutt had a bark that stunk like ash, which everyone said was proof the hound was from hell. And just as everyone expected, the coin toss proved that it belonged, by destiny, to June.

The dog's bark was all growl—heavy and low. He flashed the whites every so often so as to give off this manic look, his pupils fully dilated, his irises full of blood.

When the dog entered the ring, he pulled June and the chief of the F.U. Mordida (that bald boy dressed in black) behind him, the dog loping one giant leg at a time over the ankle-high plywood that made up the periphery of the ring.

The dog moved sprightly, although with a heaviness in commanding the space. He barked and the room shut up. Among the spectators, bookies and betters, there was a vague unease at being in the same space with this wild thing. But there was also money to be made, and everyone stayed to watch, to bet, to see if this devil-girl could never lose.

One of the bookies, some surly boy in charge of crowd control, kept his finger on the trigger of his silver pistol (just to show he meant business), the barrel pointed toward the ground.

The spectators shoved their backs to the corners of the room with the white gloss of their eyes showing in the dark. The fluorescent lights hung like operating table lamps over the blood-soaked beige carpet.

Of course, everyone bet on June's beast. Just as the bookie signaled for the fight to begin, a shot rang out. The dog's eyes split away, his skull undone.

A flash of aspirated bright, red poured out into the air and everyone's eyes were on the bookie whose smoking pistol sat snugly in his grip, his index finger extended fully so as to show everyone that his finger was off the trigger. But, of course, the shot had rung out and there was only one person holding the gun.

A hush fell over the room. And then a rumble of voices began to surge.

The crowd of dog fighters and betters and gangs descended on the bookie, demanding their money back, demanding that he should be hung from the rafters, demanding that he should be shot. And it wasn't long before the boy, frightened for his life, yelled out, "It was them!" with what he thought was his last breath as he pointed with that same extended finger to the bald boy and June. "They fixed it! They're demons. They had it fixed."

The F.U. Mordida backed away a step at a time, but the crowd descended on them hastily. It did not take the F.U. Mordida but a couple seconds to give up June as a peace offering. As the rest of the F.U. Mordida fled on foot, the crowd carried June, who fought every step of the way, to burn her alive. Fire, the crowd agreed, was the only way to kill evil. And it was well known by then that June *was* evil—the proof was printed in the papers.

June remembers the smell of it more than anything. She remembers the fire, blistering hot and fueled by trash. It peppered the air with its chemical scent that she could still smell long after they'd thrown her, head-first, into the blaze. That was after her brain went fuzzy and everything went cold.

She fell asleep just as the bottles started crashing around her, the beer fizzing up and burning sloppy-wet all over the ground. The hot air fell heavy in her lungs, each breath a sour-sweet sickness in her belly.

A bottle hit her square in the forehead, spilling its contents all over her bloody face. The rest of her body burned while her nerves froze. She remembers she put her hand to her head. She didn't even notice the big toenail of her foot turning to ash. Blood all over her palm. Another dull crack at the base of her skull and then beer pouring everywhere. Hiss and spray. Everything sweltering. And then darkness.

As June walks through sunny San Miguel now, her wagon in tow, she feels her facial scar tightening in the summer heat. She cranes her neck back to see Uli struggling to keep up, one foot slower than the other.

"You're going to break that," she says to him, motioning with her hand toward his foot.

"Think it's already broken," he says.

"It's not. You'd be wailing like holy hell if it was." June slows down just a beat, lets Uli catch up. "You know, it's kind of a miracle you didn't break anything in that crash. Looked bad. Everyone heard about it. You're practically a celebrity."

"I'm not a celebrity," says Uli. "Celebrity means you're rich."

"Infamous then," says June, trying to lighten the mood.

"What good does that do me?" says Uli, visibly soured by his pain.

June wonders if she's pushing him too hard. *No*, she thinks. *He has to learn. No use babying him.* "Maybe get you some friends," says June, feeling her scar tighten on her face again.

"I have friends," says Uli. "In Harlingen."

June doesn't know how to tell him, yet, that he's not going back to Texas. He's never going home.

A shadow delta blots out the sun. A jet streaks overhead. The sky rips apart at the seams again. From the west, June spies a thin layer of diesel smoke rolling in under the low pressure of the same front pushing sand into the clouds. The smoke hangs there on the horizon like radiation fog, separating the land and the sky. *Won't be long*, she thinks, *before the army pulls in. Maybe next week. Maybe the week after.* She remembers the last time they did. Nobody left their homes for weeks because of the curfew. Everyone who went out was arrested or shot. Every dog was simply shot.

"Would you say we're friends?" says Uli, pulling up beside her and taking a hold of the wagon.

She looks down at his feet, still gimpy. There's a tightness to the way his ankles bend that makes her want to pick him up, haul him on her own back.

June smiles at him and says, "I'd say you owe me. I hardly know anything about you."

"Well, what do you want to know?"

A long silence passes between them before he says, "I've got an idea. Let's play a game. Two truths and a lie. Do you know that one?"

"Everyone knows that one," says June.

"All right, then. I'll tell you two truths and you guess the lie. One: I didn't really crash in a plane. Two: I think your Sex Pistols shirt looks like a joke. Three: I think you're kinda cute."

At this June blushes, but there's an anger too that blooms under her skin. She feels her scar again. *Who does he think he is to play with my feelings like that?* What a horrible thing to say, whether it be true or not.

She tightens her jaw, feels her teeth grinding to a click. She feels herself shutting down. Feels the scar over her face tightening again, that rage boiling beneath her skin.

"You don't know me that well," she says all too calmly as she gets up in Uli's face so that he has to step back. His eyes go wide. The wagon handle clangs on the ground.

"You don't get to tell me that you think I'm cute. You don't get to tell me whether I'm worthy of your affection or not. I'm here so you don't fucking kill yourself. Because this city is dangerous, it's fucked. And you're fucked if you don't know how to survive in it. And all those planes crossing overhead, you see them? They're going to drop little leaflets—today or tomorrow—that say they're going to shoot the shit out of this place. And if you don't have anyone here holding your hand like a baby, by the time they do, if you don't have anyone here to keep you from fucking dying, then you *will* die. And that's on my conscience. And that's why I'm here. Not to be your plaything. Not to be your friend. But to keep you from getting killed until you can take care of yourself. There's no going back to Texas, understand? Those old friends you've got? They're gone. That old life you used to have? It's done. Your family too. There is no Texas anymore. There's no Mexico anymore. There's San Miguel. And there's everyone who lives in it. And that's it, understand?"

"Yes," whispers Uli.

"Learn then. And shut the fuck up."

June can feel Uli shrinking before her. She watches him silently break down. He doesn't make a sound. He doesn't move a muscle. He just presses his eyes closed as if willing himself to disappear.

June feels a lump in her throat. She thinks back to the woman he asked about this morning. She thinks of how many ways that woman might kill him.

June's in the right, and she knows it. Nobody else is going to tell him these things.

She spits in the dirt. "Fuck," she says to herself. "I'm sorry," she whispers to him. She reaches into the small of her back, pulls out her pistol, and presents it to Uli. "I'm going to let you hold onto this," she says in a calm voice not unlike the one she spoke in before she snapped.

"What am I supposed to do with this?" says Uli. He takes June's gun in his hand like a moon rock, like something from another planet.

"You're supposed to hold it."

"Is it loaded?"

"Do you know how to shoot it?"

"No."

"Well, then, does it really matter if it's loaded or not?" says June as she pivots away from the spot where she's standing and walks off toward the east with the wagon in tow.

She leads, he follows.

✧ ✧ ✧

That day, June and Uli scrap everything they can find in silence: sloan valves, coaxial wire, romex wire, telephone wire, electric lines, plumbing lines. They scrap old, abandoned buildings and even some buildings yet to be abandoned. There's an auto body shop that smelts the copper for one hundred and fifty pesos, which June happily forks over. She tells Uli that that's more than a fair price. "Never pay more than two hundred and fifty to smelt anything under fifty pounds," she says.

The auto body shop uses a brake drum as a mold so that the cooled copper comes out in heavy twenty-pound disks that clang once they're knocked from it with a rubber hammer.

June and Uli collect three disks in all, the last disk smaller than the first two. They wheel them in their wagon toward the scrapyard on the Eje Central, which is a long twenty-minute walk from the auto body shop. The Eje Central cuts through the middle of the city. It connects to the other end of the *periférico*, where the scrapyard and graveyard sit like twins outside the city limits, exiles leaning one against the other.

There's a chemical haze pouring from inside the junkyard that screens out the sun and filters the light so that it gives the street a pale, blue kind of tint. On the walls of the scrapyard, there is graffiti layered over graffiti stretching for blocks in each direction.

Ash billows down from the sky in flaking layers, wave after wave, onto a ruddy blue attendant's booth near the base of the wall. A trash fire crackles off in the distance. A crooked man with sinewy arms slides back the shattered Plexiglas window behind white, wrought-iron bars. He sits on a simple, wooden chair. He's seventy or eighty by the depth of the veins on the backs of his hands. He's wearing a large, white-collared shirt dinged to a crisp beige, black slacks faded to green that are cut like something from another era. Too boxy, too pleated.

"What do you want?" says the man to them through a little hole in the Plexiglas.

"We've brought you some treasure," says June, a certain familiarity in her voice as if she knows him.

The old man smiles, pulls the Faro cigarette from between his lips.

The man closes one eye to keep the smoke from stinging it and almost whispers, ever so softly as if in jest, "A treasure? All that for me?"

He eases his way down the small ramp while calculating his price.

"My name is Chente," says the man to Uli.

"I'm Uli. This is June."

"I know June," says Chente with a wink.

"Fifty pounds of copper," says June to Chente, cutting the pleasantries.

"Looks it," Chente says to Uli now. "Is that number right? Fifty pounds of copper?"

"Yes, sir," says Uli, unsure what Chente is trying to pull here.

Chente takes his time examining the disks. He picks one up and pulls something from his pocket to strike against it, something that looks like a cube of steel, but darker. Pyrite maybe. Or polished flint, Uli guesses.

Chente mumbles to himself after each strike. "Alloy," he says to himself and tosses the disk aside. He picks up another one. "Alloy. Alloy, alloy. This one too." He takes his tool and strikes each disc, looking for some color of spark or another. "Still alloy," he says striking them all again with a smile. Chente drops all of the discs to the ground before turning to June.

"I'll make you a deal. Two thousand pesos for everything."

June looks shocked at this number.

"Before you say anything, let me say this: this is good copper," Chente says, "but not perfect copper. And two thousand is what I can pay. Or you can haul this back to where you found it. Try to bargain and see what happens."

"What's wrong with it?" says June.

"There's solder in it. I have enough soldered copper."

"Only a sliver of it is soldered. Most of it's wire. Besides, it's untraceable. None of that invisible ink in it. Can't get better than that."

"I've got enough of that."

"We've already smelted it," says June.

"I'm not arguing anymore. Fifteen hundred now. Take it or leave it—it's still a good price," says Chente, his eyes wandering off toward something behind them.

Uli looks in the same direction as Chente. A military cruiser passing by, a unit of soldiers hanging onto the sides of the vehicle as it slowly manages its way over potholes in the road outside the scrapyard, the sound of their equipment jangling against the sheet metal and roll bars with each bump.

"That's not what it's worth," says June.

"Fourteen hundred then," says Chente defiantly.

"And a peek around the yard to sweeten the deal."

Chente has to think about that for a moment or two. He scratches the top of his head with his thumb, his cigarette still clasped between his index and middle finger on the same hand. A tiny sliver of hair singes at the end of the cigarette's cherry.

"Okay. Okay, done," says Chente.

He goes back to his booth for a receipt, which he writes on a waiter's ledger that looks to Uli as if it might have been stolen from a restaurant, deep, orange grease stains on it.

"Sign this," says the old man. He puts the receipt in front of June.

Uli says, "If you don't need more of what we've brought you, then what do you need?"

"Grade one copper," he says.

"Solderless?" asks Uli.

"You got it," says the old man.

"And the look around the junkyard?" says June. "To sweeten the deal."

"Deals been made," says the old man.

"I just have a few things that need repairing. I'm sure you wouldn't miss a few spare parts."

"How sweet are we talking?"

"Some refrigerator parts. *Nada más*," says June.

"Whatever you can carry," says the old man with his foot set on the wagon to anchor it in place. "That means whatever *you* can carry."

To Uli, the scrapyard is beautiful in its own vile way. From all of the things nobody wants, the homeless of San Miguel have built a city of used bricks and metal; they've paved makeshift roads with flattened cardboard that meanders like veins. There are structures on top of and between the mounds of debris, tiny homes that shoot up black plumes of smoke that pepper the air with the tang of burnt rubber.

Uli looks around but there's no human to be seen. Just a pack of dogs slinking around the periphery of one of the mounds of trash.

As they walk, the dogs mirror their every step. June takes her gun from Uli and shoots out a warning shot that cracks no louder than a firework. A little cloud of dust drifts where the bullet strikes the earth. The dogs scatter every which way. Uli, shocked, looks at June and then looks ahead toward a pile of latex dolls with a little shrine at the base of it, unlike anything he's ever seen before.

The shrine itself is aglow with Christmas lights and dripping candles shoved into the necks of brown and green glass bottles. There are sun-bleached photographs crisp and flitting in the wind. There are drawings too and pieces of tin cans ripped from oil canisters with scenes scrawled over them that Uli can't quite make out. There's a knife shoved into the ground in front of the altar, and a network of slack beads cover a statue of a skeleton woman holding a scythe and wearing a crown of white roses. The scattered dogs, regrouping now, look on from a distant hill at June and Uli closing in on the shrine.

"Why are we here? What are we looking for?"

"Another dog," says June. "But a big one. A loner."

"But why?"

"To make money with. Loner dogs are alpha dogs exiled from the pack. Not quite good enough to be the alpha dog but not quite weak enough to be killed off. They're strong, violent. They make for good protection. Especially scrapyard dogs. We'll sell it. We'll turn a profit."

"What's with the gun then? Why are you shooting? Are we supposed to shoot the dog?"

"You're supposed to scatter them. The one that doesn't scatter is the loner—the other alpha. Alphas don't scatter. They fight you."

"Well, where's he at then?"

"I'd take a guess that he's just over that hill there," says June, pulling the ears back on the gun to reload a bullet into the chamber.

She points the barrel at the ground, squeezes off another round. The birds in the sky flitter in all directions. The dogs can be heard skittering around them, the noise of their paws slapping cardboard and dirt eclipsed by the crackling sound of a roaring fire growing louder the closer Uli and June come to round the mound of latex dolls. They feel heat on their faces. Black diesel smoke screens out the sky until the wind shifts directions and the sun beams down onto a pair of glistening eyes.

Before them they see a single black dog, not unlike their own, staring them down with a mouthful of razor sharp teeth. His back arched, his ears pinned back against his skull as if ready to lunge.

"Don't move," says June with the tiniest of whispers. She moves to reload her gun, and the dog barks at her as she pulls the spring to load the bullet into the chamber.

The guttural growl from the back of the dog's throat fills the air.

Uli's eyes look past the dog to the smoke drifting out toward the cemetery. Between two, tall billows, he can make out the shapes of people surrounding a burning corpse. Black flesh on the ground. Burnt plastic in the air. The smell brings to Uli's mind the same liquid reek of the car explosion he tried so hard to wash from his hands. The people are covered in blood. The charred meat in their clenched fists is like the same blistered flesh of those bodies holding hands.

There are more than a dozen people cutting charred flesh from a dead horse that's burning over an open flame, fire blooming from the horse's ribcage where the heat has eaten its way through the body. The horse's bloody tongue hangs from her head. Her teeth grow black with smoke passing over her face.

Just then the sky rips overhead. First, one plane. And then the chopping beat of another. And then another and another.

In their wake fall thousands of pale, green leaflets over the center of San Miguel. The leaflets ride the breeze toward the junkyard, where they circle overhead in the thermal cycles of the fires burning below. Uli and June wait for one to fall, keeping an eye on the dog all the while, that gun in June's hand.

"There's your sign," says June.

"What sign?" asks Uli.

"That they're coming. I told you they would," she says and watches a rasping leaflet burn in the sky over the mare, turning to ash before ever hitting the ground and then flying off toward the cemetery.

ROT

ARACELI ROLLS A BLUNT WITH THE TIP of her maimed finger, the gangrene spreading quickly under the nail of her index. Her nerves are shot, but in the tips of her fingers, even the gangrened index, there's still an injured kind of dexterity with which she rolls the blunts. Once she's finished, she licks along the seam to seal it. She puts it alongside the other blunts that lean, one against the other, in a spiraled circle inside the cup holder between her and Iván.

They listen to the radio turned low, the Texas stations pouring in weak, full of static, over the mountains. They're roughly halfway between Matamoros and San Miguel, broken down in a tiny tourist town west of Matamoros called Potrero Chico. The town is filled with American rock climbers and campers away for the weekend. Araceli and Iván are parked outside a sports cantina with American cable, the San Antonio Spurs playing on an oversized, digital television that takes up three quarters of the back wall of the cantina and paints the entire room in a beige, digital glow.

Through the pitted glass of the windshield, Araceli watches the game as Iván scoops, with the blade of his knife, from the marijuana brick sliced open between his legs. He's got a circular grinder on his knee with which he grinds the stems and buds together. Some cornhusk to stretch it the way Araceli taught him. He tries to keep his eyes on the game, but he's so afraid of spilling the pot that he mostly listens to the static and stares at that space between his knees.

"You know they'll come after you for this brick," says Iván, grinding another circle in his palm.

"You mean us," says Araceli, licking another blunt along the seam.

"Who's to say there's not a tracking device in it?"

"You watch too many movies," says Araceli. "They won't come."

At this, Iván huffs to himself, then says, "They don't lose a brick and not miss it."

"Why does it matter now? You can go home anytime you'd like."

"I didn't know," says Iván. "I have money."

"I don't need your money," says Araceli.

"You need medication," he says, turning down the radio.

"I don't need your money."

"It'll spread, you know."

"Then let it spread," she says. "Maybe I can fix the damn finger myself with some tape and a bottle," she chuckles.

"You'd last about as long as the truck. I knew that wasn't going to last," says Iván.

"Then why'd you let me do it?"

"Maybe I wanted to get away," says Iván, his voice softening now. "Maybe I felt sorry for you."

"That doesn't make any sense," she says. "Maybe you should feel sorry for yourself. No wife, no kids. All by your lonesome in that shitty hotel."

"It's mine."

"Lonesome man in a lonesome house. An unmarried man after a certain age can be a bad thing."

"That finger," says Iván, skirting around to the subject of her health again, "is going to come off sooner or later. I could put it under the hood of the car after we fix the carburetor. Slam it off. Kill two birds with one stone."

"You wouldn't."

"I really would," he says with a weak smile.

"Then how would we make money?"

"I could learn to roll," he says, taking a sliver of cornhusk from the dash. "Here, teach me."

"It's a secret," she says, taking the cornhusk from his fat fingers. "I know how the tourists like them."

"I don't understand what's so special about them."

"They're novelty," says Araceli. "Tourists go looking for the real thing. They come to Mexico and try to find rustic. So, I give them rustic. And drugs. A winning combo."

"My grandmother used to smoke blunts like these," says Iván, picking up the knife again and digging it into the brick. He watches the glow of the television inside the cantina. A trio of backpackers step inside, their pale legs covered in dirt.

"My grandmother was the one who taught me," says Araceli. "Where was your grandmother from?"

"Jalisco," says Iván. "Autlán."

"My grandmother was from Colotitlán. That's close."

"About ten minutes," says Iván with a smile now. "We could be cousins." Iván looks in her eyes as if searching for something.

"Could be," says Araceli, licking the last blunt before taking a rest.

Through the pitted windshield, Araceli watches the Spurs with Iván, whose hands have stopped working now. He runs them through his hair before putting his left hand next to hers, and she lets him. She feels the hairs on his hand touching her rotting finger. She doesn't move it. She doesn't move anything. The sound of the radio announcer calling out plays beneath the low huff of their stale breath. Iván breaks the silence first.

"I can see why people leave," he says, almost in a whisper, his eyes watching the giant television now. "It's all glossy over there. Look at that court. Look at those players. In everyone's head a full set of straight teeth."

Araceli pulls her hand away to start on another blunt. That jangling feeling in her nerves again. She feels Iván closing in on the space between them, the console creaking under his weight. He descends on her like a ravenous animal hungry for a meal.

She opens the door to break the moment. She licks the blunt and slicks it behind her ear. She takes the hem of her dress by her ankles and pulls it up to make a pouch, carrying all the blunts she's made in front of her like a girl carrying blueberries in her dress. She hops from the car just as she feels Iván's breath, hot and wet on her ear. The earthy, cloying smell of alcohol and sweat and marijuana ash in the dark desert heat.

"You wait here," she says to him and closes the distance between her truck and the Americans, their white teeth gleaming in the digital glow above them.

Araceli makes nine hundred dollars. A little over five hundred from the backpackers, another hundred from a French-Canadian couple, and the rest from the tenants of the hostel where the French-Canadian couple is staying: a pair of brothers who can't find coke but settle for weed; a group of eight hikers too drunk to realize what they're buying; a lonesome punk rocker from Mexico City's Tabacalera neighborhood who has been camping in Potrero for weeks writing a screen play; and a girl from Austin who couldn't afford Europe.

That night, Araceli uses the hostel showers and brushes her teeth. Iván sleeps in the driver's side of the truck. Araceli sleeps in the truck bed, out in the open and dreams of her sons.

In the morning, she goes to the dingy internet café attached to the hostel. At the back of the café there's a pregnant woman sitting behind a fold-up picnic table with a fat monitor resting on it. Next to the pregnant woman, a cheap percolator brewing more condensation than coffee. The machine rests on a red, plastic *taquería* stool with *Coca Cola* written up and down the legs. Between the legs of the stool, a ten-liter jug of Epura brand water and an industrial tin of Kirkland's coffee. There's a laminated sheet of paper next to the machine that lists the prices:

Coffee: 10 pesos

Cream: 2 pesos

Sugar: 2 pesos

Pornography: 30 pesos/ 30 minute limit

Internet: 15 pesos/ hour, 10 pesos/ 30 minutes

Araceli carefully considers the list. She wonders if you can't access pornography through the internet for ten or fifteen pesos. She wonders if there's a private computer they use for that. Thirty minutes is very quick. Or is that long? Who knows?

"Can I help you?" says the woman behind the desk.

"A coffee and thirty minutes—internet, thirty minutes, I mean."

The pregnant woman takes a Styrofoam cup from the tip of a stack beside the CPU. She points Araceli to the nearest computer, which has a box of tissues next to it.

"Not pornography," says Araceli. "Internet."

"Oh, I'm sorry," says the woman playing dumb, "I have a bad ear." Without asking, the pregnant lady puts both cream and sugar into the Styrofoam cup.

"Just black, please," says Araceli.

"I already put it in," says the woman.

"Fine," says Araceli and plops down in front of the computer next to the pornography computer before scooting one more seat down for good measure.

"Large coffee fine?" says the pregnant woman.

"The smallest you have," says Araceli.

"I only have large cups, I'm sorry. It'll be twelve pesos."

"But it says ten right here," says Araceli, pointing to the sign.

"*Pues, no,*" says the pregnant lady, her face full of mock anguish as if it physically pains her to correct her own mistakes.

"Fine," says Araceli, seeing the woman is unwilling to bend. She peels out a blue twenty-peso note from the small pocket in her dress. "Here's twenty now," says Araceli. "Stop fucking me over and I'll give you the ten when we're done."

The pregnant woman does the math in her head quickly, her eyes rolling to the corners. "*Pues, no,*" says the lady again, her face full of mock-anguish.

Araceli looks at the clock. Three minutes already gone by.

"I have twenty-seven minutes left," says Araceli.

"*Pues, sí,*" says the pregnant woman.

Araceli takes the cup of coffee from the ladies' hand, swishes it around and downs half of it in three gulps. The lady sticks around a while, watching Araceli log on before she goes back to her perch behind the fat monitor at the picnic table, measuring water with a small Styrofoam cup from a bottle.

Araceli does not use Facebook but she knows what it is. She's seen her sons use it a thousand times. She knows how to Google "Facebook" and then her sons names and then "Harlingen, TX," because that's where they live. She learned that much at the Harlingen public library, where they taught her how to Google anything.

She finds Uli's profile first—blocked—before she makes it to Cuauhtémoc's. Her eyes tear at the sight of him. His profile picture is of him in front of the Pawnee. His flat head is covered by the borrowed AOPA cap Sampson, the grove boss, gave him. Cuauhtémoc's wearing his father's shades, Ray Ban knock offs from the 90s. His last update was in late May. Nothing from him since. Her heart sinks.

She looks at the horizontal bar across the middle of the window. *If his page is up, he still has to be alive,* she thinks, but she knows that logic is flawed. She scans his page. His likes, his music, his favorite books. Reading these things comforts her in some small way. He's still preserved, if only digitally. *He's still alive. Of course he is.* No internet in San Miguel—that town is barely standing. At least that's what she's heard. They barely have utilities. *That must be it. That's why he hasn't logged on,* she thinks.

Araceli clicks around. Cuauhtémoc's favorite music: RINNO. His favorite books: *Catcher in the Rye, Hank the Cowdog, The Absolutely True Diary of a Part-Time Indian.* His favorite teams: The Houston Rockets. *Dumbass,* thinks Araceli. *Fucker's never even been to Houston.* And it's then, in that thought alone, that Araceli begins to lose it.

She chuckles at first, a quick huff that blends into a heavy exhale before she makes a gasping, hyperventilating wheeze. The pregnant woman jumps up from her seat, looks at the screen over Araceli's shaking shoulders, first to make sure she's not looking at pornography before moving to the computer on the far left to retrieve the tissues.

"Some tissues? Some water?" the pregnant woman says to comfort Araceli, putting the tissues in her face now.

"How much for water?" asks Araceli.

"Five pesos small cup. Seven pesos big cup. But don't worry, the tissues are free."

Araceli thinks about it for a while before she says, "Big cup." She'll treat herself, she thinks. The woman walks away. She wants to take a swig of her coffee, but she can't even keep her mouth closed. She bawls. Her mind goes wild.

Araceli switches back and forth between the windows at the top of her browser. Cuauhtémoc's page, Uli's page—still blocked.

On the Facebook homepage, in the right-hand corner, Araceli sees the signup form: First name, last name, e-mail, password, birthday. *Do I have an e-mail?*

"Your water," says the pregnant woman, coming up behind her now. She places the box of tissues beside Araceli again, the Styrofoam cup of water in front of her.

"I'm fine with the water," says Araceli.

"Are you okay, miss?" asks the pregnant lady, her face full of anguish.

Araceli looks from the screen to the woman's belly, avoiding her face altogether. She must be seven months along. Eight maybe. Enough to feel the baby kick. Araceli remembers what it was like when she first became a mother, when she first felt it kick. That's the last time she lost a child. Miscarriage.

Please leave me alone, Araceli wants to tell the woman, although the woman's voice helps somehow. It's soft. Genuine.

"I will be," says Araceli, "once I figure out how to get an e-mail. Can you help me do that?" says Araceli. "Can you do that for me? Can I pay you to get e-mail?"

"E-mail?" says the woman, surprised, her anguish deepening. She's confounded by the question. Who doesn't have e-mail? "Yes," she says.

"Yes?" says Araceli to confirm. "You help me?"

"Yes," says the woman. "You pay. I help you."

Araceli can only send a *friend request* to her sons. By time that's done, Iván has already gone off on foot with a wad of bills in his shirt pocket, his boots popping gravel as he walks toward the one lonesome grease shop at the end of the strip to look for a second-hand carburetor.

Everything in this town seems to be connected to something else: the internet café connected to the hostel, the restaurants connected to the cantina and the grease shop is no exception. Its leaning structure of corrugated tin and wood connected to a Pemex station with two pumps and an air hose.

Inside, the shop is all dusk. Slants of light break from the warped tin roof not flush with the plumb-line of the wall. In the far left corner of the structure, a spiraled, compact fluorescent bulb shines over two men sitting on top of the remains of a transmission, their glassy eyes shifting toward Iván's direction where, momentarily, he blocks the flood of daylight by standing in the threshold.

Iván steps inside and the daylight floods past him. He sees both men now dressed in dark green Pemex jumpsuits, here and there patches of oil and light coffee stains. Each of the men carries a plastic mug of steaming coffee in his hand, the mechanic closest to Iván slinging his mug low by the handle with the cup at a tilt. He approaches Iván, tossing the entire cup into a forty-gallon barrel full of red rags.

He pauses in a slant of light that cuts his torso in half before saying, "What can I do for you, sir?"

"I need a carburetor," says Iván, scanning the floor.

"What make?"

"I think it's a Ford," says Iván.

"We've got the part then," says the mechanic. "You bring it here, and we'll fix it up."

"I can do it myself," says Iván.

"We don't sell parts, understand?"

"We're mechanics. We fix," adds the other fellow in the back.

"How much?" says Iván.

"Twelve hundred."

Iván, feeling the wad of bills in his pocket, thinks about it for a second. They could afford it, but Iván thinks of a number to counter them with. "Eight hundred," he says.

He watches the gears whir behind the young man's eyes in front of him. He sees his hard face break a little.

"*Pues, no*," says the boy. "Eleven hundred. It's a fair price."

Iván knows it's not but he's eager to get out of town. He neither says yes nor no. He simply says, "You'll have to tow it here."

"It's downhill," says the partner from the back of the shop, still resting on the transmission. "We can do it."

"*You* can do it," says the mechanic to his companion. "I'll take him to the waiting room. Keys, sir?"

Iván looks confused. "It doesn't even crank," he says.

"I know what you're thinking," says the mechanic. "But if it doesn't crank, then how are we going to steal it? You have to trust us, mister."

"I actually wasn't thinking that," says Iván.

"I'll take you to the waiting room. This way, mister."

Iván would help if his back wasn't killing him. He wants to sit down. He *needs* to sit down. *Fuck it*, he thinks before throwing the keys to the guy sitting on the transmission.

As the boy passes, Iván takes some peso bills from his shirt pocket. "Five hundred now," he says, "and the remaining six hundred when it's fixed."

The young man smiles, takes the bills and runs down the one lonesome stretch of road in town. Araceli's truck is the only one parked in the road. Iván wonders how the young guy knew which way to run. One road but two directions. He imagines the people who live here take note of everyone who comes and goes. What did his grandmother used to say? *Pueblo chico, infierno grande*. Small town, big hell.

"This way," says the young man in front of him, waving with his hand for Iván to follow him through the sundry bottles of Coke and Topo Chico and Pemex oil jugs scattered here and there toward the exit at the back of the garage. Behind it, an open field with a single cow and its calf grazing among lawn chairs sinking into the wet sand. The smell of dung. The smell of diesel from the gas station too.

"Didn't think you could raise a cow out here," says Iván.

"Can raise a cow wherever," says the mechanic, taking down a pair of clay mugs from two nails in a slab of particle wood hanging off a bolt in the corrugated tin wall.

From a blue HEB bag hanging from another hook and bolt in the shed, the boy produces a jar of Nescafé, a jar of powdered chocolate and a jar of clear cane alcohol in a Tamazula bottle. In one clay mug he pours a capful of Nescafé, a capful of powdered chocolate and a swig of cane alcohol. He does the same for the second mug, screws all the jars back up and moves over to the cow pissing a steady stream over a patch of sandy earth. The cow drinks from a trough as the calf nurses on her. With a flat palm, the mechanic shoves the slant of the calf's head, pushing it away from his mother. He takes a knee under the cow and pulls the slimy teat from which the calf had been sucking and gives it a long, hard squeeze. A stream of frothy milk sloshes into the mug. A gushing, brown effervescence spills into the next mug as the Nescafé and chocolate dissolve.

"Enjoy," says the mechanic, passing Iván a mug as he starts in on his own.

"My grandfather used to make these," says Iván, "when he was hungover in the morning. I never understood how it worked."

"They say it'll give you the shits," says the boy, "but not me, I've got a gut of steel. Ask anyone. I eat anything."

So say all Mexican men, Iván thinks as he takes a sip, the milk steaming over his face in the cool morning air. *Yesterday I was there, today I'm here, tomorrow I'll be gone*, he thinks as he eases his creaking knees into sitting position. The calf comes back around now to fight the mechanic for his share.

Though the sky is high, the clouds are low. A stratus stretched solid over the sierra so you can only see the impressions of the hills, the darks of their shadows tinged blue by the rows of agave planted along the slopes. *All those plants for what?* thinks Iván, getting drunk off the cane alcohol. *If not for tequila, then for sotol or raicilla or whatever the fuck it is they drink around here.* The alcohol makes him bitter, angry. The skin around his collar turns red as the cloud mist cools the sweat bursting from his pores.

Out of the fog, on their own cloud of diesel smoke, a caravan of army trucks floods down the road. They come, one after the other, their tires kicking up dust along the stretch. The caravan must be eighteen or twenty trucks long, each truck painted in dark green digital camo, with black tarps half-pulled over the arched skeleton haloing the truck bed where the soldiers sit. As they pass, the truck suspensions creak over the pot-holed dirt road. All of the men wear black masks, except for one soldier in each truck who rides standing upright, maskless, just behind the cabin, his rifle at the ready, his finger fully flexed over the trigger housing.

"Where's the war?" asks Iván sarcastically.

"Something like that," says the mechanic, not quite hearing him, pulling long and hard at the cow's teat, trying not to get kicked. "Calderón's little war. Peña Nieto's war now. But who are we really kidding—the Americans told them both who to fight. If it's anybody's war it's the American's. We just die for it. Anyway, the government is sending all of those soldier's to Juárez. Take back control of the city. And all of the little cities around it."

"Who says they're not under control?"

"The president," says the mechanic, shifting knees now. "But none of those cities are really under control, if you know what I mean. They run themselves. They pay taxes to Mexico

City, but that's about as Mexican as they get. The cartels give them more utilities than the government can. Right now, Sinaloa and Juárez are fighting each other and the government is trying to kill both those cartels with the army. But I can tell you right now that's not going to happen."

"Why is that?" asks Iván.

"The people aren't going to have it. They depend on the cartels. A lot of people are going to die. Even the papers say so: there are a lot more cartels than Sinaloa and Juárez. Another one will take their place. One cartel can control the routes, the army can control the roads, but nobody is going to control the sky. And every one of them has a fleet. You're going to see a lot of people die soon. The dope has to go where it has to go. You can't fight supply and demand. Routes will change, people will die, Peña Nieto can say he tried. End of story."

"They're headed west?" asks Iván.

"They're headed everywhere. Soldiers kill anything that needs to be killed," says the mechanic.

Iván is aware of his own breathing now, the sound of it cut by the fizzing noise of the mechanic filling his mug. And then suddenly there's the cutting chirp of a Nextel phone just beyond the corner of the garage.

Iván's chest is slick with sweat. He looks toward the direction of the sound. A boy in the Pemex parking lot with a phone in his hand. The boy speaks into it. Iván just hears the staccato of his little voice more than anything. Iván takes a swig, staring heat into the boy. He looks him right in the eye and gives him every dark thing in his heart. Iván thinks if he weren't so comfortable right now, he'd take the boy and stomp his head bloody into a fucking curb.

TREAD

IT SEEMS THAT EVERYONE SAW IVÁN leave but Araceli. The truck tires were the first to break fresh dirt after the army caravan flattened the road under their cheap tire treads. Iván simply disappeared into the fog as it dissipated in the morning. That truck, Araceli thinks, another part of her husband gone.

At least Iván left her things: a small stack of bills and her bags, which the hostel guards kept behind the desk. Araceli begs the receptionist for another night, if only to regroup. *Three days, two nights*, says the placard over the counter. The receptionist listens as Araceli pleads her case. Stolen truck. No medication. Araceli leaves out the fact that she's low on money.

In the back of her mind, Araceli thinks the receptionist could be related to the internet café lady. Same build, same bone structure. Same by-the-book demeanor—that little piece of shit twinkle in her eye that screams *late checkout fee*.

Araceli ends her plea just as the lady finally grasps the placard. *Three days, two nights*, it says. No exceptions, although of course that means *exceptions for Americans. Or French-Canadians. Or lonesome girls traveling from Texas*. Exceptions for white folks, tourists. Not Mexican drifters.

Araceli pleads her case again. "I'm from Texas, you know. I'm only half-Mexican," she lies.

"I don't make half-exceptions," says the lady behind the counter.

Araceli sniffs hard at the dry air. Composes herself. She collects her bags and walks out in search of a pharmacy.

With each step she feels the little wad of bills brushing inside her pocket. *Money comes and money goes,* she thinks. She'll make more of it.

She starts at the end of Potrero's one long street and shuffles all the way to the other side. As she passes the opened garage door of the auto body shop, she sees both mechanics passed out drunk on the concrete floor next to a cow laying on its folded legs. The back door to the garage is wide open, a baby calf peering in from the patch of field out back.

In the wind she swears she can hear that little chirp of a Nextel phone. She wonders if her mind is playing tricks on her. She thinks she needs some water, some food. But more than anything, she needs her medications, which she hasn't taken in days.

Past the Pemex station there's a crossroad. Araceli stands there for a long while with her bags, unsure of which way to go, when she spots the French-Canadian couple she sold blunts to zipping down the crossroad on a motor bike. She watches them pull into a fueling bay at the Pemex, their pale skin aglow from the sun and wind and sand. The man says some words to the gas station attendant as the girl hops off the bike to stretch her legs. To Araceli it looks like a good bike but a cheap one. Some sporty thing a college student would buy to impress his girl-friend.

The French-Canadian man, a sickly looking twenty-something, waves from his perch on the motorcycle. Araceli drops her bags to wave back, her little rotting finger throbbing something awful as she lifts it above her heart. She makes as if to hobble toward them, but the man motions for her to stay put. The attendant puts the gas cap back on. The girl—also sickly looking by Araceli's standards, just a whisper of a woman—

hops on back and, before Araceli can pick her bags up again, they're making their way toward her, that whiny little engine sputtering in the low-oxygenated air of the sierras.

"Greetings," they say to her in their lilted English. Araceli remembers Iván made all of the deals but this one—she sold to the Canadians. They could barely string their Spanish together, and her English was only slightly better. They did the deal in English.

"Greetings," she says, mimicking his sound.

The man makes this face at hearing his words thrown back at him, unsure whether Araceli is mocking him or not.

"How are you?" she says to him.

"All good," says the man. "Heading to Camargo today for Feria and then up to El Paso from there."

"Camargo?" she says, her eyes full of hope. She looks at the tiny slice of pleather seat behind the whisper of a woman. Enough to fit herself, she thinks. Space for one more on the back end of the tiny motorcycle. She tries hard to remember her Mexican geography. *Camargo—Chihuahua—west.*

"West?" she says to the man with pleading eyes.

"Exactly," says the man. "Northwest. You waiting for a bus?"

"Pharmacy," she says.

"Pharmacy? Are you unwell?" asks the Canadian man.

"Unwell," says Araceli, spitting his word back at him again.

"Bandages? Antibiotics? Medicine?" says the man.

"Medicine!" says Araceli, excited at having recognized this word.

"There's a pharmacy the next town over. It's just a mile from here. I could get your medicines and bring them back with you."

"I go with you," says Araceli, dropping her bags now and kicking them to the side with her good foot for dramatic emphasis.

The woman scoots forward on her seat. She pats the little slice of seat behind her.

Araceli hops on. The suspension creaks. They ride off into the dry air, Araceli's hair flying out behind her like a thousand tiny whips rasping in the wind.

THE LOTTERY

ULI WAKES UP ONE DAY to find that he's been in Mexico for a month and a half. He looks out of the bedroom window. Darkness outside. It's six in the morning, July 17th, by the date on his busted Timex watch. He checks that date against the thirty-five tick marks he's scribbled in the back of his father's Bible, one slash for every day he's been in San Miguel. In the upper right corner of that same page, another set of tiny slashes for the days he spent in the hospital in Matamoros right after he crashed the plane. At the bottom right corner, the number 50 for the days he's given himself to decide whether or not his family is coming. He's nearing that number, he knows, but there's no real way of knowing how many days he might have been in the hospital. He guesses it was about twelve days. He remembers those days were nested one inside the other inside the other. That hospital morphine haze never really left his brain. Or his body, for that matter.

Every day he wakes up like he does this morning, paralyzed in his own bed, held hostage by the various aches that come out at night to cripple him. Every morning for Uli is a struggle to move. His body is sixteen though he feels like sixty-three. Uli wonders what sixty-three is actually going to look like for him. When he feels the pains in his feet, his thighs, his neck, his legs, he imagines the way his body might further deteriorate. He imagines himself curled like a pretzel. A crooked spine, a hunched back, a sinuous slant of a person.

Maybe it's that image in his mind (like a portent) or maybe it's his wanderlust or maybe it's his desire to push beyond the parameters of the city (as if his healthy body were out there somewhere, waiting to be found), but Uli makes up his mind, this morning, that he's leaving San Miguel.

He flips the pages of the Bible to the back where he keeps his money, stuffed between the pages of Revelations and where baptisms are recorded. Eight hundred bucks left from what he's made with June. *Might be enough,* he thinks. He stacks the bills and then restacks them. Hides them between Revelations again so that they make the Bible's spine bulge, the glue starting to rip away from the binding.

Uli looks out the window and imagines himself running serpentine through the boulders in the street, his feet expertly navigating the potholes and slippery sand and crumbling asphalt as if his body were never broken. He imagines what it would feel like to be whole again. He tries to remember what that runner's high felt like. Like he might be able to run forever. Like he might run all the way to Juárez—through Juárez, through El Paso, down I-10, all the way home. Unstoppable.

Uli gets out of bed, pulls on his increasingly oversized jeans and his grey San Antonio Spurs shirt that fits too tight around the collar. He slides his sockless feet into his too tight shoes. Cold sweat between his toes. He gingerly walks past June, asleep on the couch, and eases himself out of the too creaky front door. He disappears into the still-dark morning. Just the glowing sodium lamp—the only one still working along the street—outside Uli's house buzzing against the dim glow coming from the windows of that woman's house across the street.

In the middle of the street, Uli puts the open palm of his left hand up against a boulder to ground himself. He swings his right leg back and forth. Then his left one. As he watches the shadows move behind the closed curtains of his neighbor's home, he feels the blood-bright pain inside the complexities of his knee. He feels, too, the ant-like swarm inside his capillaries—in his toes, his heels, his calves. He stretches his quads before pumping his right knee into the air. Then his left. Then his right a second, third, fourth time the way he used to do right before a race.

He'd like to follow with lunges, but he worries he'd never get back up again. He just wants to run. Wants to feel the wind on his skin. Wants to get drenched in that warm sweat that only comes from the entire body working in sync, every muscle working with cartilage working with bone working with blood working with the heart pumping to the edge of explosion.

He takes off at a dead sprint toward the end of the street. A streak of hot pain jolts from his heel to his heart. He runs through it. There's a clicking in his knee only audible through the feeling of it in his bones.

He listens to the click, like a second hand marking the passage of time over the booming whoosh of his heart. Each click comes as a new threat: a snapped ligament or a ripped joint. *Should I stop?* he wonders. *No*, he thinks. He runs through it, listens to the staccato of it that grows louder the harder he pumps his legs. He hears the slap of his cheap shoes on the pavement, then the pushed air of his lungs starting to burn, then the sound of blood in his head again, then that clicking. The feeling of his body working in sync—fiber to fiber, muscle to muscle, nerve to nerve. His skin drinks in the wind. He runs as if compressing time, as if every click in his knee were a second closer to home.

Uli knows if he's going to leave he'll need more money. And then he'll need to disappear.

Tonight, he thinks. *After we've sold the copper.* Or tomorrow morning. That might work just as well. When June is asleep. A morning like this morning. He'll slip out. No goodbyes. Nothing. Just disappear. *Easy*, he thinks. A clean break.

If he's honest with himself, she's weirding him out more and more these days. She keeps carrying that gun in the small of her back. Keeps talking about that dog that got away—that cursed thing that came out to greet them the day of the burning mare in the junkyard. Says she wants to go back for it. Says she knows how to catch it this time. Moreover, he's beginning to hate June's morning music ritual as petty as that seems.

She's always humming something that sounds like Hendrix, maybe. Or Clapton. One of Uli's father's records that she listens to real low on his father's Fender amplifier in the living room, her head beside the speaker, her eyes closed like she's dreaming.

Uli knows she means nothing by it, but he can't help but feel like she's taunting him, mocking him for his claim to his father's house (or at least the pieces of his father that used to belong to him). Those records, that amplifier. Like portals into a past in which June never belonged. He knows she feels this too because whenever he catches her humming she always shuts down and shuts off. Like it's some big secret that she listens to his father's music. But Uli wonders if she might shut down for another reason too.

Like all Mexicans that Uli's ever met—including his father (especially his father)—June acts like Hendrix is still alive, like Clapton never got old, like the Beatles never met Yoko. Uli thinks that like all Mexicans, she hums those songs because she's embarrassed of singing them aloud. Too self-conscious of her own English. She sings in the shower sometimes, and Uli gets a kick out of that. The words are never right.

Slowing down a bit in his run, Uli thinks about leaving again. A little weight comes off his heart thinking about June singing out loud. Singing that Hendrix song (or Clapton song) like she means it, like no one is judging her.

Just up ahead, the rasp of drunk laughter tearing into the morning air. The road is clogged with a military convoy half-parked in the road and half-parked up on the sidewalk. Uli ends his jog and looks inside the vehicles as he passes, hundreds of soldiers sitting under their green, digital camo tarpaulins in the backs of long truck beds. The trucks themselves are giant vehicles with long benches over the wheel hubs, two parallel benches full of soldiers (sitting shoulder patch to shoulder patch) facing each other. The floors inside the truck beds are strewn with emptied cellophane Takis wrappers and *caguama*-sized beer bottles. The women soldiers are busy applying make-up in their compact mirrors. Blue eyeshadow. Purple lipstick. The men are pot-bellied and red-eyed in their morning drunkenness. They look like they haven't slept in days. Uli gets the vibe that they're all supposed to stay put under their tarpaulins, but there's a group of young soldiers, around his age, lining up at a makeshift taco stand that's set up shop alongside the convoy.

There's the smell of a butane flame like the rotten synthetic air leaked from a soccer ball. There's the smell of tortillas warming on a comal. The smell of coffee and corn oil too.

Toward the end of the convoy, a small group of officers drinking inside a bar that Uli's never noticed before. Its sign boasts LONDON PUB up above the threshold. It is, possibly, the most depressing thing Uli's seen in San Miguel. The officers look at Uli as he passes. One of them drunkenly barks at him before falling out of his chair.

Uli watches as the officer rocks on the ground like a beetle on its back, the whites of his eyes rolling manic in his head. He stares into the sky, then at the convoy, then through Uli as if he were either an obstacle or a ghost before barking again, trying to get some reaction from Uli that Uli doesn't know how to give.

Nothing, nobody can stop the lottery, and everyone knows this. Not the soldiers in the streets, nor the autodefensa people's militia that came before them, nor the narcos who came before them. June explains that the lottery is an institution older than San Miguel, which is to say older, even, than the Spanish presence in the region. The Mexican soldiers in the street respect the lottery just as the Spanish soldiers and priests did five hundred years ago, just as the Raramuri tribe did sometime before that. And as far back as anyone can guess, it was the Raramuri themselves who invented the lottery.

June explains that the Raramuri believed in human sacrifice. They believed that the Devil wasn't necessarily evil. Occasionally, the Devil would collaborate with God to bring the people to heel, and only through human sacrifice could the Raramuri salvage their lives from endless torment. So, the lottery was invented. Human lives were given up for the common good. And the system was fair in that it was supposedly random. June thinks it was then, as it is today, designed to dispose of undesirables and enemies in the community and surrounding regions. And just like then, it pays dividends.

June guides Uli toward the *centro*, which is where he found himself the first day in San Miguel when he went looking for Atómico after he'd escaped. They walk past the highway bridge that separates his neighborhood from the next one, that pocket of San Miguel where the police station, the butcher shop and that crowd of people (smaller now, but still there) can be found. Uli remembers that same cat fishing his paws inside a bucket of blood. He remembers that same old timer with his ladder and copper screws. Those plaques resting on the ground full of names: the soon to be sacrificed.

A group of soldiers, just arrived in the city, watches at the periphery of the crowd mostly comprised of women and children. Uli assumes that, like his father had, all of the men have gone north. To Texas, Arizona, California. There's a certain buzz in the air. Above the hub-bub of muddled, middle-aged voices, there's the cutting whine of a child bowled over in pain at having struck her toe along the curb leading up to the police station. As if in solidarity, other toddlers whine too for no apparent reason other than to have their voices heard.

As the hub-bub reaches a fever pitch, the old man with the copper screws drags his ladder outside from the tin awning of the police station and begins to climb it. There's a collective rustling. Women, all around Uli, reach into their bras, handbags, shoes, sleeves, pockets to produce little white sheets of paper like the ones Uli had seen that day he went looking for Atómico.

June produces her own little slip of paper from the small pocket in her jeans.

"What are those?"

"Official betting slips," says June, looking out for the man about to climb his ladder. "I bet on the small list every time," she says, unfurling the official, water-inked slip. In the sunlight, Uli can see that the watermark is of the city seal of San Miguel. A set of laurel leaves, a Spanish coat of arms that looks too elaborate to be real and the name of the city, San Miguel.

"On the small list are the nobodies," says June. "The every-day people. There are two lists. The first list is made up of the big wigs, which include mayors, generals, public figures—those kinds of guys. And then the small list, which is mostly made up of ordinary people. Like us. The small list pays more. Twenty to one. But the big one pays ten to one. Still not bad if you're sure the mayor's going to die, or something like that. These days, those plaques are just hitlists, really. The names of the people the cartel is going to kill."

"What would you have to do to end up on a cartel hitlist?" asks Uli.

"Steal product, steal money from them. Petty stuff."

"Well, who did the killing before the cartels arrived?"

"Everyone," says June. "Some men even killed their wives, if you can believe that. Did it for the money."

Uli is not sure if June is joking or not, if any of this is real or not. "There's someone to kill every week?"

"Every six weeks is more like it. Social cleansing. The cartels always have someone to kill. Everyone lets it happen. Everyone says, 'let the delinquents kill themselves if they want to.' I think that's why the army doesn't intervene. Anyway, it works like this: the cartels put the names up on their blogs and then those same names are put up on a plaque for all the public to see in San Miguel. You buy a slip of paper for five pesos that gives you one shot at guessing who you think will die. You only get one shot, one name. But the catch is you have to put a date on your slip. If that person dies within one week, before or after that date, you win. If not, you get nothing. Get it?"

"And what's with the screws? The plaques?"

"The city makes a big show out of making the deaths official. The man goes up there with a plaque and crosses out the names in red so it's public—official. If you win, you go see him. He handles the show pretty much. That's his job. They always give that job to an old person. He does the slips, the payouts, the climbing up the ladder to take the old plaques down and put the new ones up. He's also in charge of raising the odds if a name's been up there too long. That gets more people to come and bet if there's a big payout.

"What's the longest a name's been up there?" asks Uli.

"About seventy weeks," says June.

"Who's name?"

"Mine," she says.

And before Uli can even say anything to her, a hush comes over the crowd.

A woman scolding her toddler quickly snaps her neck to where everyone else is looking. All eyes focus on the old man climbing the ladder. Silence. Just the sound of his feet creaking up the rungs, those two large plaques knocking against each other as they dangle below him from a line of rope.

The women shuffle their feet backward as the old man swings the plaques around the front of the ladder to keep them away from his body.

At the top of the ladder, there's a can of red paint and a brush. He calls out the small list—all of five names and their corresponding death dates—in his shaky, old man voice before striking through them all, one by one, with red paint. All of them are crossed off but June's.

Uli looks at her. The scar over her face. Those watery eyes. He can't help but think of how easy it would be. There'd be money in it at least. From the corner of his eye, he spies the gun in the small of her back. Takes a breath. Watches the show.

Some women cheer, others send up a breathy air of exasperation, their tongues clucking as they wait for him to put up the new list.

There are eight names in total on the new plaque. Of course, June's name is up there too. Most every other name is unremarkable except for two. CHENTE VASCONCELOS, the junkyard scrapper, and ARACELI URIAS, Uli's mother.

"Shit," says June.

Uli looks at his mother's name up on the plaque and for a moment that's the only thing in the world he sees. He feels June slip away more than he sees her. She pulls her wagon past the police station, past the bridge, past the Oxxo convenience store on the other side of the bridge, hauling ass hell for high leather to get where she's going. Or, at least, where Uli thinks she's going. To get her copper scrapped before Chente can push up daisies and leave them broke forever. To get her money. To get her car. To drive off wherever she thinks she's going to drive off to.

Uli thinks about running after her. But instead he pushes through the crowd and asks the old man with the ladder just one question: "How much for June?"

In the north end of San Miguel, in a colonia named Huasteca, there's a shuttered Spanish mission that's never been scrapped. The mission is the only solid structure in a long road of rusty, corrugated tin structures. Auto body shops, crack cell phone stands, bakeries.

The look of it is like something carved from a single slab of rock. White-washed adobe squared off at the top into a single curved gable inlaid with a Virgin Mary figure, open palms at her sides. At each side of the hammered patina door there are two busted, circular windows guarded with crossbars. Over the door itself, a mangle of padlocks.

June produces a small, black, rolled rag from her back pocket and unfurls it over the ground beside the church door. Inside the rag there are a set of allen keys and various handled needles. There's one needle with a sharp curve and another one with a slight curve. Another that's bent like a bunch of waves coming in off the ocean and another with a sloped "P" that's worn thin around the top. June expertly wields the lockpicking tools into the complexities of the pins and gears shielded behind the padlocks and camlocks and rim latches all hanging from the door, one lock over the other. They shine in their sloped deformities from being struck so many times, nobody able to hammer them with brute force off of the door.

The locks clack open, one by one by one, as June picks them and pries them from the door with a steady, steely efficiency. She holds each lock as if weighing them in the center of her palm before dropping them, slack wristed, to her feet so that they clack along the bricks. It takes only twelve minutes for June to shove the church door open.

A cool draught makes its way from inside the building out into the warm July air. It smells stale and old. Darkness pours over them as they cross the threshold.

Inside the church, the altar is still intact. There's some tagging but not a lot. Mostly it looks like time has worn down the structure all by itself. There are electric lights in the iron chandeliers overhead and a single copper pipe that runs the length of the building. A wall brace. The pipe bolted into the corners at the roof and the wall. Exactly what they're looking for.

By the thickness of it, Uli guesses it might be seventy pounds of copper altogether. Enough scrap to feed them for a month, just that one piece. At least enough scrap to feed them while June's dog recovers to fighting strength. Not that she's too keen on the idea of fighting him just yet.

"Let's make some money," says June, swinging her wagon through the aisle between the pews. She parks it to the left of the altar. In the corner, a stack of purple, lent rags four feet high. On top of the stack there's a cord of decorative golden rope laid in a coil. June unspools the coil. She snaps a segment of it to test its strength. It pops with a dry rasp, the dust from the fibers flying into the air.

"Might bring the brace down," she says to Uli. "It's long enough."

"Cord is a cord. I don't see what length has anything to do with it."

"You double it up. Make it stronger. Like this," she says and loops the cord in two. She ties the loose, tasseled ends of the cord into a weighted knot, which she uses to thread the space between the brace and the wall. She throws the knot and misses three times before she gets it through, the weighted plush cord falling the twelve feet back to the ground with a soft thud on the concrete.

With the rope fully wrapped around the copper pipe, she turns her back to the wall with the slack of rope over her shoulder and pulls with all her weight. No dice.

"It's gotta be quick," says Uli, "or you'll bring the whole thing down."

"I got it," says June, a glare of frustration flashing from her eyes through that fleshy mask.

Uli grabs a fistful of slack rope and pulls with June, the tonal stress of the tension sounding all along the length of the rope, but the copper brace doesn't even budge.

"Maybe a hammer?" says Uli.

"No. That won't work," says June.

"Well, hell, I don't know."

"Maybe one more try," she says. "We've got it here. We just gotta get it. I've got one more thing," she says.

"Pull it from both sides?" asks Uli, ready to throw an extra cord of rope over the brace at the other end of the wall to pull along with June.

"No," says June. "We'll get it from one side first. Then we'll get the other side. Easier to fight one bolt than two."

"Makes sense," he says, eager to let June try her thing so they can get onto his idea.

Uli puts his hand inside his jean pocket, feels the lottery ticket there.

He watches June tie the rope around her waist. She pulls hard with her back, tightening the rope again. Her feet angle along the steps that lead up to the busted altar of the church, the crucifix hanging heavy over her as Uli steps back to the opposite wall. When she pulls, the faintest of cracks appear around the brace's bolts before the wall shatters with a flurry of tiny fissures.

A wind pushes through the church's open doors. The powdered adobe from the wall, loose now, pours off into the breeze. It slicks about the church's corners, the pews, past Uli and then out into the street.

As June leverages herself further up the altar steps, a look emerges on her face. A mixture of relief and pride and hope as the groaning bolt comes loose from its mortar. The brace comes undone. It swings down from the wall that clang like gold in their ears. In that split second, she looks to Uli as if to say *I told you so*. But also as if to say, *we're going to be ok*. And its then that Uli looks from her head to her hand, the rope going slack in her fist as the wall crashes down onto her.

A strong gust pushes over him. The adobe grit stings his face. He half-expects to see a pool of blood, to see June just a pulp in the ground. But when he opens his eyes, he sees a thousand tiny skeletons at his feet instead, some of them no bigger than his thumb but others as large as full-term babies. A few of them still have skin over their bones, mummified in the earthy clay.

To Uli, the sight feels like an ugly portent, but also like some sliver to a larger truth. Of all the ways this church could have come down throughout the centuries (of all the people these skeletons could have revealed themselves to) it's him now watching this light fall on their crooked limbs, their death undoing June's life with the very weight of their existence.

He'd heard of this kind of thing before, from his father, but he always thought it was lore. A tall tale. Stories of priests in colonial times who would get Indian women pregnant. They'd hide their mistakes in the walls they built, figuring nobody would tear down a church. Not ever. Abortions, newborns—it didn't matter. They were all buried.

Uli looks at all those baby skeletons scattered at his feet. Bones as white as the dust. A skull, a rib cage, a femur. And then he sees June's blood spreading under all of it. That little slip of lottery paper burns in his pocket as he digs and digs, wondering if she's made it, knowing (if only in the back of his mind) that even the darkest secrets find the light of day.

ALMA

EACH BREATH FOR JUNE is like drowning in a sea of pain. She hunches over the bathroom sink, hissing through her teeth. Her hot breath fogs up the bathroom mirror. She can feel a crunching in her abdomen when she exhales. *Hiss-wheeze, hiss-wheeze* go her lungs. She feels Uli's eyes on the exposed layers of flesh beneath her peeled scar. The cool condensation on the mirror slowly disappears (and then reappears with her breath) in front of her as she works to glue herself back together.

Pale, blistery flesh hangs down from her cheekbone. She peels back a mucous-wet sliver of scar tissue just above the corner of her lip. She looks at her mouth in the mirror. She doesn't look at her blood. She can't stand the sight of it. She doesn't feel the two separate pains of her broken ribs and of her lacerated face. She only feels one pain throbbing all over her body.

"Give me—" she says to Uli, breathing hard now, "—the glue."

She waits for it with her flat palm outstretched.

Uli, leaning in the threshold of the bathroom door, hands her a small tube of Resistol and a towel. They'd go to the free hospital but it's full—it's always full. Glue will do the trick. She knows it.

Her eyes water as she holds her breath just long enough to squeeze a line from the tube along the pink edges of her scar. She has to work fast before it dries. She makes an arc around the bone of her cheek. And then she peels the layer of flapped skin up with the tips of her fingers and puts it flat over the arc of glue. She exhales a long, hot breath. Her eyes water again. She pats her skin dry with a ragged towel. From the mirror in front of her, June cannot tell what's a tear and what's glue.

She leans on Uli who helps her from the bathroom to the bedroom. She lays herself down on the bed. *Hiss-wheeze, hiss-wheeze.* She says to Uli, "I'm drowning."

She looks to him for consolation but only catches his eyes falling on her pistol resting on the nightstand. He puts his cool hand over her forehead. She only sees his wrists now. She closes her eyes.

"Just another minute or so," says Uli.

June knows the glue package says thirty seconds to dry on wood surfaces. Twenty-five seconds on aluminum. It doesn't say anything about flesh.

The pain comes and goes in waves. When it comes, her legs go up and down. She holds her rib cage. She puts her hands over Uli's hand. In her head, she can almost hear bones crunching, the sound more imagined than audible.

"I'm drowning," she says to him again.

"You'll be fine," says Uli.

"You have to go," she whispers.

"Where?"

"To get the money. Before he's murdered."

Within a block of the scrapyard, a single federal cop with his car lights flashing. A pack of *nota roja* photographers snap away at the body, crowding the cop out of his own scene.

Uli dumps his wagon. The wall brace rolls to the ground.

Chente is shirtless outside his attendant's booth. There's a belt tied around his neck, looped at the other end to the handle of the door. His belly is a map of busted capillaries and purple veins that sprawl like the naked branches of a tree over his abdomen. The belt cinches his neck so that his head is cocked at an awkward angle.

From a distance, Uli can't make out whether Chente's eyes are closed or not. The dead body is more real than anything he's ever seen. More real, even, than the car bomb cadavers.

Chente's mouth is open. There's a little trickle of dried blood on his chin. You can tell the blood poured steady when the wound opened. The trickle is still glossy wet and bright between his bottom teeth. Uli thinks of the burning mare, that barbecued creature. He looks for that big plume of ash in the sky right now. *Did I dream that?* he wonders, looking up into the sky for that smoke, but there is none. Just blue sky and the sound of dogs.

Who could have had it in for Chente? he wonders. *Who has it in for June?*

Uli kicks at the wall brace he'll never sell. He thinks about June's pain. He wonders how much longer she might last, how much longer his money might last.

Before leaving, Uli looks down on Chente one last time, the photographers snapping all around him. On Chente's left cheek there's the remainder of a green bruise, the blood having already drained from his face and pooled elsewhere. His death mask is on. He looks younger maybe, the creases of his wrinkles less defined. There's a jagged part in his hair that Uli had never noticed before. It starts from the crown of the head and wanders toward the temple. And there's a little chain and medallion around his neck. St. Christopher. For a second, Uli thinks the man might look like his own father.

Around the scrapyard, the sky is littered with moths that skitter about the light of every glowing thing, even Chente's teeth, which glow with a hue all their own in the purple whirl of police lights burning bright against his green skin. The moths do not discriminate between the sources of light. They land, two or three of them, on the curl of Chente's open lip. They gum their wings up in the blood of his mouth and stay there. They drink it. They die in it.

It takes the entire walk back to his house for Uli to get the gall to knock on the door of the woman who lives in the house across from his. As he waits there, his neck starts to itch. And then his scalp. And then his legs, crawling with the static that comes with bad circulation—blood making its way through his capillaries that are rerouting around the broken bits of himself.

He stays anchored there until a woman answers the door. He runs his fingers through his hair.

"Who are you?" he immediately asks, before she can even say a thing.

She laughs at this, breaks the tension in the air. "Who are you?" she says back.

"I live over there," says Uli.

"I know," she says. "I'm Alma."

Based on what little June's said about her, she's nothing like what Uli had imagined her to be. Her eyes are grey and soft, almond shaped but thinner somehow. Her face is round. She's heavy for her frame. Baby weight. Her face looks about forty years old, menopausal peach-fuzz on her jaw, but her hands say almost thirty. She's wearing a faded, blue dress with white polka dots. Uli thinks she could be either a hipster or a church lady. Uli is leaning toward church lady.

Alma stares at Uli as if waiting for him to speak.

"My friend is injured," he explains to her, eager for her to see the urgency of the situation. "I need your help."

"Is she still alive?"

"Yes, but she's got a broken rib. She can't breathe."

"Well, nothing can be done about a broken rib. There's food in the kitchen," she says coolly. "You're Arnulfo's son, right?"

"How do you know my father?"

"He left a while ago. Good man. You look like him. Come inside and eat," she says.

At this, Uli pauses, unsure of what to do. He feels that ticket in his pocket.

"Everything heals in time," says Alma. "Come inside. Come."

And so Uli goes in, feeling as if he's already betrayed June. Of course, June would tell him to leave. She'd tell him this woman was no good, but who else should he turn to right now that June is on her death bed? Uli thinks this is what being out of ideas looks like. But he's also driven by his new fascination for this woman who knows his father. He wonders if she has some answers. He wonders, too, if this isn't why June wanted to keep him away from her in the first place.

Her home smells like chicken stock. It's filled with religious paintings. There's one of the lamb of God and another with Jesus and a lamb. There's another one of a lamb in a pasture. There's another one of Lazarus with open wounds, which isn't finished yet, and looks more like Judas than Lazarus—not dead enough.

Her paintings are good but not great. Everywhere, scattered about, are sketches of people. Mostly men.

She sits Uli at a wooden table in the kitchen that's blistered with wet, coffee mug rings.

On the floor there are paint brushes resting in emptied coffee cans, milky residue crusting up the insides where the water has evaporated. Across the floor there are sheets of newspaper and splotches of white paint over an advent calendar in the community pages.

"Are you a Catholic?" Alma asks.

"I was raised Catholic," Uli says.

Alma places a percolator on the stove and fills it with water and a teaspoon of powdered Nescafé. From her freezer, she produces a large Ziploc bag of *pozole* frozen flat, which she opens by running a knife down the seam of the plastic. She pours the brick of soup into a nickel-plated saucepan with rivets that wiggle as the steam builds under the lid.

"Are you Catholic?" he asks her, which is, of course, a stupid question.

She doesn't answer. She just stands in silence in front of the stove.

She places the coffee in front of him in a clay mug. "Drink," she says. She lights up a cornhusk cigarette.

The coffee is too hot. Uli lets it rest at his lips for a moment.

She says, "Drink it," again, barely moving her own lips.

Uli does as he's told. He scalds his tongue.

When the nickel-plated rivet is dancing violently on the pot lid, she lifts the lid and dips a ladle into the pozole. She pours two boiling ladles into plastic green bowls with tarnished tin spoons. A layer of orange grease sits at the top of the liquid where it separates from the broth in tiny iridescent globules. She throws diced onions into Uli's bowl, cilantro too. It tastes like heaven.

"Do you like it?" she asks him. Her smile is like a mother's smile, brilliant and tense at the same time.

"Yes—God, yes."

She pours more coffee into the cinnamon-laced mug.

"My mother has one like this," Uli says. "Made of clay. She only drinks tea out of it."

"Is she from the South?"

"She was born in Aguascalientes. My geography is not too good," he says.

"Where are you from?"

"Who says I'm from somewhere?" he says.

"Everyone knows where Aguascalientes is," she says.

"I'm from across the street."

"You're from Texas," she says knowingly. She sips easy at her steaming, clay mug. A long silence. She stares quietly into her coffee before she says, "Don't worry about your friend, Uli. Worry about yourself. Understand? That's what your father would tell you. Or am I wrong?"

There's a knock at her door. Alma cranes her head to the kitchen window by the sink. Parked by a busted Volkswagen in the street is an orange Ford Lobo. She stares off into space as if considering whether or not to answer the door.

"Should I get that?" he asks, trying to read her face.

She doesn't look him in the eye as she says, "You're a sweet boy. Very much like your father."

The knocking comes again, steady and firm. All business. Uli wonders to himself if she might be half deaf. It's a long time before the knocking stops, and the engine in the Ford turns over.

Uli sees Alma ease her lips. She sets the cup down before picking it back up.

"You like to eat? Eat," she says, picking up his bowl, pouring in another ladle of pozole.

Her eyes tear up. The morning light pours in through the striations of light, making the greys of her eyes glow. Everything else is bloodshot.

"What was that?" he asks.

She ignores the question.

"Are you feeling better?" she asks, getting up to grab something from the cabinet above the fridge.

"Yes," says Uli.

"About your friend," she says.

"Yes," he says.

She pulls down a case of Cokes and a bag of hard Bimbo croissants. "Here," she says, pushing them in front of Uli. "If you're hungry, I'll feed you. I'll know when you're coming. The Lord told me you'd be here," she says.

"The Lord?"

"The Lord," she says.

At this, Uli wonders, exactly, what her relationship with his father was. Because he hates people who talk like that. Always has hated them.

Uli nods, sips his coffee.

Alma takes out a votive candle and some matches and places the candle in front of a picture of Saint Rita of Cascia kneeling before a crucifix with God's infinite wisdom pouring down onto her. Beneath the picture, a little ribbon is tied around the base. *Patron Saint of the Impossible,* it says.

Alma lights the candle and says she's going to say a prayer.

Uli doesn't know how long it's been since he's last prayed.

"Eat," she says to him. "You're staring at me and I don't like it."

But what else can Uli do but stare? He doesn't know how to tell her that he wants to pray like her. He wants to thank her somehow, even if it's only by gawking at her praying.

The orange Ford Lobo pulls up outside her house again. A frail-looking, pot-bellied man hops from the passenger seat and waddles over to the house, knocks on the door once again. And once again Alma pretends not to hear it.

Uli parts his lips to speak.

"I'll get it," she says.

Alma crosses herself, goes to the door and opens it. In walks a man, impossibly tall with purple boots. He kisses Alma on the cheek. Her husband maybe? Her brother?

Uli doesn't know why the man reminds him of his own brother. The man moves like Cuauhtémoc. He has that same look in his eye—that thousand yard stare like Cuauhtémoc used to have from looking out the windshield of a plane all day.

Alma unbuttons the pearl snap on the man's chest pocket and pulls out a brown baggy.

"Would you mind?" she asks Uli.

They whisper back and forth. Uli sees that she's almost melting under his gaze.

He grabs her ass. She takes the baggy and shakes off his grip. She brings the baggy over to Uli at the kitchen table.

"For your friend," she says and reaches into her painter's apron hanging by the canvas to produce a syringe. "For the pain. Understand? Do you know how to do this?"

Kneeling in front of June, Uli does it exactly as Alma told him. First, he lays everything out on the snare drum beside the bed: the heroin, the syringe and needle, the spoon (washed in alcohol), the candle, the cigarette filter, a shoelace, some water. And then he halves the brown lime she gave him. Alma told him brown limes work best. They're riper. They give more cit-rus juice, which dissolves the heroin faster, which makes the solution cleaner.

The heroin is brown and clumpy. Alma said that's how you know it's good. Alma calls it brown sugar. The best kind. Straight from the source, which means straight from the man in the purple boots.

He can hear Alma's words in his head. *Not too much, not too little. Not too hot. She can smoke it if she wants.*

Uli looks at June now, lying in bed, as he squeezes the lime into a ceramic bowl. Her chest moves up and down with impos-sible little pats of breath. She's sweating and moaning or trying to moan. It takes breath to moan, and June has nothing left to spare, which is why she doesn't argue. She can barely complain. She just sits there and watches.

"You'll feel good in just a minute," says Uli, scraping some heroin from the clump with the edge of the spoon and pushing it onto the snare drum beside the bed. He crumbles the dust with a heavy tamping beneath the spoon's curve. "A pile no larger than his pinky nail," he remembers the man in purple boots told him. It smells like vinegar.

He takes his pinky nail and places it beside the clump over the snare drum. He compares the pile two, three, four times. He pinches the clump between his index and his thumb like one might take a pinch of salt and drops it carefully into the hollow of the spoon. The sweat of his fingers causes friction against the drumhead so that it rasps with each pinch of the heroin. There's a rhythm to it, a steady, working groove. The snare rattles. The spoon gets fuller by the moment.

Uli lights the candle with a match and runs the needle through it two, three times. He dips the needle in the lime juice and draws, with the plunger, five units. He dips the needle into the water and draws fifteen units. He shakes the solution inside the syringe and then empties it into the hollow of the spoon, where it dissolves the heroin into dark, reddish clumps.

June hears the spoon sizzle. She feels the pressure of the shoelace cutting into the skin over her bicep. Her pulse starts to thicken. She hears the blood in her ears. The tips of her fingers go numb.

"Stay very still," Uli whispers.

She sees the flame.

Slowly, the dark burns away from corners of June's vision. She sees her own arm, from the corner of her eye, outstretched along the mattress. Her veins bulge blue-green beneath her skin. She feels the pinch. And then nothing as warmth washes over her body. June thinks it's like going back into the womb. Her breathing slows, her pain disappears. She thinks about her sister, her mother. It feels as though she's kissing them good-night. It feels like she's beautiful again, like she's never been damaged. Like the night before Christmas when she was five. She's never been this happy. She thinks, *This is how I want to feel forever.*

DESERT SPARROW

AT JIMMY'S RANCH, the Hacienda de San Sebastián, there's a cur dog that lives inside a burnt-out DC-3 with his friend, a black-throated sparrow. As far as Cuauhtémoc can tell, they've been there as long as the land itself. Cuauhtémoc thinks the sparrow is the prettiest bird he's ever seen. A jet-black beak to match the oval patch of black over its belly. The underside of him is a smoky white. Two gray, parallel streaks just above and below the eye. A tight tuft of blue-black feathers over the crown of his head. That color stretches back all the way to the raw patch just under his right earhole where he scratches too much with just one rapid foot, just like the dog scratches himself when he's got an itch behind the ear.

The bird goes everywhere the dog goes, eats everything the dog eats, perches himself right between the dogs ears so that he can see everything the dog sees. Every afternoon they play. The bird *tack-tack-tacks* about the ground and flits in the air before the dog can lunge at it. The dog grows angry at his impotence, until one day the dog takes a long, swift, unexpected lunge and pulls the bird from the sky. He gives it a fierce shake. Snaps the bird's neck. Eyes heavy, the dog brings it over to Cuauhtémoc, who has been watching the whole thing. The dog drops it at Cuauhtémoc's feet as if saying, *Fix this, please*. The dog lies down and whimpers, waits for Cuauhtémoc to pick it up.

It's the first time Cuauhtémoc's ever held a bird. He strokes its feathers, feels its warmth. Even dead it's still the prettiest thing he's ever seen.

A swift kick of sand meets the dog's watery eyes. "Get out of here!" shouts Lalo from behind Cuauhtémoc.

The dog pulls back, bounces around on his paws with his tail between his legs. Lalo shouts again. The dog takes off, his mourning cut short.

Cuauhtémoc sticks the dead bird in his shirt pocket before turning around to face Lalo, whose eyes are glassy red.

"Could have rabies, you know," says Lalo. "Jimmy doesn't give them their shots. They're good as strays. Shouldn't get too close to them. I don't."

"You got the money?" asks Cuauhtémoc.

"I do, if you've got the banking all set up."

"It's set up."

"Well, tell me about it," says Lalo, his red eyes darting between the ranch house and Cuauhtémoc, scanning for anyone who might overhear them.

"It's a Frost Bank."

"Is that a good one?" says Lalo

"It's a Texas bank. Got a big building in Austin."

"That's not what I'm talking about," says Lalo. "I mean will the volume set off any alarm bells or anything?"

"Banker told me that the limit was ten grand to set off a transaction report. We're only doing eight at a time. I'm depositing hard cash, just like you told me."

"And how much have we got in there right now?" asks Lalo.

"About seventy grand. More than enough to get you started if you want to come along," says Cuauhtémoc with a smile now, feeling the warmth of the bird against his chest. "I could show you the deposit slip if you want," says Cuauhtémoc, pulling an envelope from his shirt pocket.

Lalo takes the envelope and immediately puts it in a pocket inside his jacket.

"You're not going to look at it?" says Cuauhtémoc.

"I don't need to see that," says Lalo. "I trust you. More than that, I trust that you'll be in touch when it's time to withdraw the cash. We'll split it—fifty-fifty. I won't forget this, friend."

"You should burn that slip," says Cuauhtémoc. "Nothing but trouble. Worse than trouble, it's evidence. They'd kill us for it."

"Nobody's going to find it," says Lalo, patting his pocket. "Even if they catch me, I wouldn't tell on you," he says with a wink. "Why would I?"

"Another load?" asks Cuauhtémoc, his eyes fixed on the DC-3.

"A small one this time," says Lalo. He looks over his shoulder, then hands Cuauhtémoc a blue envelope full of cash.

By the weight of it, Cuauhtémoc guesses it's about two grand. Not even worth the landing and drive to the bank in El Paso. "A little light," he says.

"Dance lessons, violin lesson," says Lalo with a smile. "Kids don't come cheap. There'll be more next time."

"I'll remember that," says Cuauhtémoc, Lalo's eyes suddenly severe. "You all right?"

"You know, they probably already know the money is missing," says Lalo. "In fact, I know they know. It's just a matter of time before they track us down."

"Well, all the more reason to get this deposited quickly," says Cuauhtémoc, walking toward his plane on the airstrip.

Just as Cuauhtémoc pivots away, he's grabbed by both shoulders. A sting in his bicep where his jacket is pulling on the wounds that haven't quite healed. Lalo's sour breath is upon Cuauhtémoc now. His crazy eyes stare deep into Cuauhtémoc's own gaze. "Hey, listen. I know you don't have to come back.

You've got more than enough money to break free. But you should come back. Your brother is still alive, you know. Here, in Mexico. Not far. I saw him. I met him."

"Bullshit," says Cuauhtémoc, visibly angry now. He feels his blood pressure rising. His arm itches.

"I could show you where he's at. But you have to come back for me. And my daughter. Can we make that a deal?"

"He's dead," says Cuauhtémoc.

"He's not," says Lalo, squeezing Cuauhtémoc's bicep hard. "He's not. I know you think that he is, but I know someone that's watching out for him. A woman I see sometimes. He's alive."

"Bullshit."

"I have a picture," says Lalo.

From his front jean pocket he pulls out a charcoal sketch on the back of a love note signed by someone else, not Uli, but the portrait is undeniably of Uli: the same flat head, the same tiny mouth, that hair that grows out (not down) like a paint brush, those close-set eyes, that too-big forehead.

"Where did you get this?" asks Cuauhtémoc.

"I told you already. A woman I know. Here," he says, his one hand holding onto Cuauhtémoc's shoulder now as the other hand expertly folds the sketch back along its creases, placing it in Cuauhtémoc's hand. "I can only help you as much as you help me."

"Okay," Cuauhtémoc says, feeling the weight of the sketch in his hand. He doesn't look down at the paper. He just looks Lalo in the eyes.

"You come back. You come back, and I'll show you where he's at," says Lalo, uncurling his fingers to free Cuauhtémoc from his grip. "It's all coming to an end soon. You have to trust me. Come back for us. If not for me, then for my daughter."

That's the last time Cuauhtémoc sees Lalo with two feet on the ground.

Cuauhtémoc has learned to sleep between heaven and earth in the cockpit of his own plane. On two pieces of cardboard, he's drawn, in pencil, an E6B slide rule. It allows him to calculate, given the direction and speed of the winds aloft, the proper wind correction angles, the true air speed of the plane and the amount of fuel burned, among other things that make it possible for him to set the plane on course, set its pitch, power and trim and doze off with an alarm clock in his lap, the earth rolling beneath him. All of his numbers taken care of, he can let the controls go and relax.

This morning, the whirling propellers rattle the frame. They rock him to sleep with the sun flooding the cockpit, the warmth soaking into his clothes.

Behind his shut eyelids, he sees blood red. He dreams of nothing at first, just watches the purple iridescent swirls take shape. He quiets his brain by pinching his arm. A little pain to keep his thoughts centered on one thing.

When he feels dizzy, he knows his equilibrium is off and the plane is tilting. He opens one eye, looks out the windshield. The nose is too high and the stall horn spurts. He adjusts the trim on the rudder to get it flying straight, to keep those clouds over the same scratch in the windshield. He levels the plane by picking a spot out in the distance—a cloud, a tower, a mountain top—and keeping it in the same spot on the windshield.

He opens both eyes, watches that scratch stay just above the top of the clouds in the distance. He watches it for a long time. Makes sure it keeps still. He adds fifteen more minutes onto the alarm clock, checks his numbers once more, checks the scratch in the window again, messes with the trim just a smidge, and closes his eyes for good until sleep overwhelms him again.

The cold air frosts the tips of his eyelashes, and this gives him bad dreams. The skies are cold. The drugs make it worse. His nerves are jangly beneath his skin, raw like sickness spreading from the limbs in. Nicotine burns at the tips of his fingers. In his nose, the sweet rot of a stinking wound. When he touches it he remembers the prick of Jimmy's knife in his septum from last night. Jimmy's blade full of cocaine.

No sleep on my watch.

Jimmy likes Cuauhtémoc high like he likes everyone else around him high. Cuauhtémoc does everything to fit in, does everything to go unnoticed and he never sleeps. Nobody sleeps in the safe houses, especially not the *sicarios*, the murder artists, who are perpetually high. Everyone drinks and smokes and fucks and snorts, and Cuauhtémoc does too. And all the while, he can't wait to get back up in the sky again, can't wait to be alone, like he is now. Can't wait to sleep.

The sun is the only natural thing left for him, the only thing that keeps him going. When he feels the sun on his skin, he imagines those same rays hitting his brother in San Miguel—two brothers under the same sun. Wherever he is, they're both beneath it. And sooner or later he'll find him. He swears he'll find him. Lalo gives him hope.

Everything depends on Lalo now.

A squall line of wind jolts Cuauhtémoc from sleep. He sits upright in his seat, realizes he's freezing. He pulls the cabin heat on until he feels woozy. He lets the sun and the carb heat unwind his cold nerves. His body relaxes but the adrenaline keeps his brain high.

When he closes his eyes again, his thoughts start to scatter. He imagines the whir of the engines outside, a buzzard flying beneath his shadow, a sweating bottle of Topo Chico mineral water, the bathroom of the safe houses he's lived in, all of his things in a single satchel, a bottle of shaving cream and a new razor from the drugstore, too many condoms, the smell of a woman, the sour taste of her kiss, too much alcohol and not enough food. A girl in his dream looks like all the other safe house girls. Thin, faded. He only loves them because he has to, and even when he does, he wonders how many dead men they've slept with already.

In his sleep, Cuauhtémoc's altitude sickness builds. Hypoxia. A mixture of nausea and happiness like laughing gas, like grove sickness—pesticide sickness. In his mind he can almost smell the oranges. The ripeness of the blood from his father's stomach fresh in the wet earth, the vomiting of poison.

He sits with his boots dug into the rudder pedals, opens his blood-shot eyes and glances at the creosote below. He stares out over the cowling at Texas on the other side of the river. He's imagined it a million times, what it would be like to fly out that way and never come back. He knows what would happen if he did. His brother would die. His mother too. Revenge killings. That was the deal he made.

He thinks on that, huffs a short, stale breath. Pins and needles up and down his arms.

Just over the engine cowling, the sun sets high over the scrub brush below. Off to the northeast, the night-flooded caldera shimmering like so much black glass in the moonlight.

He sets the carburetor mixture rich to bleed off altitude. He yaws south by the rudders and drops the nose fifteen degrees or so. The dive angle sets his engine braying, a surge of air cooling up into the cowling. He concentrates on the power of that engine. Knows it can pull him to earth quicker than he'd like to admit. He waits a second before pulling the red throttle shaft out to idle. The propeller swings low and slow just over a thousand RPMs. The whiskey compass in the windshield does its little dance.

A flock of buzzards fly in a ring over some rotting carcasses below. Cuauhtémoc gooses the throttle to rev the engine a little, some sound to get the birds scattering. The whistling wind slips past the air frame. The largest buzzard pulls away first. It flaps its lazy wings in long, slow strokes before it pirouettes into a dive. The other buzzards follow suit. *They couldn't fall even if they tried*, thinks Cuauhtémoc. But the plane falls. It slips down from the stratosphere, pulling the wind behind it, those carcasses getting bigger in the windshield and that whistling pitch getting louder, a high whine like a tuning fork on glass. And then the pressure builds like a needle in his ear. The bodies grow bigger. As the birds scatter, the carnage they're circling appears below the spot in the sky where they flew.

Nine men strewn pell-mell along Highway 2, their blood coagulating like oil in the sand. A quarter mile south, toward San Miguel, a candy-orange Ford Lobo with its rack of headlights shot, its mostly burnt-out diesel engine smoking greasy black in the sun.

Cuauhtémoc hovers just over the scene. He levels out and eases the throttle, dumping full flaps to bring the plane to slow flight. He circles maybe a dozen times or so, the propellers loping slow as he glides down into ground effect. He bleeds off a little altitude with every round, trying to make out the faces of the dead. But that's the thing with the dead: they never look anything like themselves.

It's only by the boots that he can recognize one body spilling out of the driver's side of the orange pickup. Purple boots. Maybe ten miles out, a procession of Jeeps from San Miguel, hauling ass toward the smoke. Cuauhtémoc eases in the throttle. Leaves the flaps down to pop him up, give him more lift to climb quicker. Even from that high up, he swears those boots are moving.

SAFEHOME

CUAUHTÉMOC ALWAYS GREASES THE LANDINGS. If the winds are strong, he lands in the desert north of Obregón, on a sand strip outlined by burning tar barrels, desert oak and split saguaro cut lengthwise to catch the neon sun. But if the winds are calm, Cuauhtémoc lumbers his aircraft, an aging M20J, onto a neighborhood street in Lomas de Poleo just inside Ciudad Juárez. All of the homes abandoned. Everyone gone from the drug wars.

The neighborhood landing always warrants thirty degrees of flaps, the elevators popped low with the shimmy damper extended full to the hook and bolt, no further slack to give. The flexing tension of the wire pings up and down the length of the aircraft as it descends. You can hear it ringing like a bell in the sky from both sides of the border. From one hill, the Mexican army looks up with silent admiration for the pilot who can grease such a landing. From the other hill, the Americans look down into the city with a fixed gaze as if willing the cartel plane to crash.

Cuauhtémoc dives in at an angle, on a slip stream, with his left rudder pushed full to the carpet and his ailerons turned fist-over-lap so the plane falls fast and loud, the up-gush of wind roaring high through the idled propellers, the plane like a vulture descending crooked into the remnants of the neighborhood. Five hundred feet, four hundred feet and he'll kick out the rudder to right the plane just before impact. He'll land it clean and free onto a street named Nahual, where the crumbling tar-gravel and rock splatter up against the nickel-plated underbelly of the plane behind the thrust of the cooling twin flat-eight Lycoming piston engines still revved to a thousand RPM.

The wingtips, forty-eight feet from one tip to the other, scrape along the thresholds of the houses on either side of Nahual Street. The power lines roll up and stretch over the bump of the cockpit. All of the birds move to either end of the line, unimpressed at the smoking four hundred and fifty horse-power engine threatening to suck them in. The driver, too, waits unimpressed at the end of the road.

The driver is always the one asking questions. The driver is both Cuauhtémoc's ride home and his interrogator, his friend and his enemy. *How was the flight? Any messages to be relayed? Any peculiarities along the way? Are you sure? Are you sure?* he'll ask. Cuauhtémoc knows the routine, and he knows better than to incriminate himself on what he did or did not see from the skies.

The driver is always different but more or less a variation of the same man. Mid-thirties, severely overweight, reeking of Delicados and cheap sex and Tommy Hilfiger cologne. Probably named Chuy, which is short for something. Cuauhtémoc can never remember.

From his cockpit, Cuauhtémoc can see the driver sitting back in his pleather-covered seats, drumming his nicotine fingers on the steering wheel of the truck. He listens to the American radio pouring in from the station on the hill. He checks his watch and waits for the engines to cut. He checks his hair in the mirror, perfectly lacquered with Tres Flores brilliantine. He cracks his spearmint gum. His breath smells like Swiss cheese.

Cuauhtémoc purges it all from his mind before his boot even touches the ground. He forgets the bloody road leading up to San Miguel. He forgets the private strip in Sweetwater,

Texas, called Fraley, where he made his drop of cocaine. He purges his memory of looking down on Interstate 20 running east of El Paso. Those burning cars. Hot, greasy, diesel smoke pouring black up into a plume that screened out the sun and painted the whole scene wispy in shadows of smoke. That familiar burnt-orange Ford Lobo—the one he'd ridden in so many times before from the airstrip—gushing from the undercarriage. Blood and oil and gasoline in the sand. A body pouring out from the driver's side wearing purple boots. Cuauhtémoc knew, even from the sky, who those boots belonged to. He purges that name from his mind too.

He plants his foot on the running boards of the white Dodge Durango at the end of Nahual street and climbs into the passenger seat.

"Any peculiarities?" the driver asks him, cracking his spearmint gum.

Cuauhtémoc glosses him over. They've never met before. "No," he says.

Cuauhtémoc keeps a stolid face, but his hands give him away, his finger pulling at the long, puckered scar on his left arm where it was cut the night he was deported from Texas, the night he was kidnapped and forced to fly cartel planes.

Cuauhtémoc says nothing as he eases his body into the passenger seat of the car. He turns down the radio and clicks it to the AM band. Texas High School Football. Westlake vs Copperas Cove. He takes the driver's Stetson from the dash and drapes it over his sun-wearied eyes.

"I can't understand English," the driver says.

"I know," says Cuauhtémoc softly and lowers the brim.

The engine turns over and the driver pulls out onto a side road. The driver expertly weaves through the boulders strewn pell-mell about the streets that keep the police from navigating the neighborhood and keep the military out too.

Cuauhtémoc closes his eyes and feels his neck fuse with sweat to the hot pleather headrest. His mouth is dry. His bones are aching. The driver takes Cuauhtémoc the long way to the safe house, which looks like all the other safe houses in Juárez. A squat, pale-brown one story. Bad foundation. Meandering cracks in the walls that split jagged in the cold months like sweeping bolts of lightning.

Desert wasps make their home in the seams where the warmth escapes. They breed and die. They shred up the adobe with their lives until the house takes on the fragile look of a cracked egg, or like tempered glass about to shatter.

Cuauhtémoc eases his aching body from the comfort of the pleather. He moves to turn off the radio, but it's already off. He walks around the fender and slaps the numbers tacked on the wall of the house just for kicks. 410. All of the safe houses end in 10—2810, 510, 4510. Cuauhtémoc commits every safe house address he's tried to bring down with the slap of his palm to memory.

The door opens. Darkness pours out from the threshold. A wiry little man with ropy muscles lays out the flat of his hand. Cuauhtémoc and the driver hand over their chirping Nextel phones like they do every time.

The little man puts them in an oversize Ziploc bag and says, "I hope all is well."

Cuauhtémoc's eyes try to adjust to the musty darkness inside, but he's nearly blind. He can only feel the little man's words on his neck now, a plume of smoke that cools just above the shirt collar and hangs there at the volume of a whisper. The driver follows behind.

"All is well," says Cuauhtémoc to no one in particular, and the door shuts behind him.

Inside, there's the too-sweet smell of perfume and sweat. There's the honeyed sound of women's voices, soft like leather—the lilt of beauty queens or beautiful liars who say they're beauty queens. There's the *knock-knock-knock* of their heels against the tile, tiny women who seem almost weightless as they glide.

They appear to Cuauhtémoc behind the iridescent patches of light that burn away from the center of his gaze, his pupils fully dilating in the dark. All of the women look the same to him. He wonders if he's met any of them before.

On the long table in the living room, there are silver bowls of cocaine, an RCA universal television remote, a polished pistol reeking of Hoppes 9 oil, a sweating beer, a half-finished ham *torta* sandwich with a bag of Sabrita potato chips.

"All is well?" asks the little man again.

Cuauhtémoc takes a bite of the sandwich and a swig of the beer and repeats, "All is well."

Lalo lies unconscious in the safe house tub, his hair still tinged with the sulfury smoke of burnt diesel. His hands are smoked black and his eyes are two fiery coals peering out with a thousand-yard stare. He's barely breathing. He's soaking wet in his clothes: a blue, pearl snap shirt, a pair of Wranglers, a pair of purple Larry Mahans that have all but cracked the fiberglass tub wide open. Along the inside of the tub there are long black arcs where the heels have scuffed in the struggle. The leather of his boots bloat about the same time his skin does. His fingers turn white and puffy in the water.

Cuauhtémoc's face turns ashen at the sight of Lalo—this man he'd purged from his mind only thirty minutes ago. A million thoughts course through Cuauhtémoc's brain just then, but none louder than the questions.

"What happened? What's going on?" says Cuauhtémoc. He acts just as surprised as he should be, though of course he'd seen this coming from way down the pike.

There's a doctor sitting on the toilet in a white coat, R.M.P. embroidered on his lapel. Across from him there's a boy with blue tattoos up and down his arm, these beautiful Chinese dragons with red eyes. The boy is wearing jeans rolled up to his calves and a plastic green rosary that dips in and out of the pink water of the fiberglass tub. He seems to be holding Lalo down or at least guarding him.

The doctor checks Lalo's pulse, consults his watch and then produces a capped needle from his breast pocket.

He plunges the needle through the denim into the fleshy part of Lalo's thigh. Lalo's eyes spring open, the black of his pupils spreading like ink to chase the green of his iris away.

"I only fly planes," says Cuauhtémoc to the little man staring up at him.

The little man rubs his eyes and says, "We need to know who else. We know you were close. We need to know who."

"I only fly planes," says Cuauhtémoc. He says it again and again. He keeps repeating it like it might change something.

Of course, Cuauhtémoc knew these things happened, but he never dreamed he'd ever be part of it. He knows what's coming, and Lalo knows too. Everyone looks down on Lalo in the tub. The air is static. Lalo refuses to look anyone in the eye or speak for that matter.

"I need you to tell me where it's at," says the boy with blue tattoos into Lalo's ringing ears.

He grabs Lalo by the neck. Lalo coughs deep and raspy from the diaphragm. He looks at Cuauhtémoc finally. Cuauhtémoc looks away.

"Where's the money?" the boy asks Lalo, tired and aggressive like he's asked him a thousand times before.

Lalo swallows his own voice.

"Where's the money? Where is it? Who has it? Tell me," says the boy with a cool, unnerving calmness. A whisper. A plea. "Tell me. Where is it? Where is it?" Lalo's eyes stay open beneath the water. They only close right before a giant, pink glug escapes his lungs and clouds the tub with a rolling boil. Lalo's hands grasp the sides of the tub. His index finger points at the boy, then the ground, then Cuauhtémoc standing by the doctor.

The doctor waits a beat or two and then raises his hand. "That's enough," he says.

The body is still. The doctor rubs his eyes and puts a plastic device over Lalo's mouth that makes him puke up water until his teeth chatter, until the color returns to his lips.

"You'll get us those names," says the little man as he leaves the bathroom.

Cuauhtémoc and Lalo are left alone. Everyone knows what Cuauhtémoc knows already.

Lalo's eyes are still dilated wide, the adrenaline in his veins faster than the cortisol.

"Don't say anything," says Cuauhtémoc to Lalo, and Lalo nods his chattering head.

Lalo points his index finger to the mirror over the sink, and Cuauhtémoc looks up at it, presses his thumb to the glass to check if there's a space between his thumb and its reflection. It's flush. It's a two-way mirror.

Cuauhtémoc turns off the lights and lights the votive candle over the toilet with the single match left in his ruddy matchbook. Saint Rita. Cuauhtémoc places the candle between him and Lalo. He produces two crushed Faro cigarettes from a soft pack in his breast pocket and puts one behind his ear, puts the other at the corner of Lalo's mouth, the bent cigarette jumping up and down, up and down with Lalo's chattering jaw.

Little flecks of tobacco fall from the end of the cigarette and rest on the surface tension of the water.

"How long has it been since you ate?" Cuauhtémoc asks.

"Long," says Lalo.

"What do you want?" Cuauhtémoc says. He rubs his eyes.

"Please," says Lalo.

"Chinese food?"

"Please."

"That's good," says Cuauhtémoc, lighting his own cigarette from the flame of Saint Rita's candle. The smoke casts shadows on the wall. "That's good," he says again and takes Lalo's cigarette by the filter to light it with the cherry of his own.

He places the cigarette back into the corner of Lalo's mouth. It's wet, so it burns better at the top than it does at the bottom. Lalo takes quick puffs to keep the fire from going out. His mouth fills with hot smoke. He coughs and coughs, unable to get a breath.

To Cuauhtémoc, it's the saddest thing he's ever seen.

Some people said Lalo was queer but others said he was just like that—purple boots, those games he used to play. That one he used to do with a ten-dollar bill.

He'd stick it in a urinal, a cantina urinal, and then go back to the bar and drink with Cuauhtémoc and watch, observe, take note of everyone who stepped inside to take a leak.

He liked to take bets with the bartender: who'd be the one to reach in and fish it out? The thought of it amused Lalo to no end, his little giddy chuckle amplified by the half-emptied glass at his lip that made him look retarded.

Every so often, a patron—a nice elderly woman or a vaquero or someone—might pat Cuauhtémoc on the shoulder and say, "So nice of you to take your brother out. He looks better every day," or "Lucky him to have a brother like you. How is he doing as of late?" to which Cuauhtémoc would say, "fine, fine," and end it at that.

Lalo would take little swigs and then laugh again to himself. He taught Cuauhtémoc to laugh in those days. Cuauhtémoc would laugh only when Lalo was right about who'd take the bill from the urinal. Almost always, somebody would pay the bar with the piss bill and the bartender would know (Lalo would smell it just for proof) and the matter would be settled. If the bartender won, Lalo would cover five percent of whatever the cantina was paying the cartel that month in collections. But if Lalo was right, the bartender would pay five percent to Lalo on top of the standard fee. It was usually a wash, the odds favoring the bartender, which is why the bartender kept betting against Lalo.

For Lalo, the kicks were enough, and when he won, he'd always split the earnings with Cuauhtémoc, which is how they got talking about money in the first place.

This was in the beginning, when Cuauhtémoc was still new. Ever since Lalo had captured him, Cuauhtémoc had been lonesome in that briny way—sulking, scared, stone hopeless. For all of the lore he'd heard growing up in Texas about the Zetas and Sinaloa and El Golfo, with all their evil ideas and all of their evil ways, he'd never expected a narco to look like Lalo, who was more silly than scary and a little bit stupid too.

Within the cartel Lalo was an outcast, like Cuauhtémoc, and this made them brothers in a way. They both felt paralyzed by their circumstances. Their loneliness hurt and throbbed like a bruise. It was only when Cuauhtémoc thought of escape, of going home, that his body felt at ease. Cuauhtémoc could sleep when he dreamed of escape. He ate, he breathed, he laughed knowing that everything he did, every cent he made in this line of work, would all be put to use someday—not too far from now—once the cartel imploded and he'd find his family and go back home to Harlingen.

When they drank, he and Lalo mostly talked about how Cuauhtémoc planned to go back to his old farm in the orange groves and dust the crops until he bled black in the nose. He told Lalo about the June bugs and cicadas that come every so many years and the smell of all that chlorpyrifos raining down from under his plane like urine. He told him of other smells too. The smell of his mother's pozole stew boiling hot on the kitchen stove. The smell of tobacco drifting in off the breeze from the grove master's cigarillo, wet like rain but sweet like autumn.

"Work on a farm like a fucking slave?" Lalo would say to Cuauhtémoc. His lecture was always the same. "That's your big dream?"

"Maybe."

"That's the problem with *paisanos*, Cuauh. We're still slaves. Even in Texas, Tucson, wherever. We make *El Norte* run and we bring this country to its knees. But at least there's some dignity to destruction. Some dignity in living here. It's nice for a little while, don't you think? But eventually, I'll leave this too. We'll both leave it, you and me. *Before* this cell implodes. That's my plan, anyway."

"How?" he asked Lalo one time. And Lalo looked at Cuauhtémoc almost surprised, as if he didn't expect that question or at least the audacity of it. It was only one word—*how*—but between them both it was the most dangerous word. It was the bridge between dreaming and doing. *How* connected them at the brain. *How* was the end but also the beginning of everything. And suddenly, it was out that they were both planning, scheming against El Jimmy. They would both leave their cartel, escape it which, of course, carried its own obvious dangers. El Jimmy still knew where his mother and Uli were. It was the thing that kept Cuauhtémoc from simply taking his plane and flying off into the north. It was this fear that kept him coming back, day after day, to the desert strip or the little road in Lomas de Poleo.

"Out with it, then," said Cuauhtémoc, as excited as ever. "How? How?"

Lalo's answer was simple. "A lot of cash."

"How much?"

"A lot. More than we could ever make."

"From where?"

"From everywhere," said Lalo, and he explained how he kept his money in one place but never on him. He kept it in the base of the aluminum-lined false steering column in that burnt-orange Ford Lobo he'd drive across the border into Texas, that hollow space where drugs were kept and stored. Safe from the prying eyes of X-rays, gamma rays, whatever rays reflected off the aluminum sheet inside the steering column. Other drivers drove that pickup too, but the money was still safe. Everyone knew that to steal from the cartel was a death sentence. And of course, everyone talked about the stash in that steering column, but nobody knew who it belonged to, so nobody dared take it. The other drivers assumed it was a test of sorts, of loyalty or something.

Lalo got a kick out of that. He loved the idea of his money traveling to all the places drugs went, the places he might go some day after this: Houston, Wichita Falls, Oklahoma City, Tuscaloosa, Raleigh, New York, Montreal.

"Come with me," Lalo would say, and they'd make plans together. They dreamed of fancy hotels, fancy dinners, Buchannan's Single Malt Scotch, never having to work for El Jimmy or anyone else again.

Lalo told him that when it was his turn to drive the Lobo, he always checked on his money and it was always there, packed against the back of the column down by where the Freon hit the A/C vent. The bills were always cold, and he liked to fan them in his face. The smell, like plastic.

Cuauhtémoc remembers Lalo telling him all of this. And he remembers asking again, "But how? So, you have a lot of cash. But what do you do with it?" Cuauhtémoc remembers that crooked index finger on Lalo's hand and how it waved the bartender over with just the tiniest motion that night in the bar, the windy heat of June slapping hard against the window panes.

Lalo took a hundred-peso bill from his wallet, looked off toward the cantina bathroom, and said to Cuauhtémoc, "Let me show you what honest men will do for money."

In the bathroom, Lalo busts his chin on his way toward the porcelain lip of the toilet. He hurls and hurls, his voice splattering echoes inside the toilet bowl that rattle out at the tiled corners of the ceiling. Nothing comes up. A beaded string of spit arcs from the fleshy part of his lip to the clear water below.

Cuauhtémoc hooks his arms under Lalo's and pulls him up so he's kneeling. His chin sluices bright red. It meanders in streaks like jagged lines and stops at his collarbone. He looks as fragile as an egg and just as pale. That incredible voice, that incredible noise.

"Don't talk," says Cuauhtémoc, "Don't speak."

He takes the Chinese food from the ledge of the bathtub and places it on the floor. "Don't eat," he tells Lalo.

They look at the mirror and then look at each other. They see themselves. Lalo, the boy he used to be. Cuauhtémoc, the man he might become—the bloody mess, that pulp of a person. He looks at Lalo the way you might look at a car wreck, the way you might observe it and rubberneck because you don't want it to happen to you. He observes Lalo begging. Cuauhtémoc swears when it's his time that he won't beg.

"Please," says Lalo shivering in his cold clothes. "Please," he says reaching for the food, and Cuauhtémoc lets him have it.

He nibbles at the breaded chicken. He can't keep anything down.

Inside the tub the ashy cigarette from Lalo's lips, snuffed and bloated at the filter, spins slowly under the drippy faucet.

Cuauhtémoc takes off his shirt and ties it like a scarf around Lalo's neck. He pats him dry with the tail of it. He grabs him by the shoulders and blows out the candle.

The sodium lamps pour in through the window and light up half the tub orange. In the dark, the other half is blue. Lalo's skin is yellow, his torso cut in half. The water is green, the same shade of green Cuauhtémoc remembers so well from his childhood.

He eases Lalo's head into the water and closes his eyes. Lalo wraps his legs around Cuauhtémoc, and Cuauhtémoc lets his mind drift back in time. The warmness of Lalo's escaping breath. Like Texas heat in the summertime.

Cuauhtémoc lets his mind go elsewhere. He imagines walking barefoot in his old backyard or what he considered his backyard at one time. It's where he played anyway, he and his little brother. It's still teeming with sounds. The tick of the heat in his ears, the tick of the insects flapping from one tree to the other, ruining everything he's ever worked for.

Behind his closed eyes there are the cicadas too, seventeen-year-old cicadas humming pitch perfect in the shade of the orange tree branches. You can't see them, but they're there. And they'll die eventually, like all the other critters and crawlers and men and women in the grove—all poisoned by the pesticides.

Lalo moans and Cuauhtémoc brings his toes to a point. He's flexing his calves, he's bringing his body up two or three inches to the tree. He pulls down a switch and plucks a cicada from the branch. He pinches its humming legs between his fingers and dangles it away from his face, as far as his arm can reach, staring at its molting body. The cicada feels the same way it did when he was seven—the last time he handled a cicada—like a sliver of metal but undeniably alive.

He remembers how he and his brother would make them fight. How he'd clip their wings and set them off against each other in a dirt ring like oversized ants. Being flightless made them hostile. They circled for a long time before they attacked one another. They made them carnivores, he and his brother.

It was always a quick death. He remembers how placidly his little brother watched as one cicada would split the other open, the broken one's exoskeleton flaking like bits of fish food. And they'd talk over it just like teenage boys might talk over cigarettes or old men might talk over dialysis at the Harlingen Scott & White down the road—what is the worst way someone can die?

His little brother would always come up with the funny deaths: ants, getting killed by a hooker, getting killed by ants and a fire and a hooker at the same time.

When it was Cuauhtémoc's turn, all he could think about was shriveling to death, sloughing away like that bug—molting, beautiful and iridescent like that cicada drying in the dirt.

What a slow death, he thinks. How cruel children can be.

He thinks of the cicada and thinks of the drivers and thinks of Lalo and thinks of himself. Disposable, just like everything else. He'll molt under hot dirt eventually, somewhere in the world. In his mind he can see their skin sloughed off by zip-ties or bullets or fire. He's suddenly conscious of his own scars all over his body: the puckered red blips of skin around his wrists from when he was kidnapped in Matamoros, the pink laceration over his arm when he was made to fight gladiator-style at midnight, the serrated, bead sutures across his clavicle from when he crashed a plane for the first time with his brother.

He opens his eyes and sees that face underwater. Perfectly still. Perfectly at peace. He imagines plucking each scar from his body to lay them over himself. He thinks he can remember what it felt like to be flawless at one time.

COMFORT

ULI HASN'T SEEN THE MAN with the purple boots in weeks. It's August 1st by his Timex. He buys June's heroin from another one of Alma's friends, a guy who looks like a younger version of Chente. Same broken smile, same watery eyes. He introduces himself as Sapo. Uli thinks he tries too hard to be cool.

Sapo wears sunglasses indoors. When he meets June he shows her new places to shoot. He says her veins will collapse if she injects too often in the same place. He shows her the veins between her toes, behind the knee, on the side of her hip. He makes love to her without looking her in the face. Sapo asks Uli if he wants to join in. He asks: *Where are you from? How did you get here? Do you have any family?* Uli always answers: *deported, plane, one brother somewhere out there.* Sapo smiles at this. Uli wonders, when he leaves Sapo and June to their business, if Sapo has killed anyone before, if there is a murderer under his own roof. *Just pay him what you owe him,* he thinks.

Uli doesn't hate Sapo but he hates the way he leaves with their money. And today, Uli decides that he's going to spend a little of that money too.

He takes what little he has stored between the pages of the Bible—his escape money—and spends it on love. Because even when you're out of work, the body still craves.

Uli sleeps with Alma only to be close to someone, not because he's attracted to her in any way. Under her dress, she's bloated and saggy from childbirth. Her belly is a constellation of greasy stretch marks that reek of petroleum jelly and cocoa butter.

Before today, he didn't even know she had a baby. It's a five-month-old. Alma tells Uli that her name is Alma too. Uli tells her that he's never heard of a baby named after her mother before. Alma ignores everything he says. All business. She takes him by the hand and pulls him through the dark hallways of her house to her bedroom. Stale air. A cut of light that makes its way through the black-out curtains. A queen-sized bed with a floral pattern comforter. No sheet. Just bare mattress and the licorice-like scent of Fabuloso cleaner coming from the bathroom. Uli wonders if this isn't her real bedroom but her professional one, if that's what you'd call it. *Her office?* he thinks.

She examines Uli before starting. "This is standard procedure," she says. "You do it before taking anyone into your bedroom."

The baby is asleep in a crib off to the right of the bed.

Uli has never been naked in front of a woman before. Or a baby for that matter. He wonders what happens if the baby starts to cry. Does he get his money back? Does Alma tend to the baby? *Do I tend to the baby?* So many uncharted waters he has to navigate. This is all a little more stressful than he thought it would be.

As Alma handles him, he looks over the room quickly, planning his escape. On the other side of the bed there's a nightstand with a doily type thing draping off of it, a stack of children's nursery books in English atop that. On the TV, in the corner of the room, a framed wedding picture of Alma and some strange man Uli's never seen before.

Uli looks at the baby. *I can't do this.*

"Come here," says Alma and pulls him by the waist with her hot little hands. He's never noticed how mangled they look. Like his grandmother's hands, soft and pink and slanting to the left. He tries to look her in the eyes but he only sees the baby's features in Alma.

She says to him, "You must be a Sagittarius. Always living with your eyes open, even when you're making love."

"I don't know any other way to make love," he tells her, which is the truth, and she laughs at this. Uli feels good that he made her laugh. He calms down a bit. Stares at the doily for a little while.

"I'll show you," she says and takes his wrist. She skids his clammy hand awkwardly from her neck, to her floppy breasts, full with milk, to her abdomen, to the spade arc wrinkles of her C-section belly button, to the stubble between her legs. She makes him keep it there even though he doesn't want to.

She says, "Kiss me on the neck."

So he does.

She says, "Say something."

Uli doesn't know what to say.

She pulls on his hips and they rock. He feels awkward, animal-like. He wants it to be over. *I'll be quick*, he thinks. He feels himself throbbing inside of her.

She says, "Not yet, baby. Not yet. Think about something else. Think about the wheels on the bus going round and round."

Uli starts singing that nursery rhyme in his head. He looks over to the nursery books in English on the night stands. He looks over toward the crib. Little Alma throws her arms wide and Uli look at her eyes, like drops of champagne.

"Keep going, keep going," she says. "Think about something else, anything else."

Uli makes a list of things he has to do today:

Buy a chicken (a live one)

Buy a tank of water

Buy a case of Cokes

Buy a bottle of multivitamins, a bottle of antibiotics, a bottle of deworming pills, a bottle of Percocets—he's getting into the dog fighting business now, he and June and Atómico. June knows everything about dog fighting but she's only half-lucid these days. Uli thinks he can do it alone, if he's given the tools. And, of course, the dog.

Alma pulls hard on his hips. Instant guilt.

Uli lies on top of her, palms down on the floral print comforter. He's looking at the baby looking at him. He's reminded of the wall that crashed down over June. All those skeletons with their eyelids leathered by dust.

"She sneezes sometimes and wakes herself up," says Alma.

"You think she was watching?" he asks

"She wouldn't remember," says Alma. *What if she thinks I'm her dad?* thinks Uli. The thought makes him laugh. Desperate for conversation, to move on from what they just did, Uli thinks about telling Alma about the church wall that fell on June, but decides against it.

"She was looking at you," Alma says.

Uli can feel Alma's gut working into the curve of his spine now. He's never had straight posture and now he's glad she can't see it—how the buttons of his spine meander to the left and then the right.

For all that can be said about Alma, no one can say she doesn't love herself. She loves every grease burn on her arms, every acne scar between her breasts, every crooked finger on her broken little hands that somehow healed slanting left.

Alma catches him looking at her fingers and draws them in to make a crooked fist.

"What's the matter?" asks Uli.

"Oh, they're bashful," she says.

Alma remembers, in this sliver of a moment, that her father used to say that when she stared at his foot for too long. His big toe missing. He'd always stick it beneath the covers of his bed. "Oh, it's bashful," he'd say. It was chopped off by an overzealous captain in the Mexican army. This was the early 90s and it wasn't a secret that her father was a Zapatista sympathizer. Half of whatever money he made on the coffee plantation he gave to the Chiapas independence movement, and he raised his family on rice and stale sweet bread, which his wife would mash up in milk and serve as a porridge of sorts. There were more guns than chickens on her father's plot in Acteal and, although the Mexican military rolled in at random one day, searching high and low for guns, they could never find them hidden in the dirt floor beneath their family bed. His neighbors called him lucky, but he called himself religious. He swore by the scapular that slicked to his back when he was working hard in the sun, that brown ribbon that hung between his shoulder blades with a different cardboard saint attached at each end to keep away all evil. Saint Rita and Saint Francis of Assisi.

Some said that her father was hiding a giant tank beneath his bed. Others said that Subcomandante Marcos himself was hidden there. Many jokes about her father's sexuality and his toe were made in the barbershops and cantinas of Acteal until one day it was rumored in the halls of government in Mexico City that Subcomandante Marcos himself was, indeed, under her father's bed. At which point everyone stopped laughing.

The military trucks sailed into the village of Acteal on a black sea of diesel fumes and dirt. Everyone was massacred. They shot the men, they stabbed the women, they stabbed the children, they stabbed the babies inside of the women. All over Mexico pictures of the town were shown. An example was made of Acteal, a lesson to be remembered. Everyone was killed except for Alma, who jumped into a water well and sobbed for days, her city burning all around her.

The echo from the well drove the soldiers crazy. They all believed the crying came from the sound of ghosts coming to haunt them for their evils. This went on for three days until a soldier of the most ordinary kind found her.

From the neck down she was like a prune, her skin peeling off in layers that reeked of pus and mold. It was because of the smell that none of the soldiers touched her, except one desperate little man. This lonesome soldier who packed her up and took her north to San Miguel before dying some years later, though not before giving her a baby before he did. That's mostly what he left her. Her house and the scars on her body and every misshapen bone in her hands. And this baby that eats everything.

Next to Uli, she fingers her father's scapular hanging between her breasts. "You know, you never go to Hell if you're wearing one of these," she says to Uli.

"If you die wearing one, you mean," he says.

"You know your catechism."

"Catechism is a joke," Uli says, trying his best to sound cool.

"Do you want to tell me a joke?"

"Sure," he says. He only knows one joke: "Will you remember me in an hour?"

"Yes."

"Will you remember me in a day?"

"Yes."

"Will you remember me in a month?"

"Yes."

"A year?"

"Yes," she says again. "This is not a funny joke."

"You're not going to remember me in a year," Uli says.

"Yes I will."

"Knock, knock."

"Who's there?"

"See," he says, "it's only been ten seconds and you already forgot who I am."

June's ribs are still cracked, but her face has stopped bleeding, the glue having worked its magic as promised on the package. Still, June cannot stand not to be under sedation. Uli has taken to doing the injections himself. He knows that if she breathes too quickly, too choppy, she'll develop pneumonia. So, he tries to sleep on the floor beside her, never really sleeping. Just listening to her breathe.

She's snoring these days, which means she's getting better. Long, legato trills at the back of her throat that sound impossibly soft, as if her palate were made from cotton or something softer.

It's in these moments, late at night, that he thinks of that little side satchel his mother used to carry full of fabric samples. He listens to June's damp breath and tries to feel satin on his fingertips. From there he makes a game of it: feels the satin and then tries to smell the cornhusk blunts she'd keep in her pocket. Smells them and tries to feel the critter-soaked earth beneath his bare feet, the heat driving all of those bugs wild in their inescapable thirst. He feels them jump up to scour the soles of his feet, bathe themselves in the salty sweat of his flesh. He hears the south Texas cicadas' pulsing screech. The sun like a thousand needles in his skin, every pore opening to some ray of light. And then his own thirst ignited. Uli, just another critter of the earth.

In his lucid dreams, Uli sees Alma's face. *Do I love her?* he wonders. *Is there a God?*

No, he thinks. *Of course not.* Although there's time and she takes it. There's money and she takes it. There's fear and she takes that away too. Which is to say Alma brings order to his life, a cycle to each day which begins for Uli when she turns her porch light on, which means she's open for business. Alma segments his life, but with June everything is one endless day, one endless game of survival. And he's done playing it.

The longer June stays up on the plaque, the higher the stakes on her life will be. A thirty-to-one payout by now. In two weeks it'll be thirty-five-to-one. Of course, everyone is looking for her. Even the soldiers that the military sent in to patrol the city. In the papers it says they're going door-to-door, room-to-room, looking for someone, and everyone knows who. But no one has searched this area of San Miguel yet. Alma says because of the boulders it will be the last neighborhood to go.

"We can end this anytime," she says to Uli. "She's dying anyway."

He keeps that thought in the back of his mind. An ace up his sleeve—kill in case of emergency. Of course, he couldn't do the deed himself.

It's June's breathing that wakes him, that dissonant hiss of her vocal cords rasping ever so softly. Uli kneels beside the bed. Her eyes flicker open-shut.

"Easy, easy," he says, and reaches for the shoestring to tie around her bicep. "Breathe," he whispers. He wipes the sleep out from his eye with his left hand while his right goes back to search for the lighter.

He feels the cold barrel of the pistol pressed up against his temple. June looks down on him.

The hammer falls. *Click.* Nothing. *Click. Click.*

It takes a moment for Uli to find his bearings, that dissonant wheeze growing faster and fuller. Does she know? *Of course she knows.* He's surprised to find that the sound of labored breathing is coming from his own body, June's breath steady now as she pulls the trigger again and again and again to no avail. He knows there are bullets in June's gun. What he doesn't know is why it would jam like that. No corrosion that he can see. No dust in the barrel from his vantage point, staring straight down it toward the glint of a half-loaded bullet catching light from the window.

He takes his luck as a sign, takes it as permission.

"Why would you do that?" he asks her, emboldened now, the loaded needle in his hand.

"You," is all she can say. "You. You," before dropping the gun onto the bed, her hand wrapped so tightly around the pistol grip that an impression is made on her palm, slanted lines in red. Her eyes flicker open-closed. It's the last thing she lets go of as the heroin enters her veins.

THE ENDLESS FALL

PLANNED OBSOLESCENCE IS THE TERM mechanics use when
things fall apart; when propellers warp out of shape; magnetos
whir out of socket; ELT's short-circuit and die; pitot tubes get
stopped up with rain or bugs; altimeters spin like pinwheels
behind their circular vacuum glass, as if they were haunted by
any one of the sundry poltergeists that plague planes, those
gremlins that make them dip or shudder or suddenly stall and
fall from the sky, no more elegant or sophisticated than a rock
dropped from the heavens.

Jimmy's mechanic knows when it's about to happen, even
when there's no hard evidence to prove it—no dripping valves
or knocking engines or rattling air-frames or loose rivets or
tight yokes or cracked ailerons. Of course, every machine
comes to an end.

Pos, ni modo, thinks the mechanic. Like a doctor curing a
dying patient, the mechanic can only do what he can do. Science has no place for feelings.

Cuauhtémoc runs his hands all along the nickel underbelly,
searching for dings or dents to foul the air spoil. He runs his
hands, too, along all the leading edges—the curved bend of the
wings, the raised dorsal fin of the rudder, the variable pitch propellers which have been replaced, not a knick or dent to throw
them off balance in rotation. He checks the elevators at the

222

back of the plane. *Up-down, up-down* they go with a full-fisted push on the trim tab outside the left edge of the elevator inside the cockpit. The twin yokes inside the plane bob with the pressure, as if a ghost pilot were in the seat tugging and pulling, the rudder groaning and flexing as Cuauhtémoc pulls on that too to test its full range of motion. The pinions are all safely attached. The hydraulic brakes are all filled red with fluid. The engines are greased with oil. Everything is perfect. And with a kick to the strut, a good luck precaution more than anything else, Cuauhtémoc enters the plane and clicks on the master switches one magneto at a time until they're all whirring in sync.

"Clear!" he shouts to the mechanic, who crosses himself twice more and then steps back, watching the propellers sputter to life, chopping angrily at the slanted wind that brings with it plumes of dust that redirect in the propellers and scrape angrily along the polished nickel of the fuselage.

From the sound of her, she's a living, breathing beast, all of the desiccant pouring hot from the cabin heat vent so that Cuauhtémoc's throat goes dry, the desiccant sucking the moisture from him. Cuauhtémoc closes his eyes and cuts the engines to a thousand RPM's, testing the magnetos, one at a time, listening for the rough, cutting sounds of carbon deposits not yet burned away from the spark plugs in the engines. He feels the rumble of the propellers and imagines all the metal beneath him turning to flesh. The belly of the plane is filled with bundles of cocaine, some of it strapped down behind him too. The seat is pushed fully forward so his knees crush the yoke. In front of that, just the empty skies that roll on forever toward Texas.

On the landing strip, he lines the plane up against the wind. He digs his toes into the brakes and pushes the throttle in full until he can hear loose gravel pinging against the sheet metal of the plane, the dust piling wildly around him.

He keeps his toes dug into the brakes above the rudder pedals to keep the plane stationary and pulls the yoke into his chest to keep the front wheel off the ground to execute the soft, short field takeoff. Flaps at thirty degrees. Throttle at full RPM. He lets go of the brakes and it isn't fifteen counts or so before the plane is hovering in ground effect, that bubble of air that keeps him suspended just thirty feet or so off the ground while he picks up speed by the meter. He hovers at seventy-five knots before he eases his yoke back just a smidge at a time. His plane is overweight, and he knows that it could stall at any given moment. He fixes the trim tap to push the nose down, to keep his speed up, and not long after that that he's just a speck in the sky.

He flies over the Chihuahuan desert, San Miguel just a blip in the distance. On the dash, Lalo's water-bloated leather wallet. Cuauhtémoc looks inside the wallet for the thousandth time. No credit cards, no driver's license. Just a picture of a pretty woman cut out from a magazine, a prayer card from someone's funeral and some twenty-peso bills.

He throws the wallet out the window, watches it flay open in the wind and spiral to the ground. All of the bills explode from the wallet about a thousand feet down. Cuauhtémoc watches the bills float in a patch of windless sky. Just the sound of the engine in his head, the sound of his guts churning around his bones. Hope welling up inside him as he looks down, his brother somewhere down there.

Cuauhtémoc cools the engine just to get a little closer. He sees a lot of people. A lot of soldiers too. None of them his brother. Miles upon miles of empty streets. He thinks he could land somewhere inside the city. He could tell his boss there was engine trouble. He could run away forever, get lost in that maze of lights burning bright against the desert. He wonders if El Jimmy still has eyes on his brother. *Did he ever? How did Lalo find him?*

Don't be stupid, he thinks. *Fly on. Get the load delivered. Live another day.*

Cuauhtémoc dials a number into the VOR and then pushes the throttle in. Not ten minutes later, somewhere over Texas, a loud boom jolts the plane on its axis and a great plume of fire pounds loose from the right engine, charring the port side of the plane with a greasy jet of black smoke that sputters and bursts as it's fed from the wings. Cuauhtémoc reaches down to the right of his leg and cuts the pump to the port wing by pulling the fuel lever from BOTH to LEFT. He idles the throttle and the plane starts to yaw before rolling. He cross-controls with full right rudder and full right aileron. The smell of fuel fills the cabin. Buzzards on open wings shoot up past the catapulting plane.

One thousand feet and the plane loops over as the giant pile of cocaine behind Cuauhtémoc shifts and slams into the wall, sending the plane wobbling with the load's momentum. The bang sounds throughout the airframe, the plane jerking about the skies like a jug of water slid across a table. Fast-slow like that. Chaos.

Outside the windshield, earth turns over sky. The negative pressure pushes and pulls at Cuauhtémoc's eardrums so he can't even tell what's up and down anymore. He thinks about Lalo's wallet hurtling to the ground. He thinks on those bills scattering as he watches the altimeter dialing backwards. The stall horn squeals as the wind scatters out along the wing's airfoil.

Eight hundred feet. Five hundred feet.

Cuauhtémoc pushes hard on the rudder until his toes are bloodless. He levels the plane and then loses it as the shifting load throws him off course. Rights it again. Loses it again. Rights it again and again and again, the stall horn blaring with each successive spin. He mixes the fuel rich and then shoves the throttle in full to the red nub, his blood pressed from his fingers to his knuckles. In his mind he anticipates the pain, the memory of his first crash outside of Matamoros. In his left hand, a death grip on the wild yoke that's bruising his palm.

"Please," he says over and over again.

His controls turn mushy as he angles the nose down to gain speed and control. He idles the propeller as if recovering from a stall, but there's only two hundred feet left between him and the ground. His shadow spreads across the dirt. It's then that he takes his hands from the controls completely and covers his face with his arms.

It's the cocaine that wakes him up, his surface wounds dusted with it. His right shoulder is carved by crushed glass pushed through his flight jacket. Out the windshield, the rest of the tempered glass falls a piece at a time to the datum right in front of him. One hundred yards ahead, the wild-burning rot of a blackened engine separated from the aircraft mid-flight.

He looks around, studies the wreckage from inside the cockpit. The pile of cocaine behind him miraculously crushed the port side part of the aircraft but not his own side. The back of his seat is shredded, the stuffing pouring out from the plastic, but his torso is somehow still intact. The glass on every instrument is shattered except the spherical glass of the whiskey compass bobbing east, then north, then east again.

His brain is abuzz with cocaine. His eyes shift between the altimeter, the yoke, the gushing pain in his boot, the broken wing, back to the altimeter, back to the gushing pain in his boot. The broken toes, all of them like one single pile of hurt and not individual pains with their own unique injuries.

He presses down too hard on the pointed, brass-bracket toe of his boot and his split nail makes a cracking noise— inaudible to the ear but audible in the way it resonates in the nerves, in the skin, pinging up and down his spine so he thinks he can hear it. It feels good now in this beautiful, ticklish, numbing kind of way. From his toes pours hot blood into his boot. Hot blood that would alarm anyone else, but to Cuauhté-moc it is even more comforting than the pain—that constant that tells him he's still alive. The pain in his toes tells him he's not paralyzed. The pain everywhere else tells him that his body is damaged but still functional.

He unbuckles his belt. He pulls off his cocaine-dusted jacket, his hat too that keeps the headphones from pulling out his hair. He breathes through his shirt collar. Blood on his sleeve. He dabs it to his face. A stinging cut right beneath his eye. He dabs it again. Looks at the blood. He jumps from the cabin and limps off on broken toes toward the culvert off highway I-10 going east-west.

Fifty yards out from the highway, he looks back. A great cloud of cocaine powder dusting out into the wind like one oblong sheet of cascading snow. He looks at the sight from that distance, takes a second to soak it all in. Five hundred pounds, it must have been. Two hundred and twenty-seven kilos at ten thousand dollars a kilo. Over two million dollars, not including the plane. It smells like gasoline or ether. Something chemical.

It's then and there that he makes his decision or, rather, his decision has already been made for him: there's no way he can ever go back. No way he's ever going to repay his cartel the money. No way he's ever going to see his brother again.

His feet firmly planted in Texas, on the asphalt of I-10, he's got only two choices now: east or west. He chooses east.

Against the twilight, he spots a Love's truck stop glowing in the distance. The sun sets gold and all the June bugs come out. They swirl around the halogen bulbs of the truck stop awning, that white light making the oil-stained concrete below sheen green like the desert does under the moon. Time crawls about as slowly as Cuauhtémoc does, and the sun disappears, leaving only the day's heat rising in watery layers over the road against that dark light that hangs around as if the sun never left at all. Even in those waves you can see the June bugs fly in on the shimmering, moonlit crescents that water up until they've found their place in the heat agitated pattern of bugs under the bulbs. It seems as though all of the critters of the desert come to this place for rest at night, even Cuauhtémoc.

You can hear the dry halogen buzz cooking the glass, cooking the bugs beneath the glass. They fall to the concrete once they're burned. They fall on crisped, crooked wings. They fall slowly like drying pieces of ash, their greasy bodies strewn about the concrete.

Cuauhtémoc limps under the awning with the heat of the road in his boots. His wounds buzz with a wet heat all their own. Like the kind that comes from a rope burn or a hand caught too long on the iron. He squashes the bugs under the soles of his boots, and they pop like grapes. They spread wet until they're mixed into the oil streaks on the ground. Cuauhtémoc moves along as gingerly and crooked as an old man. Over the green sheen of the concrete. Over the tire smudged yellow paint of the curb. Over the glossy faux granite tiles and into the convenience store.

"Do you have a shower?" he asks the attendant, a middle-aged woman. Her nametag says Lizabeth. Blue eyes, box-colored blond hair. Vertical wrinkles over her upper lip.

"Five dollars," she says. "For the towel."

"That's fine," says Cuauhtémoc, dusting the cocaine from his clothes, trying to make himself presentable. She rings it up on the machine with the nub of her pencil, completely underwhelmed by the spectacle of Cuauhtémoc.

The cash register springs open and Cuauhtémoc opens his billfold filled thick with Mexican pesos.

"Do you take these?" he asks her. She points to a little yellow sign at the register with the nub of her pencil. It advertises bus fares to northern Mexico from this station: Zaragoza, San Miguel, Coatlitli, Ciudad Juárez, Torreón, Monterrey, Mazatlán, Sinaloa, Tijuana. Beneath that it says AMERICAN DOLLARS ONLY. Beneath that it has a conversion fee calculator glowing digital red. In one column the American flag, in the other the Mexican flag. Both electric displays are broken. They read digital 8's across the board.

Cuauhtémoc takes a wad of cash from his wallet and hands it to her. "I don't need change," he says. He thinks about the plane again. He thinks about all that money he owes Jimmy.

"Can't do it. Sorry. American dollars only."

"Could you make an exception?" he pleads with her, the blood bloating the seams of his boots.

"Can't make any exceptions for no one, mister."

"It's been a long day," he says.

"You got a credit card?" she says in her west Texas twang. "Or a debit card?"

"God—jeez, miss. Just—I'll give you all the cash in here. Will that do?"

"How much is it?" she says, clacking her lacquered nails on the counter, the little nub of a pencil about ready to click open the register.

"It's about four hundred dollars," he lies.

She thinks about it for all of half a second before she says, "I can make an exception this time. Fifteen minutes, hot water."

She hands him a towel and a plastic door tag with the number nine on it. "Shower four," she says and blows on her nails.

The towel is so bleached that Cuauhtémoc can feel the fibers squeak in his fingertips.

He walks into the stall and tries to unbutton his plaid shirt with all the precision left in his fingers. He tries to unbutton his jeans, unzip his fly, cradle the heel of his right boot to pull it away with both hands, but he only pulls harder at the strained muscles in his abdomen that shoot out a fatigued twitch. He falls and slaps his palm against the cool, beige hexagonal tiles of the showering room, the veins on the back of his hand flush with blood. His toe creaks. His arms bleed. Time moves slowly over him.

"Ten minutes," yells the woman from the doorway.

Cuauhtémoc pulls himself up, turns both diamond-cut acrylic knobs at the same time so that the water pours hot and clean onto the crown of his dry head and then over his clothes and then over his aching body. He watches the water swirl pink down the drain, and he cries. He cries and cries under a shower that's so hot it puts a chill in his nerves.

AUTODEFENSA

EVERY MORNING ARACELI WATCHES the buzzards ride the thermals in the far distance. She'll wake to a halo of three or four circling in the sky, but it's not long before another dozen join the circle, their numbers growing as the sun shoots high, every other star in the sky fading to blue.

In the mornings the men of the autodefensa (the militia) will patrol the three sides of the little pueblo just off the highway on which Araceli and the Canadians were captured. They're always looking for narcos. Or for regular people like Araceli. People to ransom. People to help them perpetuate their way of living. Separate from the government, separate from the cartels. Their own municipal government. Their own military. Their own war machine.

On the fourth side of the compound, the east side where the buzzards fly, there's nothing but desert. Nothing coming from that side. Nothing leaving either. But that doesn't keep Araceli from dreaming.

Weeks go by and Araceli's left hand slowly loses its color. The nails on her fingers go from pink to yellow. Her fingers go from blue to black, the dry gangrene spreading. She wraps it in the ripped tail of a blue shirt she finds under her cot. A child's shirt. Cookie Monster on the front. There were many children, once, in the compound where Araceli is kept. A small, two bedroom house. Toys, videogames, teething devices everywhere.

Now there are only two children left: a brother and sister, ages six and four, who the militia says Araceli is responsible for.

Araceli is separated from the Canadian couple who are held captive in another house, the woman's screams piercing the night sky so loud it's as if it comes from everywhere at once. Who knows what terrors she's seen? Who knows what her husband has watched her do?

The brother and sister and the four walls of the house are Araceli's world. And every day Araceli, the brother and his little sister go through their little routine.

The children come find her outside, on the porch, watching the buzzards in the morning. Then they all watch the planes landing, ten miles east of there, in San Miguel once they're tired of the buzzards. When the planes come, this is a sign that Araceli is supposed to make breakfast. Every day Araceli gets the same question to start the day. "What's wrong with your hand?" The brother is worried that the blackness of it will hamper Araceli's abilities to make them breakfast.

"It's blue," she says every morning.

"But why?"

"Because I'm related to Cookie Monster," she'll say. She'll show them the blue shirt wrapped up in her palm.

"Really?" the little girl will ask, day after day. "How much related?"

"Just a little related," she'll say. "I got my hand from my grandfather's side."

"Is Cookie Monster that old?"

"He ages well."

And the brother will nod as if he understands. The little sister will want to ask more questions, but she'll look to her nodding brother. She'll stare back between Araceli and her brother before nodding herself. Sage wisdom given from an adult.

They'll all sit in silence and watch the buzzards. And then Araceli will cook them breakfast, as she's supposed to. Araceli always asks them her same questions too: "What happened to your parents?"

"They're gone," the older brother will say.

"Where?"

"To heaven."

"To heaven?"

"They're dead," the little girl will say to settle the manner. The little girl loves saying this. It's her part. It makes her feel important. It completes their routine. Until the day it doesn't. This morning. When Araceli decides to walk away.

She cooks breakfast before the sun comes out, the stars bright in the black sky. She leaves the breakfast on the tiny plates the brother and sister eat from. She listens to the trucks from the autodefensa tearing up the cool, damp road outside. She fills a pink Bonafont tank with cool water she's boiled the night before from the Rotoplas tank that catches rain. And then she sits outside with the tank in her lap, looks into the wild nothing. Sand, wind, stars. And, of course, the buzzards circling even at night.

In the distance she can see the light pollution of San Miguel. No road between here and there. Just sand.

She takes the first step. In her left hand just the rag. In her right hand the five-gallon jug of water. The cold of night spreads across her back, sweat bursting hot from her pores before chilling across her open skin. She swears she can hear the earth groaning underfoot as if it's about to swallow her whole. She looks up into the night. Concentrates on that velvety blackness, the sky and everything in it her good luck charm. She looks up into the heavens as she disappears, forever walking home.

SKY BURIAL

ATÓMICO LICKS JUNE'S FACE one last time before she dies. Of their three bodies, the dog's body is the healthiest. He's healed nicely by now. A blue sheen to his black coat, his eyes full of energy, his jowls full of blood. No evidence of the butcher's knife on him anymore except for a faint line that runs through his coat where his fur cedes to scar tissue. He licks June's scar as she peers out from behind it, a certain softness to her eyes as she stares at Uli. *I know you're going to do this but you shouldn't.*

As Uli pivots from her bedside to prepare the heroin, she watches him, her head stock-still, her glassy eyes moving inside her skull with the glowing flame of the candle reflected in the black of her pupils. Uli takes a straw and shoves one end into a tiny glass of ice water. He puts the straw to her flaky chapped lips. He only feels her stale breath cold on his knuckles as he waits for her to sip. She just stares at him with her unblinking eyes, her mouth wide open.

"I'm trying my best," he says to her, cooking the heroin in a spoon.

He puts the glass of ice water down, reaches over her to adjust her pillows. "Does your back hurt?" he asks her. "Which way should I shift you?"

She cuts him a look that says, *Who are you kidding? Be done with it already.* Then she looks toward her dog. That is the last thing she wants to see. Not Uli.

Uli watches her lift her heavy, shaking arm to rest her palm on the crown of Atómico's head. Her lips move ever so slightly.

"A drink of water?" he asks her.

She just moves her lips as if she's praying, closes her eyes as if she's sleeping. It's only once the needle's in that her eyes roll back, she disappears into the flesh of her mask. The dog keeps licking her until she's cold. And then he lies beside her, licking at the smell of her breath that still hangs about the air after she's gone.

Alma digs her long fingers into his pockets, fishes out the last lottery ticket with June's name on it. She kisses him on the neck.

"Is it done?" she asks him

"I think so," he says.

"You didn't answer my question."

"It's done."

"And the groceries?"

"I'll get them."

"But not tonight," Alma says. "It's dangerous tonight."

"They're in my house."

"Your house is haunted now," she says as if warning him. "You stay here." She unbuckles his pants.

"Not tonight," Uli says.

"You're not in the mood."

"How much money do you think it'll be?"

"A lot," says Alma, reassuring him, kissing him on the neck again to show him he's done well.

Uli feels repulsed by the wetness of her lips. "She was going to die anyway," says Alma.

"Do we bury her? How do we prove she's dead?"

"I'll make arrangements," says Alma. "There's nothing more you can do."

That night an army of men—not soldiers—rolls into his neighborhood on a cloud of diesel fumes. They move the boulders out from the road so that the trucks, ten of them in all, can flow through. They go house-to-house, kick in every door as if looking for something or someone. *Autodefensa? Cartel? Scrappers?* Uli wonders. They break in but they take nothing with them. *They're looking for someone,* he thinks. *If they find June that would be a clean disposal. At least it would look natural,* he thinks. He left the shoelace on her bicep. He had the decency to pull the needle from her arm, and he feels good about that.

Uli watches them from Alma's kitchen window as they creep toward him, block by block. Hordes of skittish dogs escape from the homes and flood out into the street as the men kick the doors down. The dogs run wild through the complexities of the neighborhood. Packs fight with packs. The men fight with each other as they try to decide, driving through the mass of animals, whether to shoot the dogs or not.

The matter is finally settled when a shot rings out. On the other end of a silver pistol a boy no older than twelve years old stands in front of a white pickup. His hand is so firm around the handle of the gun that his rosary tattoo dances with the undulations of the muscle beneath his sweaty skin glowing in the headlights. He squeezes the trigger a second time and then a third, but the dogs don't scatter.

From Alma's kitchen, just a half-block away, Uli can see a silhouette of the boy's face. A pre-teen by the size of his lanky frame, an apple face with dark oval eyes. His bullets ricochet once, twice, a third time against the pavement. No dog that Uli sees falls. Instead, the dogs begin to surround the boy, squeezing around him like a tourniquet of flesh. The boy's trebly voice rings out before his legs are taken from beneath him, and he's buried by their hunger. Across the way, even Atómico runs out to join the feast.

As the boy is torn apart, as the trucks back out of the roads and crash between boulders and curbs and houses as they retreat, Uli catches himself admiring the sight of Atómico's filed teeth, sharpened to tiny blades, tearing at the boy's flesh—teeth perfectly suited for dog fighting. He's proud of the spring in Atómico's step. Proud of how he's nursed the animal back to life. Proud, too, that soon his investment will bring him money.

He watches the herky-jerky of dogs fanning in and out of the moonlit street. Every dog a winner, every dog a natural predator, if only for survival. It had never occurred to Uli before that flesh could be picked too—like scrap, like anything else. *These dogs will fight.* The red glistens over every dog's snout. Uli dreams of money, dreams of going home to Texas.

That night Uli lays beside Alma and tries to fall asleep. He makes lists of everything he'll buy with June's death money:

Some new clothes for the baby

A new pair of jeans (Levi's 514s)

Two Estrella Roja bus tickets to Ciudad Juárez (one for him, one for Alma and her baby)

A laptop computer

A motel room for two nights in Rincón de Waterfill where they'll prepare to cross

Two Bonafont tanks of purified water

A detailed map with railroads and safe homes

A coyote to guide them into West Texas

He makes a list of things he'll eat inTexas:

A Whataburger Jr. with cheese (no pickles)
The Cheesesteak LuAnn Platter at Luby's (with cabbage and mac 'n' cheese)
Carnitas from La Playa on Harlingen's Sunshine Strip (charro beans on the side)
An orange picked fresh from Sampson's grove (with salt)
A pint of Blue Bell ice cream (vanilla)
A plate of brisket (moist) from Rudy's
A thick stack of *mixta* tortillas from HEB
Anything from Taco Bell.

He makes a list of things he'll bring his mother:

A cone of *piloncillo*
A bottle of Sotol
A carton of Faro brand cigarettes
A wedding picture from his father's home (on their honey-moon in Mexico City)
A moldy suit from his father's closet (if only to bury).

And just as sleep takes hold of him the window bursts. A shockwave warps the air of the room into a pitch-perfect hum, the clanging of nails singing in unison as they enter the home.

There isn't a square inch of their bodies spared.

Uli only feels what he can see, which is to say he only feels the flash of the blast right before the nails pierce the soft flesh of his eyelids and then his sinus cavities, his foramen, lacerum, his vomer, his dura matter, his pre-frontal cortex, his meninges, his corpus collosum, his cerebrum and then his occipital lobe through which the nails reach the back of his skull and then slick out into the heat.

For however brief a moment, there is consciousness in the frontal lobe. Even as the nails plunge. Even as the neurons scatter their electric static into the constellations leftover from the remnants of Uli's brain, they pull from memory, for just an instant, the sensations and sounds leftover from the untouched amygdala and temporal lobes.

The instant before he dies, Uli remembers the forgotten sensation of drinking breast milk for the first time and the way water felt on his skin when he was just a boy. He remembers the swimming pool birthday party he had when he was nine, when he lived somewhere else, and how it felt pretending he was an astronaut in space just floating in the water like that. He remembers the sound of his mother's voice like tin in the cochlea of his ear as she shouted at Cuauhtémoc from above the pool's surface.

And she's forever shouting like that, her voice fading into oblivion. Words that have no meaning.

ACKNOWLEDGMENTS

Writing a novel is a tough, elusive and (at times) mystical undertaking. There's no one way to cut the thing, which is half the struggle. The other half is finding the time and means and support to keep going, to keep grinding against the seemingly impossible task of creating something from nothing. To sit down and dutifully write a cast of characters, their motivations, their anxieties, and place them in a world that gives them something to act and react against. And hopefully, if done right, those characters will deliver us to some fundamental truth about ourselves—people on this earth trying our best. This novel is a story about people trying their best, and the gravity of those outcomes under certain circumstances.

I think that verb, to try, is the story of 21st-century transmigration, but also the story of the writer too who confronts the impossible task of doing justice to those nuanced and complex characters. This is especially true of writing about the people of Mexico and especially those caught up in America's drug war there. I'd like to think I tried my best, but it should be said that I didn't do it alone. The fundamental truth is that these people, in no particular order, are the people who brought me.

My first tribe:

My wife, Sophia, who believed in me and my words from the first day and who (against all advice) married a writer. Thank you for loving both the light and dark. And for reading, patiently, every single draft with pen-in-hand. Most of all, thanks for reminding us of how far we'd come every time I thought I was out for the count. Thanks, too, for all of the free food.

My mom who always took me to get books that filled my mind with the first gems of literature. And who read me the scariest stories I've ever heard. I owe you everything good in my writing career. Thanks, too, for the Mexican citizenship and for letting me become a pilot. That came in handy.

My dad who taught me the joy of the grind, of the sustained pursuit of things that in other lives would have alluded us. Who taught me to keep moving, to stay persistent and to love the work that you do. But more importantly, to "dance with who brung you."

My big brother, Robert, who unknowingly blended the great Mexican tradition of nota roja with the absurdity of late 20th-century Texas. Unhinged stories, Art Bell, hilarious conspiracy theories, overheard conversations on scanner radios and strange things in general that so much fused the remembered traditions in our blood with our lived experiences as brown boys in Texas. East of the Rockies, you're on the air.

My little sister, Cristina, who always reminded me to bloom where I was planted and who always gives the best reading recommendations. Thanks for keeping me young, keeping my writing fresh and for letting me be your big brother, which was the first thing that defined me. In other words, we're cookin'.

My Fundamentals Tribe:

Larry Heinemann, who was my first mentor and the first writer to give me the time of day. Thanks for your humor, your guidance and your book, *Paco's Story*, which was the spark that birthed the fire for this novel.

Dr. Charles Rowell, who gave me my first editorial job and introduced me to the world of literary magazine production, but also revision and editing and the art of sticking to your creative vision.

Josh Pudnos, for your unwavering friendship and dark humor, which was essential to getting through the various iterations of this manuscript.

Helena María Viramontes, J. Robert Lennon and Ernesto Quiñonez who brought me to Cornell and believed in me and my ideas. Thank you for never giving up on me. I would have never finished this without your guidance and patience.

Ellen Duffer and Ladette Randolph who believed in my writing way early and who allowed me to share it with the world via *Ploughshares* and the Ploughshares Blog.

Daisy Parente for her critical eye and belief in me and this book despite all odds. A million thanks for your encouragement, friendship and edits. "Safe Home" and this book have your fingerprints all over them and I couldn't be more grateful.

Andrew Lund who helped me navigate the finer details of putting this book out into the world. You made this a better endeavor.

My Cornell tribe:

Stephanie Vaughn, Michael Koch, Bob Morgan, Alice Fulton, Joanie Mackowski, Debbie Castillo, James McConkey, Elizabeth Anker, Mary Pat Brady, Edmundo Paz Soldán, Margo Crawford, Roger Gilbert, Charlie Green, Lyrae Van Clief-Stefanon, Elizabeth A. Edmondson, Andrew Marc Boryga, Cecilia Lawless, Rafa Acosta, Rodrigo Hasbún,

Liliana Colanzi, Aisha Gawad, Alex Chertok, John Searcy, Sam Nam, Chris Drangle, Adam O'Fallon Price, Elizabeth Watkins Price, Emma Catherine Perry, Matt Ritger, Lauren Schenkman, M.S. Coe, Julie Phillips Brown, Téa Obreht, Dexter Thomas Jr., Rachel Coye, Elizabeth Lindsey Rogers, Orlando Lara, Hajara Quinn, Chuck Zeilenga, John Murillo, Clayton Pityk, Christian Howard, Laurel Lathrop, Sally Wen Mao, Bradley Pecore, Nancy Quintanilla, Meredith Gudesblatt, Stuart O'Nan and Aaron Rosenberg

My Mexico City Tribe: Ulices Piña, Aileen Teague, Aubrey Herrera, David Lida, Francisco Goldman, Efrén Ordóñez, Lindsay Van Dyke, Lorenzo Herrera y Lozano, Jackal Tanelhorn, Alba Sinchanclas Marín, Savitri Arvey, Arturo Mendoza, Claudia Arruñada Sala, Hazel Blackmore, Cesar Favila, Tanya Huntington and Dra. Margarita Vargas.

My Texas Tribe: Juan Pablo Lopez, Hector Lopez, Mark Haber, Leo Antenangeli, Marcus Antenangeli (for saving this novel from the depths of my dead computer—Buzzingo!), Lupe Mendez, Jasminne Mendez, Mike Emery, InPrint Houston, Michael Olivas, José Angel Hernández, Stephanie Ledesma, Reyes Ramirez, Gabriela Baeza Ventura, Eloísa Pérez-Lozano de Castelan and my incredible and brilliant colleagues at the University of Houston-Downtown, especially Robin Davidson, Jane Creighton, Giuliana Lund, Sandra Dahlberg, Nell Sullivan, Chuck Jackson, Michelle Moosally, DoVeanna S. Fulton, Ed Hugetz, Salvador Salinas and Paul Kintzele.

My Pan-World Tribe: Kyle Dargan, Nelly Rosario, Santiago Vaquera-Vásquez, Tayari Jones, Randolph Thomas, Megan Carpentier, Wayde Compton, Jason Rocha and Sherman Alexie.

My Institutional Tribes: the Fulbright-Garcia Robles Scholarship, the Cornell Latino Studies Program, the Freund Fellowship, the Pickett Fellowship, the Tinker Grant, the Mario Einaudi Center, the Cornell Latino Living Center and the LSSO, COMEXUS, the James McConkey Grant, the Freund Fellowship, Ploughshares Magazine (especially Lauren Groff), the Pshares Blog, the Pushcart Prize, the Picador Guest Professorship at the University of Leipzig, the Veranstaltungsforum der Verlagsgruppe Georg von Holtzbrinck, the German Academic Exchange Service (DAAD), the Institute for the Recruitment of Teachers, EPOCH Journal, the Callaloo writer workshops, the MFA program at Cornell University, the University of Houston-Downtown, the National Autonomous University of Mexico and the Centro de Investigaciones Sobre América Latina y El Caribe in Torre II of the National Autonomous University of Mexico.

And, of course, Nicolás Kanellos and Marina Tristán for their intelligence, patience, wit and encouragement in helping bring this book into the world. I'm so grateful to have this book with Arte Público Press.